Rooftop Soliloquy

by Roman Payne

ROOFTOP SOLILOQUY

1st Edition

About the Author:

Roman Payne was born in Seattle in 1977.

He left America in 1999 and currently lives in Paris.

For more information about the author, please visit:

www.romanpayne.com

Acknowledgments & Legal Statement:

This book is a work of fiction. Names, characters, places, and incidents either are products of the author's imagination or are used fictitiously. Any resemblance to actual events or locales or persons, living or dead, is entirely coincidental. This book is published by ModeRoom Press.

ISBN 978-0-578-03281-8

© 2006-2009 - Roman Payne / ModeRoom Press

Cover Photo: Orbón Alija

Cover Design: ModeRoom Press

Rooftop Soliloquy

A Novel

1st Soliloquy

IT WAS A TIME I SLEPT IN MANY ROOMS, called myself by many names. I wandered through the quarters of the city like alluvium wanders the river banks. I knew every kind of joy, ascents of every hue. Mine was the twilight and the morning. Mine was a world of rooftops and love songs.

For four nights we drank and feasted at the banquets in the holy square of Saint-Germain-des-Prés. Many friends of old assembled—tried companions, those long-traveled, with stories yet untold. There, we gathered beneath the broad moon that hung like a pendant on a string. We danced beneath festivity lanterns, dropping blushing light on the lawns and stones. On prosperous tables, gentle bread was laid. Brimming were the bowls. Much wine was drunk—good wine, well-seasoned, long ago pulled from ancient grapes. Golden-lipped girls with sleek hair, voluptuous breasts, and eyes slender as pearls strolled in and out in their clouds of perfume; summer sacks dangled on fresh arms burnished by the copper sun after days spent in private ways on provincial strips of shore. We toasted the city and the passage of time, and we laughed with gladness in our hearts, always merry in our ways, until nights overturned to dawns.

It was then on the evening of the fifth night that I resigned myself to stay in the rooms I kept overlooking the square and not to go out, as I desired to finish up some of the projects I had weighing on my mind. These were heroic times and I had much work to undertake.

From a solitary evening walk along the river, I came alone up the rue Bonaparte. Entering the room to which I held key, I approached the summer basin freshly spilling of water; and from it, I splashed my face to tame the heat. The mail had been slipped beneath the front door and I took the envelopes to the table to examine them. One was from Nadja, with rose-colored paper and a hand-painted pomegranate. Her letter was brief but excited. She was high in spirits. Everything was settled. She would be coming in the fall to study at the Beaux Arts.

"Sweet Nadja," I smiled and flung the window open with thoughts of that eastern beauty on her far-flung shore, her sun-cooked archipelago. Was there anything like Nadja? ...with her magnificent sloping waist and long saltwater back. Hopeful Nadja, with those subtle, upturned breasts and that firm tummy... No!, this was no time to dust my thoughts with the powdery prints women's footsteps leave behind. There was much work to be done! "All of this and a summer's eve," I muttered as I paced the floor, "The temperature throbs and, one by one, evening birds peck at the humid hours leaving spicy dusk with sweet tempered beaks." It was clear thoughts were coming fine. I knew great work would be done this night.

Filing the letters in a forgotten cabinet, I took to the desk to where I lay pen to sacred work. I wrote one line, then a second, humming my hero's exaltation.

Feel the tremendous heat! Any stopping this swelter? "Watery pitcher, water clean..." I drank cool water and approached the window to feel the draft. My feet stamped noisily on the wooden floor as I crossed the room. Bright is the Parisian sky—and crisp! Down in the square below, I observed the nightly banter beginning to form. "Holy banquets!" I shouted with displeasure in my heart, "Sacred, profane feasts! . . . Shut up!"

Down in the square of Saint Germain, I could see the growing assembly of the evening's fresh young girls, *ces parisiennes parfumées,* donning newly-cinched cotton tops. Streamers ran softly over ancient stones. The colorful paper lanterns, infused with light in the dusk, stretched across the lawns and were bowing and bobbing with the currents of summer winds. I left the window open and returned to the desk to continue my work.

One hour over-passed the next. A little work was set to stone, chiseled and arranged. Dark grew the sky and the strumming of newborn songs came from the square up into the airy room. Then there were songs, now there was laughter. Now a girl was shouting to her friends. Did *they* want to drink champagne? *She* did! Happy, one could tell, were those tender vocal cords, never once torn by rugged years. Sweet like a klaxon's song in private bows. Sweet was her chime. Would I have to shut the window? Must I deprive myself of the summer evening wind? Cannot the nightly air belong to me as well? I, after all, have a battle-worn hero who needs a lofty breeze in order to sail home.

In defeat, I abandoned the chair and returned to the window...

Now the banquet was in full bloom. Sweet smiles, I saw, laughter from sweet eager girls, dressed in tissues light, their frosted lips and braided hair, bound breasts and fragrant hips, holy tender wrists and palms, arms that raised to sing their psalms . . . "Let us end these happy feasts!" I implored madly, "Just one night! . . . For one night, I wish for peace! Silence all! . . . Do you not realize I am planning a hero's homecoming up here?" Alas, the revelers heard me not. I brushed my brow of sweat, and upset sighs I put forth as I closed the window and walked over to the piano to tick out a tune.

No avail.

With the still air—now that the window was shut—the heat, the muted sounds of the reveling outside, my hero's tale was waning. I couldn't get the poor wanderer home.

Again at the window. I sought the latch to open it anew and let in a draft. A clear view I had of all the happy gardens. From where I stood, one easily saw the crystal champagne flutes emptying themselves into delighted mouths. One could count the specks of glitter on the smooth shoulders of the ladies. Officers in uniforms, white-jacketed servants carried corpulent bottles beneath their arms. "Cursed night!" I cried, while the moon was swelling majestically to add to my frustration.

"And if I should die this very eve? If I should perish on some accidental chemist's drug, hazardly taken before your rosy dawn? You, gay-tongued ladies and men—speak up! Would you be happy sacrificing your hero's tale for the dregs of this night's wine?"

My words availed me aught. The revelers were not listening. Ceasing to speak, I kept my eyes fastened to the noisy square, all the while trying to think of how to return to my work. Now the band had stopped to allow one fiddle player the party's attention. This fiddler was a gangly type, with long bandy legs, and a *smoking*. Everyone seemed to take a great interest in what he was about to play—the women especially. All gathered around.

His fiddle began slow. Eyes darted around his uneasy movements with the first caresses of the bow. Then, as he sped up, his arms began waving rapidly like the wings of a gnat. It wasn't such a feat! I knew the very concerto, a most predictable piece! Still, his equine mallet got the proper attention and the fragrant ladies, all dewy-eyed, perched around him with mouths gaping in emotion.

It was during this show, I saw among the maids below, one young girl who struck my curiosity. She was in the group, among the others, though somehow apart from everyone. A young girl, shorter and more fair than her fellow ladies. Her shoulders sat upright like fruit on a tree, and her breasts swooped down like two birdlings learning flight. Those shoulders were bare and smooth and bronzed like amber resin forever preserving youth. Around her small neck of rosy skin she wore a pretty band of peach silk. And from that silk, hung a golden locket or bell, which appeared to ring each time her soft neck pulsed. And every descent that violin took, from major key to minor, her chest heaved and her neck it trembled and that golden bell it rang.

"Senseless to think I own the night!" I sighed in defeat, shutting the window anew, wiping the summer dew from my humid crown. I realized now that staying in this coop would truly avail me naught. It was time to find my own girl… I had clever Adélaïde I could visit. That fair doe with her collarbone of pearl. A famous dancer at the Palais Garnier. Her famous body smooth as fresh split ivory—and long too. She would be waiting for me now, this very night, this very hour, in her sweltering loft overlooking the grandeur of the lawns of Luxembourg. I imagined her well: her low cut dancer's top, thin and pressed with summer wetness against beautiful alabaster breasts.

2nd Soliloquy

Sweet eve sang softly as I wandered along. Sweet eve touched me gently!
It was nice of me to leave off my work again to enter anew the vibrant life
of the festive streets. I passed quickly through the Place Saint Germain
without stopping to smile at friends. I walked up the rue des Canettes,
past St-Sulpice, on up the cobbled rue Férou. Adélaïde would welcome
me gorgeously on this balmy night.

When I came inside her courtyard, I saw the windows of the
concierge were open, blowing wild-patterned sheets with spicy smells of
Portuguese cooking fires. Her children were babbling away in the
kitchen. I took quietly to the discreet stairs. Up on the top floor,
Adélaïde greeted me...

"Lover of old!" she cried, the gentle fawn.

"Lady of youth!" I sang with outstretched arms.

"So long to see you, Aleksandre! Would you like tea?"

"Good girl, no! . . . Just wine."

We kissed each other a timely hello with long ago thoughts, and
then we sat at a table laid with summer fruit and gentle wine. Adélaïde
nodded happily to me and poured the glasses. Her forehead shined with
summer heat. In due time, we prayed: "Give us this night our nightly

wine…" After we had drunk, I stood and went to the window overlooking the silent trees of Luxembourg.

"I'm going to take a bath, Aleksandre."

"Fine, fine," I called back to the far-away voice. I heard water filling the tub. I turned back to the pleasant window, back to my soft-chilled wine, back to the garden beyond, back to myself drifting farther away from the city below me. Streams of traffic on the rue de Vaugirard poured in and around me; and the great garden came to resemble, now a sea of black tar encrusted in bronze, now a gulf of obsidian flung amongst the city's copper lights. As one wanders bravely alone in a forest after finding oneself suddenly strayed from one's companions, curious as to what might be found, so my mind went off alone in errant ways as now I was alone at the high window. I began to wonder what I had to be glad about. True, it was summer; and after all, I could travel. It would soon be August. I was surrounded by friends, my work was immense, and pleasures were abundant. Life, now, was unfolding before me, constantly and visibly, like the flowers of summer that drop fanlike petals on eternal soil. Overall, I was happiest to be alone; for it was then I was most aware of what I possessed. Free to look out over the rooftops of the city. Happy to be alone in the company of friends, the company of lovers and strangers. Everything, I decided, in this life, was pure pleasure. Aye!, these were empirical times! Each moment making its own singular impression, either in thought or in vision, odor or sound… Yes, I could travel, or I could stay in Paris. I had the season of summer. Then after summer would come the even better season of autumn. After that would come the winter, followed then by the fragrant spring.

It was while I was making my peace with my life that Adélaïde bathed her delicate body. I returned to the table to drink the last of the cool wine. I then went out onto the balcony to take a breath. Adélaïde had finished her bath. When I came back to the room, I saw she had cast her towel away and was lying naked on her damp bed, allowing the summer heat to dry her. There on the bed where she lay waiting, I poured oil in a Constantinian lamp and lit the ready wick. Upon her body softly stirring…

Stirring softly, her skin took the sweet oils from my hands and the summer songs dropped from my giving lips. In the niceties of July, I fell deep upon her with silk and sweat, and lifted her high with the palm of my hand on the small of her back and felt the little tips of her well-known teeth upon me, the gentle arch of her tender feet and the strain of her creamy legs, shuddering long like a tremolo string.

Afterwards, we lay torn and battered like bruised animals.

"I'll be leaving for Vienna in a week, you know…" Adélaïde breathed this softly, while smoothing my hair with her dovelike hand. "When I get back, I'll have moved."

Vienna, I thought. That's right, I'd forgotten. Adélaïde would be going for three months to dance at the *Wiener Staatsoper*, illustrious hall. When we would see each other again, it would be in the cold months of winter.

"Where will you have moved to?"

"Just down to the quai. I found a bigger place. Next time you come to visit it will be down there."

Thus hearing, I looked around her little place at Luxembourg I knew so well. I thought then that I might miss it, though I never would. Three months, she would be gone, I considered. Let me savor then her body now, laced in humid midnight hours. With strength and skill, I brought her into me anew. We breathed and were blown like ships on windy seas. Afterwards we lay silent. Panting fresh. Adélaïde ended the silence with sentimental words…

"Do you remember what is was like when we met?"

"Yes."

"Tell me about it."

So hearing, I spoke thus, inventing a poem on the spot to recall a time two summers past:

We met in the courtyards of night.
I brought you a strip of silk

while you brought a slender key,

tied to a strand of perfumed cloth.

By a prosperous fountain we kissed.

Our noses were filled with the fragrance of summer.

You took me upstairs to your room.

We had to be silent, your sister was sleeping.

We made love on the balcony stones.

Ours was our youth in that long-ago time…

"Yes, it was a beautiful time," Adélaïde whispered, the dew of passion gathering on the corners of her lips, "It was then like it is now. And it was sure romantic of you to show my sister to the train station the next day."

"I just don't remember why your sister was sleeping here in the first place, or where she was going to on the train."

"To Montpelier, where she lives with my parents. But you remember!" Adélaïde paused, and then resumed… "Aleksandre? Will you come to see me the day I get back from Vienna? We can sleep together in my new place."

3rd Soliloquy

In Autumn, after the silence of August, many things had changed. Adélaïde had left for Austria. The drizzling rains began. In public houses we drank coarse seasoned wine and wondered privately about the coming winter and the new year. I woke early some mornings to walk in the damp darkness along the rows of *animaleries* along the quai de la Mégisserie. There I would come to meet a melancholy group: a man named August and the younger one, a Russian immigrant, called Pavel. The two shared a loft and worked downstairs in the 'Bone Shop.' The shop was an old brocante tucked between flourishing poppy nurseries along the banks of the Seine. I'd passed the shop one day and saw a sign posted on the window that read: WE BUY METALS. So on a later morning, while on my way to the aéroport to fly to Denmark, I stopped in to sell some silver.

August, the bald-headed proprietor, was hunched over in his chair identifying stamps. He was a simple-faced man with a small chin and forty-five years. Dressed in a drab grey topcoat and a foulard around his neck. Pavel, handsome and shining of youth, sat nearby arranging tin snuffboxes in a display case. August paid me cash for several ounces of silver, asking me first for the customary identity papers that are used to provide the information that is copied into the tax registry during such transactions. I produced some well-constructed documents.

"Dmitry Marcovik," August read, "resident of Belgrade."

"Resident of Paris, as well," I added, not bothering to feign a Balkan accent. The papers were beautifully crafted and didn't require a lot of theater to pass them off. I was proud of these papers. The last time I'd used them, I recalled, had been many years prior in Italy—the time when I met Pénélope. Back then, I always went by 'Dmitry Marcovik.' Neither Italy, nor Pénélope, knew me by any other name.

"Do you buy gold?" I then asked, procuring from my leather sack three ounces of beautiful gold and two half-ounce gold coins.

August shook his head. "Unfortunately, I'm not in a position to buy gold."

"That is unfortunate."

"I'd have to sell a lot of snuff canisters before I could buy your gold."

"Very unfortunate."

I returned the gold to my bag and turned to leave. As I was doing so, I stole a glance at the young Pavel. He had finished with his display case and was now sitting in a corner jotting something in a leather book. I noticed the way his hands trembled as he wrote, as though he were ill. He had a fine face for a young man, an appearance at once noble and filthy—Adonis stricken with plague, a prince dressed in rags.

"Take it," I said, turning back to August. I had reached on impulse into my sack and took out one single half-ounce gold coin. I presented the gold as a gift. "Take it. No, really, please do."

"Too generous!" August protested, pressing wet palms to a damp forehead. Pavel looked at me with caution.

"It's nothing for me," I said, waving my arms, anxious to end the dispute. I left the gold coin on the table and went to leave the shop. The two men rushed to their feet and then made as if to drop to their knees before me.

"No, get up please! No, do not thank me . . . Yes, yes, it is a gift! In return, you ask? Nothing! . . . Or, just pay me back by sharing a drink with me when I come back to town, that's all I ask. I'm flying to Copenhagen today. A big party there. Have you been to a party in Copenhagen before? I'll stop by your shop when I return and we can all three take a drink together." All the while I was speaking, I asked myself what my designs were, if any, on these two men.

"Of course you must come back to drink with us as soon as possible!" they gushed, "Please do come by the moment you are back!"

I assured them that I would, and I did in fact visit them a week later…

I had just arrived back in Paris. At the rooms where I worked in Saint-Germain-des-Prés, I found a letter waiting for me from Pénélope. She was in Paris, staying temporarily with a friend—a girl whose family-name was apparently 'Gauthier.' The envelope bore an address from the rue de l'Odéon. I quickly drafted a reply to Pénélope, saying that if she needed somewhere to stay, she should go to a place called 'The Bone Shop' on the quai de la Mégisserie and ask for August and Pavel. They would help her with whatever she may need—money, a roof, friendship… She could ask anything of them. They would deprive her of no service.

That night, I found Pavel and August at their place on the quai. The shop was closed and the windows were dark, but I rapped my knuckles on the window and August appeared in a nightshirt through the darkness. He opened the door and beamed a smile and quickly invited me up to the loft for a drink. He roused Pavel from the little cot where Pavel slept and insisted that we all sit at the table and drink together. They had some whiskey of tolerable quality. I thought to myself that the next time I came to see them, I would need to bring better whiskey. We drank and talked. And once we were drunk, I told them I would make them the heroes in a great opera that I would one day write; and I invented the opera on the spot and told them the narrative. They swore to me that they could think of no greater honor than to be written into an epic opera and vowed to be the happiest men alive should I one day sincerely write it. I gave my word and they praised me, realizing that I'd awarded them with both kinds of honor one can give a man: *timé* and *kleos*. *Timé* through my gift of gold; and *kleos* by promising them that through my epic, men and women would sing their names for centuries to come. Feeling in debt, August and Pavel persisted in weighing up our favors and commenting on the imbalance, telling me they felt ashamed, they asked what they could do for me. I told them that the greatest service they could do for me in this world would be to take care of a girl named Pénélope, who I said was my little sister, should she ever come to them in need. That they refuse her no service, that they too be as brothers to her. They gave me their vow.

After many more hours of talk, I took leave of the two men. We embraced and said a joyful goodbye as comrades do when properly drunk, and August and Pavel repeated again and again that they would refuse no service to my dear little sister, Pénélope, should she ever come to them in need.

The next morning, I woke in fever and abandoned work after coffee to go to the address from where the letter had been sent from Pénélope on the rue de l'Odéon. The gardienne of the building was a fat Portuguese woman with teeth that were hooked like the curly horns of a ram. She claimed that there had never been any tenant with the name 'Gauthier' living in the building, and certainly no Pénélope had ever stayed there. She said that the building was inhabited by cripples and agèd convalescents, and the letter was a mistake or a fake. I found the situation absurd and left in haste.

"I wonder where she is?" I asked aloud as my long legs sped over the breadth of Saint Germain, "A wasted morning! At least last night was productive..." I recalled in a flash all of those beautiful scenes of my opera I'd invented in the loft of August and Pavel. "Those two men earned that half-ounce of gold I gave them with the epic they inspired me to write. I must be sure to write it someday and not forget any details." I gave thought to the memory of the night sky I saw through the window of their tiny loft on the quai de la Mégisserie and how beautiful it had looked as the whiskey was swirling in my head. I recalled the way the moon had risen out of that window once I'd finished telling my story. Never had I met such melancholy men, I told myself. It would be for the memory of those two melancholy men that I would map the autumn moon in the key of G. As it will be for them that I one day write my great *Vermian Opera* in D minor. But that will all come later.

It also happened that autumn that I came to meet sweet Katell—fair castaway child who'd wandered awhile, and then settled on the Boulevard Magenta. This is how it happened:

I was obliged to meet with a certain German composer staying in the north of the city. The whole thing was against my better judgment, and I thought to cancel the meeting, but something that I read that was printed about him in *Le Monde* made me take a liking to him. It was said that he only spoke French and German but didn't like speaking his native language, that he didn't like other composers, that he hated artists in general and had a distrust of all foreigners. This, and the rumor that he only composed songs late at night when crudely drunk, made me change my mind.

I found myself the night before at the Café L'Entreacte across the street from the Opéra. I decided I would stay in the neighborhood rather than wander back to Saint Germain where I'd been working. That way I could take my time in the morning and wouldn't have to take a taxi to meet the German.

I found a simple hotel on the boulevard Magenta and booked a room for the night. The girl working at the desk was the fair Katell, an itinerant youth. She had made a deal with the owner that she would work the desk without pay, in exchange for the room she lived in upstairs.

When I entered the hotel, Katell was reading a magazine and wore a citron yellow décolleté top. She also wore a hint of bright yellow on her lips and eyelids, and this freshness came out in gleaming rays of sunlight, slyly beaming from eyes that were light brown; lynx-shaped eyes that seemed to follow whatever object was moving in the room until they would come back to you and bat themselves coyly, with confident timidity. Katell was as short as Adélaïde was tall. Her coquine lips were naturally and seductively swollen and when she looked at you, they would come together to smooth her shimmering lemon lip-gloss.

Katell turned her back to get the key to my room and I noticed her back was small and beautiful shaped and deeply suntanned without the slightest blemish. We talked and she told me she'd been all over. She left home at sixteen to travel, had worked for a year in Asia, had met all sorts of people, and never returned home. She'd liked Greece the best, though she didn't like the smell of the little streets and the churches. But she liked the smells of the cafés and the songs of the musicians who played there. She like the bravery in the Greek tales and songs. She'd read Homer in French and was trying to read him in Greek. She liked the valor of Zeus, she liked his promiscuity, and she admired the craftiness of Athena. She also liked Artemis, although she was convinced her chastity wasn't intentional. "It's like Mary," she told me, "You know in the original Greek, Mary wasn't described as a virgin. She was just described as 'a young girl,' but not 'a virgin'. . . somewhere, someone got it all wrong!"

Katell said she would always be catholic. She said she believed in God and loved him (she insisted that *him* be spelled all in lower-case), and would always love him, though she didn't like his books. The characters in the Bible were sorry people, she said. "They're horribly meek!" she told me, "And worse, they're proud of being meek! . . . Can you imagine?!" Katell liked Jesus but she preferred Achilles.

I asked for a room and furnished priceless papers to ensure the young miss of my honest identity. The passport I presented was one I used in all hotels scarce of amenities, in want of luxury; rooms I planned to stay in a mere night and no more. It was a weathered passport, and had to be smoothed out to be read correctly.

"Monsieur..." she began, trying to make out the type.

"Frederic" I helped her, "Frederic de Quincy."

"Frederic!" She looked wildly at me. I liked the way she pronounced that strange name with her tender lips.

Later in the evening I sent for wine and she asked to drink some with me, and I asked her if she wanted to hear a new song. "It's a heroic piece," I insisted, and she was glad about that. I asked if she had an instrument.

"There is a flute downstairs."

"A silver flute?"

"Yes."

"That will do fine."

Katell went to get the flute and when she came back we went to *her* room and played and sang and she learned the words to my song. Her room was bare, even for a hotel room, and when it was late and we thought to sleep, she asked if I had any toothpaste or soap. I didn't. I was traveling without luggage and had hoped the hotel would furnish such toiletries. She blushed when I told her this, and said she hadn't either these items and said she always seemed to have trouble *'taking care of the necessities,'* as she put it.

Katell then left to the hall and called one of her girlfriends to come over. It seemed she was helping a friend with a place to stay while the hotel owner wasn't around to object. The friend was called Julie. She was a dark-haired creature with shy, cervine eyes. She was obviously less experienced than her older friend Katell. Julie brought toothpaste and soap and the three of us washed and sang and played the silver flute and kissed each other's lips and were happy until, at the blue light of dawn, we fell asleep—all three of us tucked in a tight-sheeted bed. When the hotel maid rang in the morning, I rose and pressed my lips to the girls' sleepy foreheads and snuck away to meet the German.

4th Soliloquy

Winter came quickly that year. I hadn't remembered how much I enjoy the chill of late November, but when it came I was glad. Many things changed but much stayed the same. I saw friends of old—writers and actors, scholars, bankers and merchants, loafers and peddlers of pleasure—we often gathered in private houses where we feasted on hot soups and fragrant wines. Nadja had finally come to Paris to study as she'd always wanted to, and I was doing my best to introduce her around Rive Gauche Society. She took a fortunate place in a golden-heated room on the rue Jacob, near the École des Beaux-Arts; and she spent her days there amid towering easels—or in the museums where she copied the Impressionist's lilacs and sketched the marble beauties. I often saw her at night.

Katell too was back in Paris after having wandered away. She now had a place on the avenue de l'Opéra. Her kitchen lacked soap and salt but her bathroom was furnished with scents and creams and she had acquired furniture too. They were prosperous times for young Katell. She had gone to Rome for a few weeks and had returned with a good amount of money.

The invitation came on a Wednesday. Katell had cooked and asked if I was hungry and if I could bring some candles. I wrapped a well-knit scarf around my neck, found a coat in the armoire, and descended to the Place Colette and up the avenue.

In her tiny studio, Katell and I sat at a well-made table, laid with good bread and ample wine. A generous radiator brought forth heat and the sky outside the window gave night. Katell had been reading from Herodotus. When I arrived the book was set by an old aluminum Bialetti kettle that chugged as it cooked coffee on the stove. We ate with great praise for the delights of well-prepared food. There were sturdy bowls piled with hand-rolled semolina cakes stuffed with cèpes and chevre cream. Blushing oils were strung over tender cooked legumes.

After the rich meal, Katell and I rinsed the plates with clear water. I then went to the window, as was my custom after a meal, and I began to wonder about all that I had to be glad about—now, again, in my life, in the world. Everything, I decided. They were joyous times. I had the pleasures of wine and prosperous meals, the lips of sweet Katell. This, and I had the fortune of solitude. That, and the season of winter: blessed time when one can walk out into the peaceful morning and find silent streets steeped in frigid darkness. Blessed empirical season! No one could say that my life was lacking...

Sitting softly on the edge of the bed, I sang to Katell with an old wound guitar. We then clasped hands and kissed, and when the shards of moon out the window passed by and the frost on the sill was black as an unused hearth, I took to her bed with wool and down and made love to her. We slept warm that night, and close beside.

I woke early the next morning, before daylight broke, and left the sleeping girl to dream. In that tender room, a little brass mantle clock ticked along the fifth hour. Into the basin, I drew water, warm, and washed my face and shaved. I cooked coffee in the kettle and drank it silently at the window. Those candles I'd brought, I lit anew, yet they did hardly a thing to light upon the dark wood floor where lay scattered pieces of Katell's clothes. No longer citrus-hued cotton tops; now it was winter. The beige straps of Katell's bra showed like muddy rivers running along the burnished earth that was her long burgundy scarf. Her winter stockings were rolled and set about her shoes: black heels, pointed like javelins. Books were scattered on the floor. I saw she had been reading from *Cities and Countries;* it lay face-down to mark the page. I walked again through the silent room to the window to inspect the dawn. It threatened not to be light for a long while. Before I left Katell's room, I sat beside her and studied her in the darkness. She spoke in her sleep and I kissed the soft down of the back of her neck and she clung to me for a moment and then let go. I took my winter frockcoat from the closet, and dressed in my leather gloves, my scarf of winding cashmere. After buckling the sturdy leather satchel where I kept my papers, I descended the stairs and headed down the Avenue de l'Opéra. A winter wind was howling.

Back at the room to which I held key in holy Saint Germain, I drank my coffee and opened the letters that had been piling up beneath the door. A wax-stamped note had been delivered by the fair Adélaïde. She was back in Paris after much success in Vienna. She now lived on the quai Voltaire, and had new clothes to enjoy the cold. All this and she wanted to see me right away. I looked at the calendar and thought of the season. Days were over-passing. I realized I had much to accomplish if I wanted to seal the projects I had started. Ambitious projects they were. It was still early in the month but there was no time to waste. I was in heroic form, strong of mind with a fine-formed body. There were no limits to the greatness I would create on that hearty desk where I lay pen to holy craft. Still, I had to avoid the company of women for awhile.

5th Soliloquy

The "Noëlesqueia" Soliloquy

Splinters of frost grew like cold dust on the dead and stood huddled like armies of winter soldiers, until frozen gusts of December winds came to lift them up and carry them down the desolate street and away into the dark carbon depths of the city. The tenebrous watchman on the rue Jacob was pacing the sidewalk and slapping his leather gloves for warmth, longing for relief; his shuffling footsteps on the pavement came with the whistling wind through the cracked windowpane in the narrow stairwell where I climbed the steps hurriedly to reach the golden heated room on the top floor, where Nadja was undressing.

She called to me from her bed, so long, as I opened the door. Softly stirring, she turned in her nest of blankets. The skin of her exposed belly was taut and shone like the gently-curved stem of a brass spoon, tawny in the lamplight.

"Aleksandre?"

"Aye!"—the final dose of frigid stairway air flitted on my neck as I pulled the door closed behind me. A sturdy mat lay below. I patted my frozen hands and tapped the frost from my shoes—"It's cold out there!"

With my topcoat on, I crossed the room to the bed and fell down dressed on top of the unclothed girl. After we had spent a few silent moments together, I told her I had a gift for her. In my pocket, were three Argentinean candles. I set them on the table and lit them with a match taken from her bejeweled matchbox. "Take your coat off," she said.

Once we had made love, Nadja heated water in a pan on the stove. The steam fogged the window and the lights from the facing apartment rooms across the street could no longer be seen. In the morning, early, the window was coated anew, but now it wasn't steam but was the frost of dawn—such that inspires thoughtful men in wintertime.

"Thank you for the candles," she said as I was leaving. Then asked, "Where will you be for Christmas?"

"In Petersburg," I lied.

"Really?"

"No, I'll be in Galicia… in the prison."

"Tell me true."

"I'll be in Paris."

I clicked the door closed and went out into the stairwell and down through the glad street that cradled the dawn the way a peasant cradles a meal in a headscarf. Back at the room to which I held key, I put my coat on the hook and walked over to the desk to begin my work. The day was Thursday, and that night I was to see golden-lobed Daphné. She lived close by, on the Boulevard Saint Germain, above the bookseller by the cathedral. After eating my solitary feast at the table by the bed, I paced the room a few times thinking of this and that. I leafed through a book in the bookcase. I opened the window to feel for moment the cold air. The evening music had begun in the restaurant down below on the street. A group of mad gypsies were playing plywood fiddles and pewter horns. The restaurant owner paid them in food and sparkling wine. The old swindler kept cheap *crémant* in a champagne cask.

From the window, I peered down to the street and saw a handsome couple studying the menu card posted outside. "No choice in the matter," I told myself, "I'm going to have to go out tonight." I found a shirt in the armoire and coated and scarfed myself for the jaunt up the street to call on Daphné, favorite daughter of a far-away father. She was a soft-faced girl with dark and wondrous eyes, healthy thighs, and pale cheeks to match the winter sky.

A tidy elevator lifted me up to the fourth floor.

"Is that you?" she asked as I entered. She was sitting at her dressing mirror rubbing oiled milk on her face. Strangely wild-eyed for the season, she sat by the glass and hung globes of ore from gentle ears. Drops of misty perfume fell with her hand to her breast. Now was dark but for two candles alight on a thrifty table. The good girl had cooked and had dressed. A fine meal, abundant of sauce, and hearty of bread; moulds of cheese and sweet wine.

"Fair Daphné!"

"Fair Aleksandre!"

"I brought you a gift. Something for the cold of winter." So saying, I handed her a small wooden box taken from my bag. She opened the little latch of the brittle box and looked inside.

"Incense."

"Livani incense. And good charcoals. We will burn some."

Wild-eyed Daphné lit a charcoal and set it in a dish and we watched the sparks travel across its surface. A moment later the coal was hot enough to receive the good resin. Smoke billowed out: strong smoke, and spicy too!

There was a dry windstorm that night. After we had made love in her bed, I lay awake a moment listening to it. The wind resembled the crying of a winter bird who is forever bound to the sky, though weary from travel. I thought of how I too had been bound so long to this traveler's road from where I had come, and I thought of the previous seasons of my life until I fell asleep again at last, the warm skin of the girl against me.

I woke early to an empty bed.

Daphné was crouched on the floor in her slip, using a hot iron to remove some wax that had dripped and seeped into the cracks of the wooden floor. I stole behind her and seized her small pale shoulders. Tender breasts…I kissed…Tender mouth.

"When will we see you again?" she asked as I was leaving.

"In a week."

Out on the boulevard, the spindly sticks of the trees once had leaves, twisted and turned with the flight of the wind. I whistled a snatch with a glad heart.

Back at the room to which I held key, I began my work of the day. 'Happy to work,' I thought, 'Good pleasurable work—and above all, winter!' I searched in my wardrobe for a sweater and opened the window and let the cold air in. It was nearly quiet in the street, but of course it was just early morning.

I worked well and long, then at nightfall when the quiet turned to ruckus (the gypsy band had begun their nightly romp in the restaurant below) I went to the window to look outside. Well-dressed ladies on the arms of paunchy men strolled past the restaurant, down the street, past the closed-up shops. The door to the restaurant was opened for affectionate couples to enter, all in turn, as they waved their reservation tickets. The gypsy band whined like a Spanish wagon selling trinkets.

"Insupportable!" I called out my window; and, turning away, I walked briskly to the wardrobe and in it found my dark coat and wrapped about me a well-knit scarf. I paced around the room a few times, studying my shoes' effect on the wooden floor…

"Insupportable!"

I'd had only to get my keys and go to the elevator down the hall.

When I was out on the street, I turned left on the rue Jacob. It was the night for young Katell, cast-away child, who'd wandered awhile, and settled on the rue de Verneuil.

A snow started to fall while I walked. Always a dry snow beneath a pale pink or grey sky. I carved a fervent path, thinking of the pleasant things she would have waiting for me when I entered her room: sweet breads and hot wines, soups and chocolate medallions sent from Ghent; other treasures too, like brandy with coffee, and the "Nocturnes" played on an old machine . . . Oh, pleasant night it will be!

Up the discreet stairs I climbed. The hall and stairwell were heavy with cooking smoke. It was coming from Katell's room. The poor girl had tried to roast a pan of salted stuffs, oil of nuts and seeded things; and all caught in a flame and a cloud was spread over her hapless den. She called to me from within...

"Is that you?!"

"Aye, good lady! What have you done?"

"Cooking!"

I opened a window, and watched the boney fingers of winter tear the smoke from the room. When we were seated at the table, she lit the candles and a slice of *Papier d'Arménie*. In the pungent place we sat and dined on her good things. A solitary wooden chair creaked in the corner.

"Where have you put the furniture?"

She answered by way of reminder that she was moving to Berlin at the beginning of the year. I had forgotten. "I have a gift for you," I told her, "Some things to get you by till then." So saying, I pulled out a cake of soap and salt. She admired them and took them to the counter by the sink.

"I have wine left," she told me.

"Good."

We drank off a glass and I stroked her hair and small forehead where she lay on the bed. Fair Katell, she now wore only a small skirt with the strap of honey-yellow panties showing through. Her nipples were large and brown. Her lips were soft and I kissed them.

"Do you want to see," she began as she pulled the strap off her panties, away from her hip bone. I have a little rash here..."

"The elastic," I said, looking at her braided skin, a little swollen. So it was.

"Stay with me in the bed," she implored. I stayed beside her while I finished the wine and stroked the sweet strands of her hair as she fell asleep.

Late now, I left young Katell in her nest of dreams, and went to sit in the chair. It was in that chair I fell asleep and stayed the night.

It was still mighty dark when I woke. The street-sweepers were beginning to climb up and down the neighborhood. I got up, boiled water for coffee, and went to the window and touched the cold pane. Katell was still asleep.

That afternoon I was happy to be alone in my quiet room to work. It was getting close to Christmas and the city was emptying itself as the denizens sought their families in the provinces, and each day was quieter than the one previous. By nightfall, however, everything had changed. The ragged gypsies started up again in the restaurant downstairs as soon as dusk turned to night. I walked to the window and opened it up to peer out and down at the street. There, new throngs of tender girls in eveningwear, their perfumed hair poised over finely powdered faces, their arms balanced on the arms of well-spent men. So much could be imagined. The restaurant door opened and shut and the sounds of the gypsies' old guitars whined and wound around.

"How can one work with this cajoling!" I demanded with an upset heart. "Sweet faced girls and music. And if I want to work?! . . . What if I want to stay in and compose an epic tonight? A real hero's tale? Shall I not be permitted the peace of mind to do so? Shall I be wheedled into going out take a woman in my arms? If it must be then..." So I spoke; and taking from my wardrobe a heavy coat, I went out the door and started off down the hall with the aim to visit Adélaïde, who was now back in Paris.

I traversed the quarter in the direction of the river and found Adélaïde in a room on the fifth floor, in a building lost among the quais. She was knelt down on the floor when I opened the door—not stretching, mind you, but scrubbing like a maid, a spot from the corpulent rug.

"Aleksandre!" she turned to me, sponge in hand. Her poor knees were red and scuffed.

"What have you, good girl?"

"I just spilled it a moment ago," she shamefully called over to me, "…and I've added soap and sprinkled salt. It will go away!"

"Listen to me, fair Adélaïde," I began to say as she invited me in. I went over to her and swept her from her perch. "My snowy beauty…"

"Oh, Aleksandre . . . you always," she started to interrupt, but I cut back in…

"*Adélaïde* and *Aleksandre!* How our names rhyme! They rhyme like two fruit-bearing twigs on the same leafy branch. One would say they are two children walking beneath the watery moon after having made their love. One would say they are… Oh, never mind, Adélaïde, I've brought libations!" And with those words, came from my hands a skin of wine—good wine, long ago pulled from ancient grapes.

Adélaïde brought a bowl of sour leaves and sweet agrumes. We sat at the table and began to drink.

"Do you like my new apartment?"

"Yes."

"We haven't seen each other since summer. Don't you think we've changed since then?" As she questioned me thus, she touched the red spots on her cheeks with her pink fingertips. I listened for a while and then answered her with fueled words:

"Changed? Why, Adélaïde, you are etched in marble! And me, I'm healthy as a horseman! . . . in the prime of life, sturdy in the heart, strong in the chest, only those gods on high—who run swift across the broad sky—can rightly steal these things from me!"

"So you believe in gods now?" Adélaïde made an ironic laugh.

"Listen, Adélaïde, What am I?"

"Um..." she faltered, "What, you ask? What are you?"

"Yes, *what* am I?"

"Um... *A man?*"

"A man. Yes, a man, but what else?"

"A composer of songs?"

"Yes, a composer of songs! And just think, Adélaïde, of all the composers of songs who have lived in modern times, say the last two-thousand years, of all of them who are worth even a brief mention, well over ninety-nine percent of them are dead. Yes, over ninety-nine percent of them are dead . . . While I am alive! Alive and in my prime, I say!"

Adélaïde smiled with pleasure and refilled the glasses.

"And just think," I continued after a large swallow of the wine, "of all the ballet dancers that have ever lived, most of them are dead, perhaps two in five hundred of them are still alive . . . and of that number, perhaps only one in ten is still able to dance!"

She smiled even more wildly at this.

"But even more..." I lit up. I was getting ever more fueled in my speech, "let's take it even further and say you are holier than a mere ballet dancer, Adélaïde. Rather, you are a female creature who dances. You are a female creature who dances, and if you were to take all of the female creatures who ever did dance, and turn them into the fish in the sea, and by means of a patient hook select one out to live on the earth among the blessed, and be conscious of it all, and in all the seas this hook was tossed, among all the fish there are, it would pull *you* out. *You, Adélaïde!* That is the mere chance that you are alive this very moment!"

"And for this you believe in the gods! I see!" she smiled the clever girl.

"Good girl, bring me your well strung mandolin. I will play you a heroic song." And thus I did, and she loved the song. And I sang and then we drained the skin of wine and fought a wrestling bout on the salted floor.

Back at the table… we sat, sighing short breaths. Adélaïde was dressed in a low cut black top this time—her white one discarded.

"Adélaïde? Why is the radiator dripping so much?"

She looked over at the radiator, then at the frosted window above it, and pulled her scarf up from the chair to cover her neck and said, "I can't believe how cold they're letting it get."

Soon, we were again in the corner of the room. I took the sweet girl and I drew all her clothes from her like spindles of silk. I detached her underwear as though they were the tendrils of green ivy. She blushed rose in the cheeks. Her legs opened like petals of skin. Her body quivered; and after we made love she sighed with heat in her breast while I lay waste to her falling limbs.

Then, when we both lay panting like two torn and beaten animals, she leaned her long back behind us, without stirring me from her breasts, and brought forth the pitcher of fresh water that sat not far off. We drank and nourished ourselves with the gift of clean, tasteless water, and then we fell asleep in a heap of sweat and skin.

I woke before dawn, as was my custom, and carried gentle Adélaïde to her bed. I laid her down and tucked her within, and smoothed the strands of hair that had clung to her pale forehead; and sleeping she remained as I quietly stepped out the door and down to the misty quai. Then with a glad and rested, morning heart, I made my way up the rue des Saints-Pères. This, I say, was a day to be alive! And what work I would undertake!

Evening again…

Again, all my projects had to be abandoned when the cacophony of the night started up in the restaurant downstairs. Some old tinny piano had been dragged in from somewhere, and a stream of ladies in rabbit fur hats and lynx collars had gathered outside to watch. I noticed now red and green festivity bulbs were freshly strung up over the shop windows on the street. "Devil take that restaurant!" I called, …and take those sphinx-eyed ladies examining the menu board with too much joy, pressing seamless gloves to dark *couches* of winter makeup used to conceal light, tender winter-cracked lips . . . those holy little mouths! Could it not all end? . . . "Maybe one is etching a knot in eternity up here!" I knocked impatient knuckles on the windowsill as the cold air flushed my face.

It was then, peering down at the street, I saw among the scarfed ladies in the crowd, a young girl who struck my curiosity. She was well-covered to the shoulders. Around her small neck, which was bare, she wore a neat band of black crêpe. From the crêpe, hung a little silver-colored locket or bell which appeared to jingle with each fervent pulse in her pleasurable little neck. She was standing in a group of people, watching through the restaurant window the festivities hidden from my view, and with the emotion of the song and the climax of that singing gypsy's voice, her hands began to clap and her little bell-shaped mouth began to gasp and deepen in color, and the soft white skin on her neck pulsed; there the little band of crêpe trembled and the silver locket bounced on the bone above her breast, and all was lost!

"Senseless to think I instruct my hours," I sighed, taking my coat from the wardrobe. Time it was to call on my own girl—that clever doe with the collarbone of pearl. She would be waiting for me now, this very night, this very hour, in her wintry nest on the river's edge. I thought of her low cut shirt pressed against tiny alabaster breasts . . . her table, her wine, a pirouette, bodies rubbed in scent and sweat; a feast to the humming wind, beneath a dripping radiator dial.

Bitter weather outside.

Let me sing of that night I chanced away down the lamp-lit quai, far past the place I sought. Head held low to fight the cold, deep in thought and making plans, I stumbled along the quais quite far, and went through snowy passageways, cached and unfamiliar. I turned and stopped and looked to the place from where'd I'd come. The lights on the Île de la Cité flickered in the distance. I realized now the time had crept up and knew that Adélaïde would be growing impatient. Having overstepped my jaunt, I turned and started back along the quai in the direction from which I'd walked. Soon I came to the quai where she lived. It was an area unlike my own. Here I may have known every street, yet not every stone in every street. The grey zinc rooftops caught the flaking snow and held them, whereas the black waters of the river simply drank them.

From across the wide street, I stood, stopped and glanced up at the window on the fifth floor of the building where my dancer lived. A lamp was lit with a glowing shade, I knew that she was waiting. It was just before I started across the street to overtake the apartment house, long about came a girl walking beneath the streetlamp a few paces away. She was so close, in fact, I could have taken her arm. I looked at her as she passed with her head bowed low, seemingly in an effort to block the wind. She was poorly-dressed for the weather, uncovered neither by scarf, nor coat, nor hat, just a thin knit sweater that was open in the front and cinched up at the shoulders, leaving her arms bare. At the moment I saw a large flake of falling snow land on her naked neck and melt and wet the skin, I stopped her by means of a wayward phrase...

She turned and looked at me: a young woman, perhaps nineteen or twenty years-old, with a very pretty face, large mistrustful eyes and thin lips that seemed to tremble like leaves on a tree. Her stopping completely allowed me to survey her, and I noticed the little white jupon she was wearing was dirty at the hems. The fabric was yellowish-brown where it brushed against her ankles. Despite the cold, she didn't appear to be shivering; though I, myself, was frozen like winter sod. And with my heavy frockcoat, I had not the excuse of being dressed in a ribbon. Strange thing was, I had time to study all, as she wasn't any longer hurrying on . . . those eyes of hers, haphazardly etched with makeup, watched me while we stood beneath the light of a streetlamp.

Did she not know that I too was on my way, and hurriedly so? I broke with her gaze to look up at Adélaïde's window. The light from the window shined on me, welcome as a lighthouse that shines on a sailor who's been lost among the swells of the dark sea with longing to see the shores of his native land.

There in the window, a dark object passed to block the yellow light of the lamp. I believed Adélaïde was staring down at me, wondering why I was standing in the street, late as I was to arrive, and still not hurrying to meet her. I watched the window until a thin dust of floating frost—call it snow, though it was as powdery as the dust meant for a woman's cheeks—fell between her window and the streetlamp and I saw then merely halos of snow, winter clouds of floating light. I turned back to the unknown girl standing in front of me and gave her again my attention. She was looking at me, almost about to step away, it seemed. She pulled her scanty woolen sweater across her breast and her neck as a gust of cold wind blew across the river behind us.

"Listen," I finally said to the girl, "we have been standing here now looking at each other for over ten minutes. And twice now you have tried to take my hand. Or at least it seems as if that were what you were trying to do. And I would let you certainly, or I would take yours gladly for you have an incomprehensible beauty, but dear girl . . . have you no coat?!"

Hearing my words, she turned and pointed past the edge of a narrow apartment house across the street to a small, rather concealed passage where there appeared to be a night café. Over the arched doorway, hung an old-style gas lamp and a sign too distant to read. She flashed her eyes again at me and said, "I left my coat in there," and then looked down.

"But then why were you coming from that direction?" I wanted to ask. Or perhaps she was going back to get it? Although it seemed she had rather been heading in the direction of the bridge crossing the river, not at all in the direction of the café. The two of us stood rooted in place, looking at each other. I felt an urgency to get her away then from that sidewalk, or at least to move down a block or two, for I distinctly heard a window opening in Adélaïde's building across the street. I took a couple steps to the right to let the dark branches of the willow tree over-hide me overhead. Noticing my shift in position, the girl looked at my feet as if she were expecting me to move again and were curious to see how I would do it. She gave a little wave of her hand as if to ask for an explanation, but before I could speak, she turned her back towards me and peered again over at that little passage where the frosty sign and the sanctuary lamp hung over the arched wooden door.

"I'll come with you," I said suddenly and rather distinctly, surprising myself that I, neglecting to remember the open window on the fifth floor within earshot, had spoken thus. Now I heard it shut; and with it, I imagined, all of the warmth of the city was pulled into that holy apartment overlooking the Seine, and all of the cold of Paris sunk down with a sudden drop that shook the willow branches overhead. The girl standing in front of me finally began to shiver.

"To get my coat?" her voice quivered.

"How so?" I countered, realizing I had been involved in a little imaginary scene and had lost the train of conversation.

"You will *come* with me to get my coat?"

I didn't bother to think, I recall, I just touched the girl's shoulder, and she flashed me her eyes. She then turned with me and we hurried towards the night café. Stopping once in the middle of the street, I first checked to see that she was indeed following me, or coming at least, which she was; I then peered up to the fifth floor window and saw the light was now switched off in Adélaïde's place. I gave it a moment's thought and understood that it had grown very late and I wouldn't be calling on my fair dancer on this night.

By the time I reached the doorway, I was in a bit of a fever and didn't trouble myself to look around me. All I knew was this girl was by my side and the other girl, the one whom I had wanted to see, had set out to see—pale Adélaïde with her sweet thighs and beautiful breasts—was now certainly contemplating my absence.

A swift rush of heat…

I found myself entering into a night café. The unknown girl from the street installed herself at a small table near a window and immediately began warming her hands over the candle on the table. I sat down across from her and observed. I noticed then how small her hands were. Her nose too was small, and young, and upturned like a winter leaf. She kept her head bowed, watching only the candle that warmed her hands. The café was empty of patrons.

We stayed silent—she warming her hands, I observing. When the proprietor came over, he brought another candle and the menu carte and we ordered a demi-carafe of wine. The girl took out coins that she had in a little knit pouch on a strap that had been concealed beneath her sweater and laid them on the table and began to count them   I asked where her coat was and she said quietly that it was hanging up in the back of the café.   I decided that she had been in this café before and had only gone out to take some cold air, and thus stumbled upon me, a stranger—though I had no way to be sure and decided I wouldn't question her on it.   Seated silently, I watched her slowly arrange and rearrange the coins she was counting on the table.   They were large ten-franc pieces and some small centimes and her fingers passed over them finding intrigue in the serrated edges.   She made lines and geometrical shapes—now a tarnished constellation, now a metallic honeycomb.

The proprietor brought the wine and I filled the glasses.   The girl I was with looked up long enough to take a sip of her wine.   When she'd set her glass down, she gave a quick inhale—more of a gasp—and looked at me and said softly that she was sorry she didn't say 'to our health' before drinking, that she'd forgotten.   She then resumed counting her coins on the table.   I saw that she had just the right amount to pay for the wine and it was then I insisted that I would pay for the wine and she could keep her coins.   She looked up as I said this, as though very surprised.   When, after, she went back to get her coat, I learned from the proprietor that the wine had already been paid for.   It turned out, as the girl would come to explain moments later, that she was living above the café . . . or *staying* rather . . . that she had paid for a month's lodging, and some money on top of that for expenses in the café; that her father had come to visit from the provinces and had helped her in the way that fathers do, and now he had left again and she was on her own.   When I made reference to the sum of coins on the table, she again seemed very surprised and I realized that this whole time she had not been counting them at all, but had rather been arranging and aligning them out of nervousness.

She started shivering again and brought her hands over the candle.   The sleeves of her coat came close to the flame.   The coat was nicer than I had expected her to possess when we had met out on the street—a black peacoat with large buttons.   The proprietor came once more and he addressed her by the name of 'Anne-Sophie.'   He'd come to tell her that, by-the-bye, he'd received a letter for her that day in a small envelope. To this bit of news, she took almost no interest. She told me, while the proprietor was still standing there, that she had been coming to this café most nights, or rather, *every* night; and that it was pleasant and she would continue to come every night for as long as she was living upstairs; and then, suddenly, she waved her hand and said she actually didn't know—or *couldn't know*, rather—and blushed when she noticed I'd taken particular interest in these last words.

I asked the proprietor for some coffee, but he sadly shook his head and claimed that the machines were broken and there was none to be had. After he'd gone, she admitted that 'Anne-Sophie' was in fact her given name but that she preferred the name 'Victoria.' She clasped my hand for a moment and her palms were cold and the wool sleeve of her peacoat brushed my wrist and the sensation was pleasant and the joy remained after she let go. "Where would you go?" I said of all things, "of all places?"

"Of all places?" She lit up at my idea for talk, and gasped with an eagerness that I found peculiar. "Only, I think I would like to visit Place Dauphine before morning time when the people arrive and the automobiles come. I imagine it still dark, but almost light. And when lightness would begin to seep in, I imagine the streetlamps would still be lit and it is this I would like to see too!" And then she frowned, "But I'm afraid I can't wake up early enough to get there before dawn. I am so tired in the mornings—hard as I try! But sometime I will. I will keep trying."

To this, I smiled, delighted by her innocence. She asked me if I wanted to leave to find coffee and I said yes, that there was another café in St-Germain I liked and we could go there.

"Oh!" she exclaimed, as if innocently frightened by the idea of another café. She expressed a wish then to see where I lived . . . or *how* I lived, rather, was how she put it. I told her she could see how I lived, that we could have coffee there, and she agreed but said she had to go upstairs to her room first.

"Would you mind if I come in twenty minutes?" she asked. I didn't mind, and I explained how to get there (she claimed not to know the city). I wrote down the code to the outside door and told her the floor number. She said she would try to not get lost. I laughed, saying she had better bring her coat along with her, and she asked that if she were to get lost, would I return to find her this same night at this same café. I said of course, but that it would be hard to get lost in a neighborhood such as St-Germain where the streets are laid out in such pristine order, and that I would see her in twenty minutes and got ready to leave; when she added, "But maybe sooner!" almost with an imploring tone. I uneasily stood and as I did, she reached and pressed my hand to hers, and with the touch of her cold hand—a soft touch carrying that desirous sensation so often dreamed of and hoped for, and so rarely found—there came a gentle fever to my head. I felt an age of triumph in that empirical touch.

Outside in the street, I found myself in a slip of vertigo. The cold air smoothed itself sweet and ominous on the drops of sweat that beaded up on my forehead as I walked along. Each stoop of every doorway seemed to look the same on this night. I studied their bricks, their rubble, while walking down the cobblestones. Over there, a closed-up bookseller. Over here, a boarded-up wine shop. Twice I found myself heading in the wrong direction and was surprised by my sudden disorientation. I wanted so to be back at that café with the unknown girl who'd named herself Victoria and was deep in flight. "I left in the night," she'd said, "Just like that!" giving her reasons for coming to Paris. It was only weeks later she would come to write a letter to her mother and father in the provinces, telling them where she was. "I will cherish her," I thought aloud, and suddenly felt strange for mumbling thus.

Now, back at the room to which I held key, I stepped out of the elevator and walked down the hall and entered the room that was steeped in golden radiator warmth. I switched on the silver lamp and looked around the bare room. I suddenly felt tired and even more feverish and thought to lie down while I waited. "Strange, Anne-Sophie," I said aloud, thinking that, if I *were* to lie down, tired as I was, I should open the door to the hallway a crack so that she could find it easily and let herself in.

The light was off and I stretched out fully-dressed on the bed. I felt that strange painless, though oppressive, pressure beginning in my head—that which comes at times after days of not sleeping properly. I had a strange thought, one of those visual thoughts whose homes are made in the darkness, in that place where life meets dreams on a creaking fence. I realized I was flitting away. More so, I felt keenly aware of that young woman whose presence I was awaiting. I knew then for sure that this strange woman would conquer me, should I not be careful. Reaching for the tablet in the shadows on the desk where I lay pen to work, I began on a clean sheet to write a phrase on the paper thus:

IF I AM FOUND NO LONGER ALIVE, IT WAS AT THE HANDS OF A GIRL NAMED VICTORIA.

...Just so that she would get away with nothing. I signed my name.

I folded the paper and crawled from the bed in the dark to the wardrobe and opened it and hid the note beneath a stack of clothes. I took another sheet of paper and wrote the same message and folded it and hid it elsewhere, behind the wardrobe. After, I crawled back to the bed, still fully-dressed, and felt myself now surely falling asleep.

I was stirred suddenly, warmly, not by any crackling fires, nor by footsteps on the wood, but by her warm body huddled and firmly wrapped in clothes cast down upon me, lying on my chest. Dark it was, yes!—but light enough to see the outline of her face. It was her!—she had come! A long while, I had slept, no doubt. Yes, she was late in coming, but now she was here and upon me and her tender mouth was pressed against mine, sweet and soft.

After she kissed me, she pulled back and said earnestly that she was late. She had been distracted at the café against her wanting and was very late indeed. She informed me that when she entered the building to see me, she saw a band playing downstairs. She was surprised that there was a restaurant there, and, of all things, open on this night in particular. I said yes, that the scornful restaurant was open all the time, that there were these gypsies who played all night, every night, and that we shouldn't concern ourselves with such rascals. While saying this, I pulled her close into me. I pulled her in and held her and desired again to feel her lips on mine but I couldn't find them for they were cast between the bone of my jaw and the lobe of my ear. Motionless, I studied the warmth of her breath passing over my temple. Soon to cease the silence, she spoke thus, quietly but distinctly in my ear…

"We will forget this nonsense about all of these little notes, okay?"

"What did you say?" I asked, finding this startling to hear.

"It's just nonsense you're hiding notes in the clothes and behind the furniture."

I felt again that fever and my fluttering eyelids and that strange pressure in my head and felt myself falling asleep again, though I wanted badly to remain awake, despite her wild words; to feel her against me, to taste her mouth again, to even hear those words again, though strange they were. But I let it go and let her go, cast all aside and out I fell, and thought it was just as well; for even if not awake, I could sleep now and she too would sleep and be against me, our bodies pressed firm, entwined and wrapped in winter wool, and with that I was gone.

I awoke before dawn. I was alone, dressed and on the bed. I looked around the room to which I held key and saw all was as usual: mostly empty, tidy. The door to the hall was open and creaking. Had I left it open? The tablet and pen I keep on the desk was oddly on the floor near the bed. I sat up in the predawn darkness and lit two gentle lamps and leafed through the tablet. All the remaining pages were blank. I felt pleasant, as though I had slept a healthy sleep. Outside, it seemed light was soon to break. The sky appeared heavily clouded, though still all was dark. Standing, I opened the window and felt the coldness on my face. The zinc rooftops bore the plates of ice formed by a winter night. Listening, all was silent. The gypsies had stopped their playing downstairs for another night. If I watch these rooftops, I thought, daylight will soon throw itself upon them. It wasn't until after all of these impressions and realizations that I remembered the events from the night before, that I remembered the encounter with Anne-Sophie. Thinking of her suddenly, I flushed with the memory of her having come to my bed, that particular set of visions, and was surged with a great desire to find her immediately and to know what had happened. I walked quickly to the wardrobe and took out a heavy coat. I put on a scarf and goatskin gloves. I searched for the notes I had hidden but found none. Had she come in the night through the door I'd cracked open for her, found those notes before kissing me, and took them away with her as keepsakes? Or had it all been a dream, even my writing those scraps of nonsense? Before starting out the door, I went back for the tablet of paper. I leafed through it again but couldn't tell when I'd last used it. Sighing a full breath, I put the tablet with the pen in my pocket, in case I would have to leave a note—if she were to be absent.

Outside the wind twirled with the clean dust of ice that bites at knees through woolen trousers. I wandered the streets I knew so well for some time in the bluish darkness. Strange, the morning never broke. The early dark hours dragged on. Strange, I lingered along the quais, trying every streetlet, every discreet passageway. Alas, I could not find the café. Scornful fever I recalled had kept my foolish brain from marking and remembering my way after I'd left the evening before. I searched every quai in St-Germain as well as the Faubourg, down by the bridges and museums, up by the gilded *coupole*. Alas, the café was nowhere.

"I renounce!" I cried, and started back towards the apartment where lived my dancer, Adélaïde. But before I reached Adélaïde's building, I stopped again and began anew to look for the discreet passage that had cradled the elusive café where lived above, the winged Victoria. No renouncing! I coursed again all of the abandoned streets and desolate morning passages. Still, the holy café where I'd drunk wine with that fair strange beauty only hours before never appeared. Continuing past the bridges, I noticed the blue cut-out shapes of the apartment houses on the island in the city and decided I would go immediately to Place Dauphine. It was almost dawn. There we would find each other! My intuition said that of all mornings, this would be the one she would be awake to make it to Place Dauphine before dawn as she had always planned.

I crossed the frosty stones of the Pont Neuf and entered the Place Dauphine. Winter trees were brittle with black trunks and grey twigs. Cold morning winds brushed their branches against the sodden earth floor of the square like hired sweepers who stroll beneath streetlamps, between park benches, collecting leaves like the corpses of time. A crisp and hollow place it was on this morning. Empty, neither Anne-Sophie nor anyone else was there.

I stood awhile in the darkness, marveling at the streetlamps glowing like winter gems beneath a sky that threatened to grow light. I looked at the perimeter of the square, the streets empty of automobiles, the barren sidewalks. It was then I came to see a light flicker and illumine in a nearby café. Now there was someone, some person, outside the café. I squinted to see clearly, to discern her face. There I beheld a woman: a tall creature with a weather-beaten face and heavy hills for shoulders. She was hunched over, pushing a crude broom across the grey stone sidewalk in front of her golden-lit café. I approached from across the square…

"Dear weathered woman, let me come in out of the cold!" Pressing these words into the fabric of my scarf, I seized the door-latch. The broom-bearing maid followed me into a blistery warm room and observed me taking a seat by a large wood stove erupting blue flames.

In a café that was empty but for the two of us, I sat. From a fortunate kettle, the woman poured coffee, black. On a wooden tray, the coffee was brought. Holding her own cup in drowsy hands to remedy sleeping eyes, she spoke thus, issuing forth from winter-chaffed lips…

"I wasn't expecting customers today, it being Christmas and all."

"Christmas?!" Lord, I see what day it is! And here I come to overtake this good woman's place on a holy day, and not in the clothes of a saint. I flushed with embarrassment for having come at a tender time, and so stood to take my coat.

"No, please!" the woman started. Then she added calmly, "I beg you, stay awhile."

She sat down near me and began to explain that she was alone. Her mother, who owned the café, was ill upstairs. The old woman had taken to bed the day before with a fever and a rattle in her throat and it was something to bring worry. For a time we sat and talked and drank coffee together. We mused on the morning waters of the nearby river, the sanctuary stillness of the Place Dauphine before dawn, before the automobiles and people come; and we talked about travel and the long passage of time. Then, abandoning the cups and kettles, the woman started the weary walk up the stairs to check on her sleeping mother.

I muse on this sometime later, when outside the day has risen. With the cold sun in its zenith, I sit by the sacred stove which pours pleasant blue flames. Now and then I gaze out the window at the deserted square—always silent and empty of automobiles and passers-by, always the army of morning streetlamps glowing gold, dissolving into a sky swelling with lightness. In the blistery warm café on the Place Dauphine, I sit and think of Anne-Sophie, once called Victoria. And on my tablet of fine birch paper, with my own heroic pen, I write the events of the last night past—a singular time I will always keep tucked in my mind, as I go my wandering way.

6th Soliloquy

In the Mountains…

In the mountains my spirit was as vast and as still and free-moving as the shafted firmament of sky above bearing the moon's happy shards. Like a plywood painted stage for cloth-sewn shepherds with ready flocks abundant of fleece, cotton for wool, and carrying good barrels to drink, so was this scene of the cutout mountains passing slowly by as I, a winter voyager, walked the snow-caked road on that January night.

Now was my birthday. I might have had thirty years, though I may have been infinitely older or younger. The moon was full and white as a drop of clear water. The road I walked down ran high over sheer cliffs leading down to a valley, the mountains of the Haute-Savoie steeping on either side. This was a glorious life!

Beneath a bridge I o'er passed, walking along in the moonlight, ran a brittle mountain stream. How to command the quality of such a stream? I had no way, though I believed it was brittle.

7ᵗʰ Soliloquy

Back in Paris after an alpine revelry...

My train piled into the Gare de Lyon. It was ten o'clock at night: that singular hour, peculiar and undistinguished. The métropolitain zipped fast underground. I surfaced to the streets at the Palais Royal and started off towards the Left Bank. I walked like a winter stick on a balance beam across the Pont des Arts, on past the golden *coupole* of the Institut de France. I was headed to call on the beautiful Nadja in her apartment on the rue Jacob. She had hailed me in the mountains with a gracious invitation the way the shore hails the sight of a weary sailor when favorable winds are abound. Pleasant stairs took me up to her lofty room.

"Aleksandre?" she called from behind her easel.

"Aye, good girl! Let me see what you're working on."

I went to have a look.

Nadja smiled and showed me her picture, saying that I had inspired the theme. *The Death of Calypia*, she called it, after one of the operas I'd composed. In it, a young girl with blood-burnished legs was draped over a cot in a clearing of woods.

"I wanted to walk down to the bridge before you came," she said, "but it was too cold. It gets so cold in Paris!" Nadja had a peculiar fondness for bridges. "…Never mind that. I cooked for you."

She had indeed cooked for me: well-cured foods from her native land. A winter meal heavy of sauce, fine of spice, and not lacking in wine. I kissed the fair girl as she placed her brushes aside to attend to boiling pots. Sweet hopeful Nadja… she had paint dabbed on the backs of her elbows and on her wrists. Sapphire-eyed and supple-skinned Nadja… when I had met her, her skin was copper like silt in the twilit summer sun. Now she'd traded her gold for winter white. Thinking back of that time when we met…

It was long about summer, a year and a half ago, on the rocky beaches of Croatia. Nadja was alone by the water, sitting. The way she reclined on the sand, her glistening bronze body balanced on her elbows, wrists set pressing softly against sun-browned hips, her body making no effort, having no anxiety. Her long legs, like the stems of golden spoons, were extended outwards. Her back sloped magnificently as she looked out over the water, squinting to see, or not to see, in the bright sunlight. One guessed she was studying the sun's effects on the waves rippling across the Adriatic, or was looking blankly in thought, or was not thinking of anything, but just allowing the healthy oil-dark sun to play on the surface of her skin. Her hair was made straight and almost black with a semi-matte sheen from the saltwater. Every few moments, she'd take her gaze off the sea and put her golden chin down against her collarbone to examine her tummy which was small and firm and went in a gentle slope to where it disappeared beneath the taut elastic of her bathing suit. She wore no top as she tanned. On her body, her breasts rose and sat firmly and beautifully on her chest—one would say drops of sweet honeycomb wax were dripping from a candle. As the sun dropped over the horizon and shade was cast upon us, she covered her bare breasts with her bikini top and it was only then we spoke for the first time.

She said she was on the coast traveling with her father. They had a summer villa alongside a tiled road, on a sunny stretch of land beyond the ruins of the Roman palace that crowned the aquatic city. Her father, she said, was a serious man who stayed in to work all days and throughout the evenings, while she, Nadja, spent most everyday at this beach trying to make her skin as evenly dark as the sunburnt rocks along the shore. She told me in her manner of attractive indifference that she was planning to go to Paris to study painting, and she was happy to learn that I lived there. I gave her an address of where she could write to me and said I would be happy to familiarize her with the city, if and when she came; and the two of us walked up the road to a peninsula where some strange flowers were growing. She walked barefoot, with a light yellow cloth wrapped around her waist, hips swaying as rhythmically as a dancer's, as effortlessly and unconsciously as only a very young girl walks; her top stayed comfortably bare but for a bikini on a thin strap. I wore pleasant sandals on my well-traveled feet and felt the hot sun on my own skin as we strolled along. At a restaurant on the peninsula, we sat on the patio together and ate dinner and drank cold sweet Dalmatian wine. Nadja's suntanned throat swallowed with tranquil pleasure as she looked out at the wayward sea and talked coolly to me. She talked then as she talked now.

Now that she was in Paris studying painting as she had said she would, she often came over late at night, or invited me to come, and hear tender words about her pleasures. She told wild stories, often making references to things past, always over wine or coffee or a lip's embrace, her mouth loved sensual joys. On her first night I visited her in the apartment her father rented for her on the rue Jacob, we made love and laid long together. My hand rested gallantly on her hip bone, knowing that no other raptures could be as fine. she told me of the house she had to herself with a walled garden in a city of tiled rooftops and winding canals—a city far east of the islands of the breezy Dalmatian Coast where we'd come to know one another. She mentioned too having had a lover back home, a young man of a sensitive nature, who had come to a tragic end somehow or other—something involving a revolver and a basement room. As I find such generalizations about suicides to be vulgar and in poor-taste, I always changed the subject when she spoke about it.

Then a false spring came in February and lasted a week; and each morning Nadja would walk up to Montmartre to paint watercolor scenes of the warm, sunlit cobbled streets. She came to see me often after with a pouting mouth and a look of defeat.

"I will try again tomorrow if it's sunny," she would say.

The first painting she was happy with, she presented to me as a gift. She kissed me on the mouth and slid it under the bed, asking me to promise not to show it to anyone. I told her it was beautiful and gave my promise, saying I would show it to no one.

PLATE 01 – Nadja's Triumph in the False Spring.

8th Soliloquy

The "Coming of Spring" Soliloquy

At last, the true spring finally came and the first warm days of April brought the lofty trees of the Parc Monceau to sweet flower and leaf. Glory is the light on the crests of the trees; glory is the light on the ancient rooftops scattered about this holy city!

In the room where I came this season to set mighty pen to holy craft, I stand at the window and look out at the spring day, feeling the bright sun refracting off the retinas of my eyes. Look there! Look down at the flowering leaves near the Roman temple in the garden. Look at the colonnades! Look at white-hatted girls being carried along by the wind!

I turned from the window and poured a glass of clean water from a pitcher to drink and asked myself… "Why stay in on this glorious day to slave like a draught-horse over admirable tasks? Is it not the coming of spring? I should go outside!"

So saying, I vowed to dress in boyish clothes and run outside and across the boulevard to the Parc Monceau; there I would find a sunny *pelouse* beneath a colorful tree. In such a place, I would dash off a carefree line or two.

So I was convinced, and dressing in white clothing, I sought a slice of fresh paper to write an ode to spring. But, heed me now, I would not bring a heroic pen . . . No! I will only bring a simple crayon, a stripling's pencil, a child's chalk. And beneath a simple tree, I will dash off the first lines that come into my head. Thus I was resolved, and wrapping a Swiss foulard around my happy neck, I ran out of the door and down the stairs and out into the street, I crossed then into the garden.

Beneath a gentle tree, I wrote my ode to spring...

Not to waste the spring
I threw down everything,
And ran into the open world
To sing what I could sing...
To dance what I could dance!
And join with everyone!
I wandered with a reckless heart
beneath the newborn sun.

First stepping through the blushing dawn,
I crossed beneath a garden bower,
counting every hermit thrush,
counting every hour.

When morning's light was ripe at last,
I stumbled on with reckless feet;
and found two nymphs engaged in play,
approaching them stirred no retreat.

With naked skin, their weaving hands,
in form akin to Calliope's maids,
shook winter currents from their hair
to weave within them vernal braids.

I grabbed the first, who seemed the stronger
by her soft and dewy leg,
and swore blind eyes,
Lest I find I,
before Diana, a hunted stag.

But the nymphs they laughed,
and shook their heads.
and begged I drop beseeching hands.
For one was no goddess, the other no huntress,
merely two girls at play in the early day.

"Please come to us, with unblinded eyes,
and raise your ready lips.
We will wash your mouth with watery sighs,
weave you springtime with our fingertips."

So the nymphs they spoke,
we kissed and laid,
by noontime's hour,
our love was made,
Like braided chains of crocus stems,
We lay entwined, I laid with them,

Our breath, one glassy, tideless sea,
Our bodies draping wearily.
We slept, I slept so lucidly,
with hopes to stay this memory.

I woke in dusty afternoon,
Alone, the nymphs had left too soon,
I searched where perched upon my knees
Heard only larks' songs in the trees.
"Be you, the larks, my far-flung maids?
With lilac feet and branchlike braids...
Who sing sweet odes to my elation,
in your larking exaltation!"

With these, my clumsy, carefree words,
The birds they stirred and flew away,
"Be I, poor Actaeon," I cried, "Be dead...
Before they, like Hippodamia, be gone astray!"
Yet these words, too late, remained unheard,
By lark, that parting, morning bird.
I looked upon its parting flight,
and smelled the coming of the night;
desirous, I gazed upon its jaunt,
as Leander gazes Hellespont.

Now the hour was ripe and dark,
sensuous memories of sunlight past,
I stood alone in garden bowers

and asked the value of my hours.

Time was spent or time was tossed,

Life was loved and life was lost.

I kissed the flesh of tender girls,

I heard the songs of vernal birds.

I gazed upon the blushing light,

aware of day before the night.

So let me ask and hear a thought:

Did I live the spring I'd sought?

It's true in joy, I walked along,

took part in dance,

and sang the song.

and never tried to bind an hour

to my borrowed garden bower;

nor did I once entreat

a day to slumber at my feet.

Yet days aren't lulled by lyric song,

like morning birds they pass along,

o'er crests of trees, to none belong;

o'er crests of trees of drying dew,

their larking flight, my hands, eschew

Thus I'll say it once and true…

From all that I saw,

and everywhere I wandered,

I learned that time cannot be spent,

It only can be squandered.

Thus I finished my ode to spring and was not at all unhappy about the way it turned out. There were a few details to touch up, a couple rough lines in the antistrophe, but that could all be done later. I had to think now of how I could use it in my hero's tale. How could it be sung in such an opera with so many sweeping laments? I knew it would have to be while my hero is wasting away on a far-flung island. He'll be given a reminiscence of youth and springtime grandeur. There, he will set out on discovery and return to sing his findings. Perhaps at the end, he laments the passage of time. Better clarify...

Beneath the tree, in the grass, I picked up once again my childish chalk with the aim to write, paused a moment . . . then feeling a fresh dose of April air, I sighed and set the pen down again and peered at the sun coming through the branches overhead. It was a sacred day! No, let it not pass . . . but if it must pass, let me wander again to prolong the joy, if I only could...

All this while inspiring and expiring, a rustle in the grass could be heard to my side. I looked over then and noticed a new girl was sitting not far off on a little torn blanket. I looked away and then again. She was dusting crumbs from her lap. Her lip was full and drooping. At her solitary picnic, she sat deflated in grief. I squinted to see closer . . . Aye!, she was a lady, sweet in years; young yes, but no mere girl . . . "Young lady!" I called over, "Why are you pouting?"

The girl turned to me but said nothing.

"Why are you pouting," I repeated myself, "for is it not just now the coming of spring? And besides, you are past the age of pouting!"

"We are never past the age of pouting!" she called back to me.

"Dear girl!" I cried, and with this I stood up and went to charm her. Rather, to enchant her into feeling a bit of joy on this singular day. Did she want to read my ode to spring? No? Well, we could walk together...

This, I suggested. One could easily find a pleasant terrace nearby. We'd need only to pass through the gates. Was she coming?

I took her hand, held it a moment, then let it drop. Her face fell like the shadows on the poplar trees when a cool cloud passes beneath the generous sun. The day was still young in years and growing warmer. I had more exploring to do, alone on my own.

Whereat the sun sat in its zenith, I wanted to call to it from a solitary place. There and only then could I truly finish my ode to spring. Besides, although this girl was sweet: tender of face, with youthful breasts, excellent in their form; her countenance was rather fallen and grim for such a grandiose season; and I knew from the pallor of her thighs and the tint in her eyes, that while we might know passion, we would not know the kind of youthful love as is fitting for spring. Thus I let her go...

And wander far, my dear! . . . With words such as these, I found myself turned away and passing on my own beneath the stones of the great rotunda.

Out on the boulevard, I walked again as absorbent as ever. I was fully aware that the sun was soaking into my blood stream at a pace that no human had ever before experienced. Only an accidental meeting with someone I knew could pull me out of this blissful state. Just then, it happened! I was tramping down the Boulevard de Courcelles, happily alone, when I heard the voice of familiar fawn pass over my shoulder...

"Well if it isn't Monsieur de Quincy!"

At first these words meant nothing to me. I kept at my pace.

"Frederic!" the high-pitched voice called again. I then realized some female had spotted me, and was addressing me by one of my more seldom-used identities. I turned to see who it was...

"Good girl!" I cried, "I thought you were in Berlin!" It was sweet Katell. She was holding a silver makeup case and a tiny purse.

"I forgot something!" she laughed. She looked fresh. Her eyes were brushed with yellow powder like the legs of a summer bee. I kissed her. "Will you walk with me?" she asked.

I nodded and lent my arm and the two of us began to walk towards Clichy.

"I just have to get a couple things from an apartment up here," she mentioned, after we were well on our way down the Boulevard Malesherbes, "Did you get my postcard?"

I told her I did.

"What are you doing in the eighth?"

"I was in the seventeenth a minute ago. You led me over here."

"Oh! So I did!"

"I was in the park, writing and thinking. When are you going back to Berlin?"

"Tonight," she said. And did I want to come?

"Good girl, no! You know I never leave Paris."

"But you just sent me a card from the Alps!"

"Did I really?" I asked. I was surprised. "Well, maybe it is so. But I only leave Paris when I'm dragged away without my knowing."

"Tu dis n'importe quoi!" she laughed, "Let's take a drink here…"

The two of us sat at a terrace at the Place Saint-Augustin, in full sunshine. I ordered drinks and Katell ran off to get some things from an apartment nearby. I closed my eyes and felt the sun warm my eyelids; and, with joy in my heart, I thought of the work I would undertake that evening. My hero's tale was abloom in my head. I knew exactly where the warrior was. He was prospering fine.

Katell came back a moment later and stood before me holding a papier-mâché parrot, traveling bag, and a silver bracelet. "Do you need some métro tickets," she asked me. "I have some."

"No thanks. I prefer to walk in the spring."

"Do you know what this is?" she asked, pulling a burnished metal stick from her bag. She held it up.

"A strigil?"

"How did you know?"

She sat down beside me and we both pulled off the cool lotus-seed wine from tall glasses. Katell explained her strigil, telling me the story of how she had wandered away from Rome. She found herself in a strange neighboring city where the people spoke no language at all, but only made sounds, like: *bar-bar-bar!* She tried to find out what kind of people they were, but no one could understand her when she greeted them in the many languages she knew. "Barbarians!"

...It was while she was walking down a dusty street fashioned of cracked clay, that she came upon a dark little doorway. She peered inside and saw there were some women inside, dressed in muslin sheets. 'At least they are women,' she thought, 'Here I may be safe to sit until I figure out where I am!'

It was here in this room that an old woman with sun-baked skin tried to wheedle her Italian money from her. Katell gladly gave one coin, but that was all. The woman led her into a dry room that was hot. Chars were glowing in a crude furnace. Sweet Katell was asked to lie down, which she did; and the woman proceeded to instruct her on some useful thigh exercises. With the heat and the exertion, Katell sweated a great deal; and when she was done, a robust old hag came in to dust her skin with purple spices.

I listened and had a good smile imagining young Katell all dusted with purple spices on her bare breasts, tiny buttocks and soft calves, all colored in sweat. "But it was really grimy!" she said, and told me how she was caked in mud and spice and sweat and dirt and all kinds of filth, and standing naked in this dark hot room, the two old women began to scrape the grime off her with these strigil tools. They scraped her off and flung the grime on the walls, to where it stuck and fastened like plaster; and then she felt cool and clean and light as they began to dust her with cold water and white powder. Following this exercise, Katell was dressed in a robe and was led to a bright open courtyard where she was offered a place to lie and dry in the sun. The women made up her face, dusted her eyes with color: lemon yellow, as she requested. The queenly Katell, upon leaving their care, had the audacity to ask to keep a strigil tool for her future travels. The old hag handed it over and young Katell skipped away fresh and beautiful. She found Rome later without any trouble.

"And how do you like living in Berlin?" I asked her.

"I'm moving to Turkey next week."

"Of course you are."

"Really though! I was just at the Turkish embassy for my visa before I ran into you. That's the main reason why I'm in Paris." She said all this holding out her proud and long-traveled passport for display.

"Why Turkey of all places? Is it that you want to go find the sacred citadel of Troy?"

"How did you know?"

"Clever girl," I laughed. We smiled and we drank and felt the cool lotus-seed wine softening our spirits. I kissed her and she squeezed my hand and asked if I would consent to leave Paris to visit her in Turkey, and this time I said, "Perhaps."

"We have a house in the desert there."

"Who is we?"

"My friend Julie, me, and her aunt."

An aunt, I considered, and slowly my thoughts drifted away. An aunt in the sand and heroic thoughts of the far-tossed Turkish desert made me forget for a moment this idyllic vernal day…

"What are you doing later?" Katell put forth suddenly to interrupt my thoughts.

"Laboring through the day," I said idly, "Laboring in the spring." Then, "Wait! Katell! Just a moment!" I had an idea. I left the terrace and ran into the café and over to the zinc of the bar to ask for a slip of paper, since the one sheet of paper I'd left the house with was covered, every speck, in the ink scrawls of my ode to spring. The barman furnished me with a clean sheet and I took my pen from my happy pocket and immediately began to write these lines…

Not to waste the spring
I threw down everything,
And ran into the open world

To sing what I could sing...
To dance what I could dance!
And join with everyone!
I wandered with a reckless heart
beneath the newborn sun.

I then paused and wrote...

Not to waste the spring
I ceased my laboring,
and ran out in the open world
to join with everything!
To dance what I could dance!
To sing what could be sung!
I wandered in an open door
wherever there was one.

I set down the pen and examined what I had written. 'This!' I thought, 'This is more correct! . . . Not, *I ran out in the open world to sing what I could sing* . . . No, not that! Saying this would mean I am performing, when actually what I wanted to express was that I was a spectator . . . I ran out in the open world *to join with everything!*'

I smiled to myself and took another look over what I had written at first, beneath that tree in the park. 'Wait!' I stopped myself, taking a closer inspection. A vague feeling that something was awry crept over me. 'Indeed,' I thought, '*Ceased my laboring* is closer in meaning than *threw down everything,* for I didn't really *throw down everything,* I just ended my indoor labors. Yes, *threw down everything* was not quite accurate in meaning. Accurate, no, but closer in feeling! Do you see what you've done, my good poet? *Ceased my laboring* is too dry to express the feeling of leaping outside to experience the holiness of spring. There's that and also . . . but wait! The second version *is* better. I ran out *to join with everything.* Not just *to sing what I could sing.* Singing is an exhalation. I went out to inhale as well as to exhale . . . to inspire and expire. Singing expires audibly but only *silently* inspires. My inspirations were greater at that moment that what I exhaled.' With these thoughts, a feeling of defeat began to seep in. 'No,' I thought, 'The first version was better after all! Wait! Perhaps, *I threw down everything, to join with everything.*' I paused. 'Throw down everything to *join with everything...*? Utter nonsense!'

"Complete nonsense!" I exclaimed aloud, crumpling up the paper, rapping my fingers on the bar, "It was better the first time!" And with a fallen heart, I left the zinc of the bar and returned to the terrace to reclaim sweet Katell. She was busily sitting out there unpacking and repacking her traveling bag.

"What did you find?" she asked.

"Nothing," I replied, "absolutely nothing."

Katell then began to talk and tell me a story, and while she was busy talking, a last idea occurred to me...

'This... *I wandered in an open door, wherever there was one.* This is gorgeous! I must keep these lines. But *wherever there was one* must be preceded by *sing what could be sung.* But if I *throw down everything* as was decided, I have to go into the open world to *sing what I could sing.* As I can't very well *throw down everything to join with everything*—that is nonsense! But I *sing what I could sing* up there, I can't *sing what could be sung*, later on . . . thus, *I wandered through an open door wherever there was one* must be proceeded by *to dance what I could dance, beneath the newborn sun . . .* That's it!' '*...To Dance what I could dance! / beneath the newborn sun! / I wandered through an open door wherever there was one.*' A short-lasted feeling of triumph surged my breast. I realized then I'd not found the key. 'Nonsense, again! If I was happy beneath a newborn sun, why on earth would I wander into doorways? What is beyond doorways besides shade? Good poet, you are losing the sense!' Was it the wine that was making me lose my skillful thoughts? I yearned at this moment to be back alone at the desk where worked I with goodly ink, bearing no trace of wine in my brain; only then could I resume my admirable task.

'Leave me now to return to the world and the moment and forsake any modifications to that which was perfect to begin with!'

...So thinking, I left off thinking and returned my ear to sweet Katell...

"...And he had the nerve to put it on my plate!" she roared with laughter, "Can you believe it?! . . . Everywhere in Africa where I went, there were peppers stuffed in the goat meat, and the meat itself was covered in hair. As if they didn't pluck it! Can you imagine?!"

No, I couldn't, but it sounded interesting what fair Katell was saying. I was sorry I'd missed the beginning.

Shade cast itself over the Place Saint-Augustin as a swift cloud o'er took the sun, and coolness fell on the brow of the powerful iron Jeanne d'Arc on her leaping bronze steed. I looked to the cool sky and missed the warmth that perhaps I'd only imagined. I looked at my watch. It was the eighteenth hour, that roguish hour that seems to steal earlier, fresher hours with almost imperceptible stealth. What have I missed?, I wondered, and turning to Katell I asked her...

"Good girl, what are you going to do before you leave tonight?"

"I have to take a coffee with a girlfriend in the fifth."

"Sure," I said, "well I will be off, I have much work to undertake." And so I left it, kissing Katell and wishing her well until the next time we would see each other. I flew off, off towards the Madeleine, my head spinning about my shoulders as I tried to spot the sun.

"Not only is it behind a cloud, but it is behind the buildings as well!" I cried, feeling as though I'd missed something of the coming of spring . . . as though when the sun had shone in the day my eyes were not as open as wide as they could have been to receive its light . . . as though my body did not receive the sun's heat to its fullest potential. Had I missed something? Or was that it? That couldn't have been it! For the first time I felt spring had come and set in without the rush. It had rained in the weeks before, petrichor had scented the air, but I hadn't felt the delights of spring. Then I thought it was just a matter of the sun. Today it shone vibrantly, I sought it fervently, I felt it but I didn't meet it! I wanted to become like that sun—ancient and ageless.

…All the while my thoughts were rambling on, I was walking on, looking around me I passed a spray of columns—Doric, Ionic, Corinthian. How did I get here? Over there is the Opéra! And here is Place du Pont Neuf! How am I already at the Place du Pont Neuf? I will just cross the Pont Bizarre, and then I will sort things out. At least it is only April. I will have time to work tonight and fathom the comings and goings of spring later on.

It was while I was passing the bouquinistes' book carts along the river, I felt a draft of strangely warm wind. It was a dry city wind, so arid that it sifted apart the white flowers that had gathered beneath a bouquiniste's stall. These wind-dried petals flit across the pavement, dusting it like patisserie flour dusts a bakery board. The warm wind passed me and seeped into all around me—sweet plants in the river, garbage on the street, the wood of the rocking boats beneath the crepuscular bridges—and new and old fragrances filled me, reminding me of the past, of ancient cities where I'd walked, of strange countries I'd wandered through, of conversations I'd had with old and newfound friends on ship bows, in unfamiliar houses, on fast traveling trains, and far-flung fields. And I knew the grace of spring was around me, but like a tender untrained maid, like a wild steed one rides on a sandy ocean shore, it had to be listened to and known. And now it was already gone, but I carried with me a single vision on up the rue des Saints-Pères where the café owners were dumping the day's eggshells on the sidewalk: that of the fragrant white petals, floury and soft, dusting the garbage along the edge of the river. I recall that strongly now that night has fallen. Now that we sit on the moonlit terrace with our wine, talking wildly of things to come.

9th Soliloquy

The "Victory Horse" Soliloquy

Let me sing of an evening in spring…

The sweet month of May had begun, and a lofty breeze was blowing warm winds through the trees along the quais of the Seine. I was walking alone to assemble with friends to feast and celebrate those new pleasant nights that follow blue-skied days. It was a holiday throughout the city and the shops and markets were closed. The restaurants too were closed and it seemed like everyone had gone to the country or had otherwise disappeared.

At the Palais Royal, I met with long-tried friends. In the square by the métropolitain stairs, we stood and planned our evening of victory. All were inspired by the arrival of a good friend: clever-tongued Mich, who had just flown in from Madrid where he'd almost married a tender-lipped Spaniardess, daughter of a well-groomed father who knew of vast land and fortune.

"We'll drink on the terraces at Place des Vosges," some proposed.

"The city is empty for the day and night," others sighed, "the chairs will have been brought in, and there will be no one to serve us."

"We can feast on the riverside, at the Place du Pont Neuf, near the emerald garden, on the well-worn historic stones."

"There will be no wine to drink!"

"That's right, the stores are all closed."

"And the restaurants too. Nowhere will we find a bottle."

It was then, that I devised a heroic plan. "Come, men," I said to the group, "Let us walk to Saint Germain. We will have our wine and our feast amid the river tides and the emerald leaves of the garden!"

So saying, I led my good friends away; well-tailored Niels and clever-tongued Mich among them.

When we reached the rue des Quatres Vents in Saint Germain, I bid my friends wait outside. I could hear them whispering amongst themselves, anticipating the plan. All the while, I slid up to where I could creep to the high windows above that tidy organic wine-shop: *La Crémerie*, where the honored Pierrot, man of many crafts, sold goodly wines, so sweet to drink.

Pierrot was in his nest asleep when I tapped on the windowpane. He crossed his bedroom in his night-hat and opened the pane...

"Good Pierrot-le-fou!" I cried in a hush, clasping my hands, "I have a rowdy band outside, and the city is closed down. Nothing to be had elsewhere. We must find libations for our celebratory feast. Help us out with an array of your sweet and ready wines!"

...So saying, I procured from my waist a small stack of crisp bills, newly minted money, rich in colored inks, the kind that pleases all men. Patient Pierrot, man of many crafts, took the offering and bid me climb down to the courtyard and wait for him to dress and descend. So I did, and passing through the street, I signaled success to my waiting comrades and disappeared through the shadows into the long courtyard.

Out back, in a courtyard that resembled a stable where beasts are kept, I awaited for Pierrot to arrive. He quickly appeared and led me out to a place where the floor was packed of straw. A door of wood led down to the wine cave. Near the door, there were several large casks of wine.

"Will this do?" Pierrot asked, motioning to the casks. And what casks they were! Rich in wood, immense in stature and breadth; five casks in all, all bearing brass handles and inlaid lids.

"Pierrot!" I exclaimed, clasping my friend by the collar, "See what you have done! A mighty bacchanal will this wine fuel. I will take all five!"

"How many are you?" he asked. And I stopped to consider my friends who awaited. There was Mich, our clever-tongued guest, and thoughtful Niels, man of foreign lands, and swift-footed Aurélien among us. There was another too: a hefty Dane, hailing from Copenhagen; he had appeared quite suddenly among us, claiming noble kin. Apparently he was the nephew of some flowery Danish princess. He was tagging along our merry group, which made us five men in all. The rest, gentle women included, would be summoned later when we'd arrive at the Place du Pont Neuf with our new-found wine.

"Will you be joining us too?" I asked Pierrot.

"No, my friend. I have to work early tomorrow."

I looked at the fruitful casks. It would take two men to carry each one, so vast were they, so heavy in form and tall in stature . . . yet two casks alone would not serve the feast I had in mind. I had to develop my stately plan.

"Have you any wood?" I asked Pierrot, "wood for building, sturdy nails, and rope for binding too?"

Looking at me kindly, patient-minded Pierrot said, "I have plenty of wood! . . . wood, good for building; with sturdy nails, ropes and tools too."

Hearing thus, I told Pierrot I would go fetch one of my men. Only one, though, for the pounding of nails disturbs no city-dweller at night, but the commotion of too many men does cause fear in urban hearts.

Out on the street, I retrieved strong-handed Aurélien, and the two of us returned through the shadows of the courtyard to the place out back. There, Pierrot was waiting with nails and tools, wood and ropes to tie with.

"What is your idea?" asked Aurélien as he calculated my words.

With his question, I set forth to explain my idea to build what I called a 'Porte-Tonneau.' . . . "It will involve large uprights shafts," I said, "cranes to carry each tonneau. Each cask will be tied by the rope and slung around the top-most crest. All of this will be compact—two casks on each side, and one trailing. The Porte-Tonneau will be on sturdy wheels of wood. Two men alone, it will take to wheel these five casks. A third will be stationed behind to watch the load and the other two men will make merry. All together, we five men will usher these five casks through St-Germain until we reach the statue at Pont Neuf, and from there, we will set one man to guard the casks, while the other four take trips descending the stone steps to the riverside place where we'll feast with the celebratory wine!"

"Some idea you have founded!" exclaimed my friend, swift-footed Aurélien, as he smiled wide at my ingenuity. The two of us then set about to work. We hammered long and hard, sending slim nails flying into moist wood. We set the shafts upright and secured them, set the crane above those. Fatedly, when we hoisted the casks onto the crane, calculating Aurélien forgot to firmly fasten the crane over the shafts.

Once these tasks were achieved, we had the wheels to firmly bolt. This was done by means of stout wooden pegs. After, we said good night to my generous friend, patient Pierrot, man of many crafts, and he wished us well in our revelry. And, setting off, we began to wheel the Porte-Tonneau out through the long courtyard towards the street. An ingenious machine, it was light enough for two men to wheel, though its load was not light... five industrious casks full of gorgeous ready wine!

Aurélien and I wheeled the great Porte-Tonneau out into the rue des Quatres Vents. The band of merry men, clever-tongued Mich, well-tailored Niels and the hefty Dane, were huddled on the corner awaiting us; and all came to meet our bounty with glad hearts and outstretched hands.

"Some feast this will fuel!" they all cried. And, with our spirits high and ascending we all set out to wheel the great Porte-Tonneau through the rue des Quatre Vents, past the closed up markets of Saint Germain, off towards the quais of the Seine.

On the rue de Montfaucon, strong-handed Aurélien took over watching the flank of the great wheeling Port-Tonneau from the backside, while our royal Danish foundling took over the weight on the right side. Those savior casks of wine wobbled only slightly on their hefty ropes tied to that crane, strong as the neck of a fine-bred steed, and the wheels rolled nicely over the cobblestones. Foreign-born Mich, good at fierce tasks, pushed on the left side of the Porte-Tonneau. With all of this, I was freed up to observe all that passed on the narrow streets.

Passing down the smooth stone streets beneath flickering gas lamps, our singing group marched, proud of the feat we had achieved. I looked to the left and saw a tall wooden house with a closed-up bakery on the ground floor. Next to it was an open cobbler's workshop. A heavy-handed cobbler in an apron stood in the doorway hammering out a pair of animal-hide shoes in the darkness of night. What a sight! Was this a medieval town-centre, or modern-day Paris?

On the rue de Buci, we passed a blacksmith stoking a fire to hammer out glowing rods of iron. On the rue de Seine, we saw peasant woman taking a child to leave it to be exposed. Somewhere along the way, thoughtful Niels, man of many myths, procured a sort of tin canister with ridges; and, using a small wooden baton to swipe at its side, he made a rhythm that we could all march to. We all had our hearts set on the great feast that would be made with our wine down along the quai.

Down the rue Jacques Callot, our mighty Porte-Tonneau, machine of *my* clever invention, rolled smooth and ardently, and we could see the quai in sight, just beyond the rue Guénégaud. We had only to cross the wide street, veer to the right, and dispatch our machine to the midway point of the old Pont Neuf. It was when half of this plan had been achieved, that the grim moment of the journey befell us.

Alas, good Aurélien, clear of calculations, left his watchful post behind the rear flank of the Porte-Tonneau so that he could walk beside the machine and sound a festive melody through the pipes of a long tin flute. A merry song it was and it brought us even more joy to hear swift-footed Aurélien's goodhearted song; still, our clever friend, so good at careful tasks, had obviously been thinking more of the feast that was to come than the task at hand back when he and I had constructed the Porte-Tonneau, because he had forgot to firmly fasten the crane over the shafts of the machine. So, while Aurélien piped his merry flute, and clever Mich and high-born Niels were occupied with playing the canister and singing; and while the hefty Dane and I were on either side of the Porte-Tonneau pushing for the benefit of all, and guiding the machine along, that careful and ingenious Porte-Tonneau began to deconstruct at the top-most part.

It first happened that the crane, thick as the neck of a well-bred steed, toppled down from the shaft. Immediately after, the first sacred cask of goodly wine on the Dane's side fell and stretched the rope taut. But the rope wasn't short enough for such a descent, and that ill-lucked cask was dashed upon the street; its plies of wood split and the moist contents were spilled! With that weight of that cask gone, the rest of the evenly-balanced load was thrown off and the remaining four casks followed the first. Their magnificent bodies, so wide of girth, fell on their ropes and struck the bricks of the street, spilling purple wine across the ground.

To tell now of the great and silent gasp we men made when those casks were dashed upon the street! As the vessels simultaneously fell and cracked open on the bricks, we good men all leapt back, eyes cast wide, and great horrible sighs of lamentation escaped our heroic mouths. To tell of the wine that flowed... rich and fragrant wine, all lost upon the street. Such horror men do not often see. Not *one* prosperous cask of fragrant wine was spilt; no, *five* casks in all! Five hearty vessels of wine were thrown from that machine. And we men were helpless there to watch it. As hard as it is to watch a mother spill tears over her son who is laying dead on a battlefield, tears like hot rivers streaking down her miserable cheeks; so heartbreaking it was to see that dark-hued wine spill from those bursted containers, those once stately casks.

For many moments, we said nothing as the dark arrays of wine flowed by our feet, as swift as the torrents of the Seine itself, which flowed just over the railing beside us.

"Men!" I finally said, "such is our grief! Surely some god who runs across the swift sky have we angered to let this fate befall us." So I spoke, and my men's descending hearts gave heed. "Let us forget all and wander now to the place to tell the news to any revelers who have gathered in anticipation of our feast." The men stood before me with bowed heads, keeping their eyes closed to keep from seeing the sad sight of that river of wine flowing along the banks of the Seine. My own gaze drifted up skyward, and I saw the stout crane of the Port-Tonneau, now free of burdens, dangling with its torn ropes overhead. Thoughtful Niels asked that we all close our eyes and share no more in that miserable sight. "Come men," we all said, and all heeded our words, "Please let us forget this." And so saying, we all set about to deconstruct the great Porte-Tonneau, so that no latecomers or passersby would get insight into our clever device. Swift-footed Aurélien, good at vast calculations, set about the hardest task of freeing the wheels and the shafts from the heavy base and moving them to the steps leading down to the river. He labored hard in lament of his error of having forgotten to firmly fasten the crane to the shafts back when he and I had built the machine. I knew his lament was unfounded, no guilt was his, for surely a jealous god led him astray during the construction of that fated machine. Calculating Aurélien was a man of careful measure. Had we initially sacrificed that odd cask to the thirsty gods, the other four would have surely remained whole and in our possession. Four casks of wine can feed a mighty feast. But in our hubristic greed we were robbed of all!

Thus, with the Porte-Tonneau dismantled and scrapped along the quai, with no more wine for a bacchanal, we set about to walk unhindered to the Place de Pont Neuf, that stretch of historic stones beside a garden of emerald leaves. There we would inform the men who had heard rumor of our heroic plan and had arrived for the feast.

At the Place du Pont Neuf, several tried companions had gathered—men rich in years and some youths too. They were waiting for the feast to arrive, as they'd heard rumor of the great caravan of casks trailing through St-Germain. They said women were to arrive soon and described them: beautiful demoiselles, slim in form, colorful of dress, of the kind that give men pleasure to see. Women whose words men enjoy listening to, for the sounds of their voices are high and soft, lofty as the ripples of wind over the wings of some high-soaring bird.

"Shall I call them off?" asked an eager friend named Cedric.

"Aye," we said gloomily, "There will be no feast." And all bowed their heads.

Walking back through the Latin Quarter, I noticed the hefty Dane had taken leave of us . . . So are men who are not tried as friends quick to stray when a feast is befouled. He had slipped away without saying farewell. Us four men, Niels, Aurélien, myself and clever-tongued Mich, continued up Saint Germain as the dark of night deepened in hue and tone. After some time, we noticed Mich was dragging behind. I looked back twice and saw his feet taking clumsy steps.

"You are tired?" we asked.

"Yes, I haven't slept or eaten since Spain. Long trip . . . I think I will go to my hotel and sleep." So he said, our newly-arrived friend, and we of understanding bid him goodnight and turned to continue on.

"He is a good friend, clever Mich," I told my men once we were farther up the boulevard, "I am sorry that we couldn't give him an honored place at a feast, as he has just arrived in Paris today."

"It would be good to do something nice for him," said thoughtful Niels.

Aurélien suggested that we host a daylight feast soon, in his honor, a banquet at the Chalet des Îles in the Bois de Boulogne. This idea brightened our path, and we continued on. Eventually we came to the gates of Luxembourg and my companions turned to me.

"I'm off this way," said Niels, pointing to the Panthéon.

"And I go here," said Aurélien, pointing to the sky.

"So you're both leaving too?" I asked, "Well, I admit there is no point in continuing the evening." So saying, I shook the men's hands and bid goodnight and we all were off in separate ways.

Alone now, I thought of the quiet room in Saint Germain to which I held key. There, I vowed, I would drink a bitter tonic to sleep and try to let the night drag on into a later morning. Such were my morals. Worse was, that it was springtime; and at no time should a man have loftier morals than in the spring. But nay, I was tired and disheartened.

It was then the coincidence occurred…

While I was dragging my weary self across the Place de l'Odéon, head hanging low, a possession took hold of me and forced me to look up. There on the other side of the street, I saw someone I once knew—someone from long ago. As he drew close, and I became certain it was him, a pleasure beyond all comparison charged my veins. My blessed heart ascended.

"Philippe!" I cried out, making swift steps to cross the street. "So long it's been!" He was shaken. He looked at me as though he were one with soft eyes coming into the light after so long spent in darkness—as if he couldn't understand what he was looking at. He seemed bewildered, scattered. His suit was nice, cut in the Swiss fashion, like in long-ago days, but his hair was disheveled and his forehead gleamed of sweat. His handsome face, which in previous times had always appeared as though it were chiseled out of supple stone, marble quarried from fresh northern shores or from the salty beds of the Propontis, now appeared ragged, as though a terrible injury had befallen him.

"Old friend!" I cried as I overtook him. The dullness from his eyes faded as he became aware of whom it was he was seeing. He addressed me by an old-fashioned name, and a great smile leapt across his face. We then clasped arms as do fond brothers when the ripening years bring them to reunite after the long and carefree seasons of youthful travels have reached their inevitable end.

"To think of seeing you here!" we simultaneously rejoiced. And with our rejoicing, all the lamentation for my cracked Porte-Tonneau and the spoiled feast swept out of me and my high spirit ascended. I was instantly flooded with happy memories of those now-faded times we'd spent together. He had been like my brother, Philippe. And those two girls, half-sisters by birth, they had been like our own dear sisters, as well as our fond lovers. Long ago it seemed, now. Many were the friends I knew back then. Many women was I close too. All now mostly faded, yet those two girls would continue to draw my thoughts. I recalled my youthful Pénélope. And her older sister: delicate Themia, born of the same father, though sharing not the same mother's breast.

Here now on the street, with my old friend standing in the light cast by a streetlamp planted in the darkness, it was night. Yet before my eyes it was day, and I was steeped in visions: I saw youthful Pénélope wandering along banks of the Seine, across the bridges, thumbing the amber pendant she wore on her neck. Visions of our travels together: mornings at the window of that little hotel on a Scandinavian street. Later, the ancient piazzas and the beaches in Italy. I remembered our dreams, I remembered our wars. I thought of the sojourns abroad, and that damned rowboat on the Black Sea. I would sit in the boat and work, scribbling notes in preparation of the oeuvres I would one day compose, while Pénélope would row the boat; her head tilted up to take the sun. I recalled the slow waves lapping against the wood of the oars and the gentle line of the shore far in the distance. Oh, great fortune to be reminded of all this!

Then Philippe stirred me from my thoughts…

"Which way are you walking, brother? I'll go with you…"

Philippe clumsily clasped my arm and we began to head down the rue de l'Ancienne Comédie. "Very strange," he said, "I just arrived in Paris this morning…." He seemed out of sorts. He began to explain that he'd been in Monte Carlo on some kind of business—some botched land purchase. He then went on to ask a nervous question, seemingly unrelated, about whether or not I still owned some hat which I never owned. The perspiration was foaming on his forehead. He said he was staying in a hotel across the river and was on the Left Bank quite by accident. "Quite by lucky chance!" he shrieked, wiping the sweat from his eyelids, "Lucky chance! . . . I wasn't supposed to be walking through

Saint Germain tonight. I'm here by pure fluke, etc." His words dropped out and stumbled over each other. He reached into his pocket and withdrew a couple crumpled tickets and started to smooth the creases out with his hands."

I started to feel worried for my old friend. What misfortune has struck him? Has he caught the worm of madness in such a mild season? His eyes resembled two bulbous larvae trembling to grow into winged things.

"Brother!," I exclaimed shaking him, "Have you visions of the present? Speak of the girls! You have recently seen our dear sisters, Pénélope and Themia?"

"Of course," he issued calmly, "I was down on the Mediterranean just a few days ago, visiting them. We were just talking about you! Pénélope is…."

Oh, to hear him mention those two! "…And they are well?" I interrupted him mid-sentence, tossing questions to this and that and therefore… "…ever so long it has been, I have wanted news from you. Recount your story, Philippe, every adventure. Don't leave out a single tale!"

"Old friend," he replied, "even if I had pitchers brimming with potent coffee to wake my thoughts and pry my eyes wide, I couldn't stay awake to tell you every tale. For this business has wearied my limbs through and through. Yet, you are in Paris tomorrow? Let's meet in the morning, near my hotel. We will have breakfast together and tell of our recent pasts, for I have many stories that will make you smile . . . Is the sky turning red? . . . No it's not, I thought it was…

"Anyway," he resumed, "we will plan a trip down to the South of France to see them. They are on the coast, not far from Saint Tropez. Themia is considering buying a large property down there. She wants to settle down. Pénélope will stay with her. Do you want to go see where they might live?"

"Saint Tropez, you say?! So they've returned to France? Did Themia sell her house in Spain? What happened to going to live in Greece? To buying a house on the Peloponnese?" My thoughts raced to the delicate Themia. She always spoke of wanting to settle down in Sparta or Corinth, or on a windy Argolic island, to live by the ever-flowing Aegean Sea.

"I'm afraid Themia gave up on Greece," Philippe responded, dripping anew with milky sweat, "She's in France with Pénélope. They're down on the coast. I'm happy to say they'd like to see you as soon as possible. We can go south this coming Tuesday. Did I say Tuesday? Yes, Tuesday! I am obliged to stay in Paris on business until then. But Tuesday we will go south together!"

"Oh, such a good news this is!" I cried with pleasure abound in my breast, for I thought then I would see Pénélope again in just a few days. My mind drifted back to the last time I saw her…

It was in a room on the rue Montfaucon where I set pen to glorious page every afternoon that summer, writing a tragedy. Pénélope had been sleeping in my bed and was now leaning on the windowsill. The incoming sun washed her face with creamy light. She was naked, except for a white pair of panties and a necklace clasped around her neck. She was proud when she was nude, with her unblemished body, and never tried to cover herself. The necklace was something I'd given her. It was a Russian winterberry encased in a drop of amber. I'd purchased the pendant in St. Petersburg; then, later in Copenhagen, I bought a chain of white gold, thin as gossamer, and presented the pendant on the chain to her when I returned to Paris. The winterberry reflected the sun on her tender chest where it rested as she stood on the bed in her bare feet, leaning her elbows on the windowsill, smiling at me in her pale innocence, her beautiful dark hair tossed across her naked shoulders. I remember those long and slender legs, firm and very young; and that sweet and gorgeous mound encased in white cotton between her legs. It swelled with hot wetness when I touched her. I kissed her lips and her tiny ears and said I would be leaving Paris for a while and we kissed again. Then she dressed and left my room on the rue Montfaucon and I never saw her again after that.

"Oh, such memories I have of us," I sighed to my friend, "Philippe, it is a good plan you speak of. I am counting on you to lead me to those girls. I must see Pénélope again. Tomorrow, we will meet for breakfast, you and I, and plan the affair. Tuesday, we will go to Saint Tropez. Think of it! All of us, together again on a sunny golden shore. What it the name of your hotel?"

"The name of my hotel?" inquired Philippe, scratching his eyelids, "Oh yes!" He took a crumpled paper from his pocket and swiftly wrote the address of the hotel. I looked at the paper:

87 BLVD BEAUMARCHAIS

'...Boulevard Beaumarchais?! What was my friend doing staying in this wasteland?!' . . . I watched him as he licked the wetness on his lips and repeated the address over and over. His eyes swelled strangely as he spoke. His right pupil inflated, while his left eyeball rolled around and wandered here and there.

"Never mind brother," said I, "Until tomorrow! I will come at nine in the morning. We will tell our stories and plan our Tuesday voyage. Until tomorrow!"

"I'll see you at nine! Until tomorrow!" he cried, and flung his hands towards the great concaved sky, and thus disappeared into the dark shadows on the winding boulevard.

"What a night it is!" I sang aloud, once alone, passing the cathedral. I started towards the Faubourg Saint Germain. "Look at these leafy bows tenderly brushing the ivory crowns of these stately houses. Oh, to be a neighbor of this fortune!" Happy I was, walking through the Faubourg, back towards the room to which I held key. I knew great work I would undertake that night! . . . Work of unsurpassable merit! . . . Work of the kind those ancient geniuses tried to buy with hecatombs of grazing kine surrendered in smoke to Calliope's maids . . . Stop! Time to breathe. Time to look around me...

Time to take a glance at my own modern age in a tender European metropolis where gilded skies are dark with storms at night. Nightingales step on loosely-strapped heels out of sleek automobiles. They *click clack, click clack* their sweet little feet across terrace stones braised by hot rain drops. "Bonne soirée!" They wave goodnight, "Je vous embrasse!" … "Bonne nuit!" Then they are gone, off… *vers leurs abris de lune…* is it summer so soon?!

No place ever inspired me to compose illuminated psalms as did the Faubourg Saint Germain. What a beautiful night to go vagabonding through antique Parisian streets… A gorgeous night to breathe the fresh air of creation on balconies, on rooftops, the sky draped over a siren's moistened braids, the stars are pearls nested in her hair; and I laugh as she kisses me. How happy I am tonight!

Vagabonding through the street, all these joyous inspirations flooded me, and I let them build in my happy heart—for I knew that when I returned, I would fall upon my work madly—just as that crazed philosopher fell with his joyful elbows on sprawling piano keys, howling at Dionysus after a lifetime of sober work. I would do like he once did!

Back at the room to which I held key, I looked at the clock on the wall. Two in the morning. I would meet Philippe at nine. In between I would work. A warm wind came through the open window. At the sturdy desk where I set pen to holy craft, I sat before my oeuvre. Sweet ink, run swiftly, I called; sweet ink, drink me gently. Froth on the muse's tongue, black as the lair of the squid in the ocean's depths, milky dark ink of my fair muse, swim well across my happy page…

I worked beautifully for many hours. My hero's tale had now taken the form of the most perfect of all creations. "How glorious is my art!" I rejoiced in the night, "Holy and sublime!" I laughed euphorically as I read over what I had penned…

'The voluptuous voices were singing in unison to announce my hero's long-awaited homecoming. Piloting a swift ship, he skiffed across the jeweled sea from his far-flung island. There he'd been stranded for most of the spring…' …fault of my own, I admit, for I'd been lost a lot of the spring myself in wine-drunk revelries of the most maddening sort. Too much cheer to hear my hero's pleas. But now that a new happiness sat on my lap, my work of art soared like heaven-bound birds in the sky…

'The long-tried hero's ship careened over the ocean swells. Strong were his seaworthy muscles, hoisting the sails. Glad were the songs he sang to triumphant melodies. And the billowing clouds brought forth winds sending him along to his homeland and family, who had been waiting years for his return.'

I walked to the piano in the corner of the room to pound out some thunder in the night. My happy elbows colliding against the piano keys sent shards of lightning to lick the waves, while thunder sent winds that blew the boat landward by night.

'When our hero awoke on the calm sea in the blushing light of early morning, he could see his native land not far off; and there on the land, he could see cooking fires burning and stately cypress trees growing. These things he'd often dreamt of when on his seafaring journey, exploring the world and fighting in distant wars. Around the fires, people were gathered playing pipes and roasting food. Sweet music could be heard!

'As our hero's boat came into shore, he could smell the savory smoke from the fires. With such a glad heart he watched the flames toss lofty billows of smoke into the peaceful sky. The pipes played on and he knew he was home! Stepping onto land, our long-traveled hero dove upon the fertile earth and kissed it plainly, embraced its bounty, rejoicing in the taste of the mineral earth that had given him life!'

I woke up sometime later. I didn't know I'd been sleeping. It seemed an advanced hour. I felt, pressed to the flesh of my tired cheek, the crisp pages covered in wild flourishes of ink, strewn and ruffled. I had been working late, it occurred to me. Then I remembered... I had worked until the little-morning on my hero's homecoming. After, while I was sleeping, I dreamt that I too was traveling by careening ship. I'd come in the night to the faraway land where, in long ago times, my own cradle is fabled to have been perched next to a thriving hearth. I too leapt to the ground upon my homecoming to smell the soil that had raised me and gave me strength. Now awake, seated at a desk in wood-furnished room, I had the sudden fear that I actually was in my native land, that my body was no longer in Paris. "But *my own* 'hero's journey' is not over!" I cried with great alarm, and looked around the room to which I held key. I saw the French electric plugs in the walls and gentle relief crept over me, for I realized that I was still far from my own native land. My wandering had not come full circle. Pleasure filled my soul.

That relief was short lived, however. When I pried my body from the mess of papers on the desk, I recalled I had an appointment to meet Philippe that morning at nine. What time was it?!

I leapt savagely from the chair and ran to see the clock... forty minutes after eight! I had time yet, but I needed to hurry!

Taking a ring of keys and a roll of paper currency to get me along, as well as my traveling pen and some scraps of paper in case I were to come across some ideas on my way, I ran out the door and down the street to cross the river. In a flash, I was on the métro line-one, feeling the cool wind blow through the empty cars as it shuttled along towards Bastille. Come Tuesday, I thought, I will be far from here—on the Côte d'Azur kissing the sun-coated skin of youthful Pénélope.

The métro stopped on the aerial platform at Bastille. I ran with quick steps out of the station, leaving the Opéra Bastille in a peripheral blur. Up the Boulevard Beaumarchais, my good heels made way: number eighty-seven.

It was a shabby hotel from the looks of it. I buzzed the door to the office and let myself in. Inside a dirty little lobby, the attendant was absent. A cat was perched on the desk, when it saw me, it hissed and bayed.

"Come cat!" I called, approaching the desk with an outstretched hand to tame the beast. Yet the feline did not like my gesture, and hissed louder, swiping with its claws in attempt to tear the flesh off my hand. It growled. I thought then to reach for the beast with both hands and seize its little head and snap it at a right-angle, so as to dispatch its soul down to Hades; but before I could let that pleasure fulfill itself, a little fat woman rushed into the lobby from the back room and threw a magazine at the cat to make it scatter. She looked at me and said...

"Gentleman, I'm sorry! My cat nearly gnashed you to pieces! She nearly shredded you to a pulp! Let me see that, is your hand bleeding? No, it's not? . . . Oh, if she had gnashed you, you would have been angry at me. And, I have enough problems without that already. Guests are making a havoc of my hotel, eating my food supply, destroying my linen and property, and leaving without paying! It is a sad couple of days I have been made to pass! Well, no matter. What can I do for you, my good gentleman?"

"I'm here to meet a friend for breakfast. One of your guests. A gentleman from Monte Carlo."

"*Bon Dieu!* I know the one you mean! He is no gentleman, your friend from Monte Carlo!" As she spoke thus, she wrung her hands and spat on the unclean floor. I took a step back and listened, curious about the story but certain she was mistaken about something.

"Let me tell you about your friend from Monte Carlo..." she went on, "...He checked-in yesterday, early in morning. I didn't ask for money up-front because he looked like an upright sort of fellow. It seems I'm too trusting. He said he was in Paris on business until next Tuesday. At all kinds of strange hours, he'd come in and go out. Then, yesterday afternoon, I went to my icebox, that just over here you see, and I found a trout was missing. What would he want to steal a trout for? Most bizarre! But that's not all! . . . Last night, I could hear him crying all night in his room. He had come in late, very late! His clothes were rumpled and he was sweating and nervous. I eyed him suspiciously on account of the trout, but said nothing. He hurried past me and went straight to his room and began weeping and stayed like that the whole night. It was most shameful! I decided then first thing this morning I would go ask for the money for the room and suggest he find somewhere else to lodge. But when I knocked at his room, no one answered. I opened the door and found your friend had gone! He left without paying! His suitcase and clothes were gone! He also soiled the linen and tore the drapes down to build some kind of hut in the middle of the room. I figure he owes me six hundred francs counting all the damage. Then one has to think of that trout! I'd say seven hundred is closer to reality...."

I listened to the old hotelkeeper as she wrung her hands and spat and swore about my friend. I couldn't believe my ears. Had he done all of that? I didn't care about the fish but I thought of my old hardy friend crying all night in his hotel room.   Then I fully realized something terrible... *he had gone!* That was the consequence of all of this!   My friend had left Paris early that morning without giving me any word.   But we were to eat together and plan our trip to the south to meet Themia and Pénélope!   How would I find him now?   I turned halfway around as if to leave.   I didn't want to hear any more about the seven hundred francs he owed the hotelkeeper.   Someday soon, I thought, Philippe and I would meet again and laugh about that old hotelkeeper.

She kept on...

"But don't you think he's going to get away with ruining my hotel and leaving without paying!" she spat, "He signed the register!" With that, the old woman hobbled over behind the desk and withdrew a clipboard and pointed at it.   "Philippe So-and-so, you see, from Monte Carlo.   I have his name right here and I'm going to call the police.   He'll spend some time in jail for ruining my hotel!"

I was brought to full attention with these words of the hotelkeeper, as I find all talk of police to be vulgar and in poor-taste.   So she had his full name, and the town of his birth.   Did she have the number of his residence?   I could benefit from such information.   She didn't?   Still she would call the police anyway and let them track him down.   I couldn't let her do that.   Thus, forsaking all hopes to reunite with my friend that day, and hopes of future meetings with our delightful sisters whom I knew to be basking away on some unknown southern shore; and feeling great benevolent altruism in my heart, the desire to help a friend, I spoke thus to the hotelkeeper—uttering not the truth, but weaving a crafty lie so as to free my friend from shame...

"Listen, Madame," I said, touching her shoulder, speaking caressing words, "I can explain the incident with my friend.   Actually, it's my fault.   I drove him up here from Monte Carlo.   I'm a psychiatrist. Maybe you've heard of me, Doctor Bjørnstad, of Stockholm.   I've published many famous papers.   You have heard of me?   No, you haven't?   Well, I'm an old friend of Philippe's family.   Your initial impression was correct, he is an upright fellow, from a very old family. His father was a horse trainer for the Prince A— of Monaco.   Anyhow, I have been treating my friend for severe manic depression for over a year now. He had been sinking deeper and deeper into a state of despair. It got so bad last January, that I suggested he take some pills—some lithium—to balance the affect. Well, he wanted no part of drugs. You see my friend has unshakable morals!

"...He refused the drugs, but his depression wasn't getting any better. He would lie in his room for weeks, just thumbing the lampshade, groaning. As a friend, and professional who understands the efficacy of modern psychotropic substances, I decided to give him the lithium anyway. I told him it was simple magnesium. 'You don't have any moral objections to taking magnesium, do you? Uh, friend? No?' So he agreed to take the lithium disguised as magnesium and immediately he got better...

"...Well," I continued. I could see the hotelkeeper was starting to take great interest in my story. "All went fine until last week when we drove up from Monte Carlo. You see, he had some business here. He was looking for an apartment for his little sister. She'll be starting college soon, and he's a thoughtful older brother. So we came up here: I to treat patients, and he to look for an apartment. It turns out he wasn't feeling good physically last week. He didn't tell me about it, but went to the *pharmacie* complaining of headaches and hypertension. They sold him ibuprofen and some diuretics. Those don't mix so well with lithium! But he didn't tell the *pharmacien* he was taking lithium because he didn't know he was taking it, you see. He thought he was only taking magnesium. You see where it's my fault!

"...He started behaving strangely after that, cold sweats, bizarre outbursts. I watched calmly to see if it would pass. Then he told me yesterday over the telephone about these diuretics he was taking. I grew alarmed! I said, 'Stop taking everything except your magnesium, do you hear?! Good! We'll meet tomorrow for breakfast and discuss your health, etc." . . . Well, had I been more responsible, I would have rushed over here to help him immediately—but you see I got distracted by some other patients. My poor friend was just having a drug reaction, good lady! And he didn't even know he was taking any drugs! That's a victim, for you!"

"Oh, I see, I see..." the hotelkeeper gushed, pressing a moist cloth to lidded eyes.

"I am ashamed about the whole thing," I continued, "but you should know that all that madness, his crying in the night, building a hut on your floor with the linen, the stolen trout . . . all of that was just a reaction from the medication. He really is to be pitied, my friend!"

"Oh, I do pity him!" The hotelkeeper was growing ever more soft to my well-constructed tale. "You are a good man, doctor!" she said to me, "A good man!"

"I'm afraid I could have done better in this situation, my dear woman. And you and your poor hotel suffered as a result." I reached then into my pocket and withdrew the roll of paper currency and began to count it out. I had brought less than I thought. "Listen, I don't have seven hundred francs with me. I have some euros, rounding out to about four hundred francs. I can come back with the rest...."

"That's alright," the hotelkeeper murmured, taking the money I held out for her. I pressed the bills in her hand. "No, that's alright, please. I'll just take the four-hundred francs. Don't worry about the rest. I just hope your friend Philippe gets better. He is a poor man. I knew all along he had a good heart, a real honest soul, etc., etc... I knew there was something wrong that wasn't his fault. The medicine explains it all...." And with these her words, she took a permanent pen and crossed his name from the hotel registry, soaking the paper with black ink until there were no more records of his having ever stayed there at all. While she acted thus, I thought to mention the trout again, but realizing no more good could come from that, I kept silent and bowed my head. After, I thanked the woman for her understanding and watched her press again the moist tissue to her tear-swollen eyes.

"Goodbye, Madame, and good luck."

Out on the street, I headed my way down to Saint Paul. I crossed the rue de Rivoli and was soon at the river. The sun blared overhead. Hot is the breath from the mouth of heaven!

It was early still, but the clear sun was sweltering as it soared towards its zenith. Such blue skies. I wished that I'd sleep. My eyelids felt as thin waxy membranes sealing the hermetic jar that was my body, empty save for a dry and jingling fruit pit in the bottom—how one feels hollow the morning after a sleepless night!

I wandered up the quai on old Île Saint-Louis. In the brightness of day some workers could be seen lifting planks with a crane to construct something on the river bank. It made me think of that Porte-Tonneau that had started this whole affair. The men dropped the plank and it clanged on some steel chains. When one hasn't slept, every sound shoots through the ear like a stinging needle—or stinging *nettle*?

"Look there… French laboring men. And look here… a prim young mother pushing a babbling babe. Should I just go back, I wonder, and try to sleep the day?" I had every reason to feel miserable about my circumstances. Perhaps one day I would run into Philippe again by pure chance, at a time when he wouldn't be losing his mind. We would actually get to travel together. He would lead me to where those clever girls were cached. Youthful Pénélope, and gentle Themia. How much farther they were from me now, with Philippe—their gate-keeper—gone astray, gone a-wandering in the mental peaks and valleys in the shadows of madness.

"Too much lithium, Philippe! Ha! Too much magnesium! Ha-ha!"

An old woman who was munching seeds nearby turned around when she heard me talking and laughing maniacally to myself. She had been sitting by the river. I took my hat off and bowed to her. No, impossible! I had no hat on my head!—just the clear yellow rays of the sun dancing in my hair…

"Look around me!" I cheered, "What a beautiful day!" …And should I have been sad about that Porte-Tonneau after all? . . . that failed device that led me to a chance encounter with the phantom of my old friend who flit by me like a shade in the underworld, carrying in his knapsack the two fair-skinned sisters? No! Life is progressing wonderfully…

Look at these laboring men hoisting their planks. And beside them, another man, a stonecutter, was chiseling a stately sculpture erecting itself proudly on riverside square. What a horrible sound his chisel makes! Never mind, look at the people wandering around in the sunshine. Look at these little shops with open doors. Watch the trim ladies step in and out with their shopping bags, gabbling like schoolgirls. It was no mistake to have spilt that wine. Look at the life I am a witness too now! It was no horrible thing to have found my old friend. Good that I was able to clear his name from the hotel registry. Just four-hundred francs and a fabricated tale—a story contrived with genius, I must admit, after so long without a good night's rest. Someday Philippe and I will laugh about that. "Good friend! Do you remember that batty old hotelkeeper up near Bastille?" . . . "The one with the trout?" . . . "Yes, friend!" . . . "Ha-ha!" . . . "Ha-ha-ha!" . . . "Great lives we live!"

Now, please just stop your chiseling, monsieur stonecutter, it's hurting my ears! No, do not stop. Keep on with the busyness of life. Keep on people! Look at you all and let me just try to explain the sheer joy of being alive in such a world as this, a place where we are all running around doing things just for the pleasure of doing things: cutting stones, hoisting planks, buying clothes, and learning crafts so that we may feel passion and inspire passion in others; to make others sing in the morning and cry with joy. Why, how great it is that in this world people don't lie around doing nothing, but rather work and strive—all of this work being done, building rafts and towers and bridges, constructing statues and the like . . . and the most wonderful part about it is that no one knows why we do it! Look at this man counting the money in his wallet. He wants to take a sweet lady to dinner tonight. Maybe they will go dancing. She is off somewhere getting ready now, buying a new belt. Everyone is working, creating things, I have my papers back at the room gathering no dust but shining with the heroic songs I penned last night while the trees in the parks were sleeping. Look at us all running around working and creating things, and no one has a damned clue as to why we do it. We just do it and praise what we do, and the good ones don't just praise it, but they sing it and dance it and rejoice in it—yes! The great ones have no regrets for collapsed plans or lost friends, rivers of spilt wine and abandoned hotel rooms. Us great ones praise everything we do and everything we live and experience and never feel like anything is not sacred or is unholy. Ours is the ultimate joy to live. It is while we are at play that we are free. That is what the crazed philosopher wanted when he banged his elbows on the piano, jabbering to old Dionysus who himself was busy rolling on the rug with two nymphs.

I was now walking up along the River Seine, myself not jabbering but singing, not serenading old bearded Bacchus, but rather serenading white-armed Calliope with her milky breath. She, I knew, would help me arrange all of this as soon as I returned to the room where I set pen to holy craft on that quiet street in Saint Germain. But before I would reach that room, I would come to spy a pretty girl strolling along the quiet quai on the Île Saint Louis. She was wearing a linen dress and well-coiffed hair and had amazingly full lips. I approached her…

"Pardon me, mademoiselle…" I went on to address her using the polite *vous* rather than *tu*. I feigned the voice of a confused traveler, unfamiliar with his surroundings, who may freely accost anyone to get help and directions, for all he wants is help and directions, no special favors. I said…

"Pardon me, Mademoiselle. Do know you the area?"

"Mmm, yes."

"Good," I said, "It's good to know the area." And that was all. I started to walk off, quite pleased with myself. The demoiselle seemed confused at first, and then she laughed a charming laugh and motioned towards me, obviously wishing to continue the conversation…

"Do *you* know the area?" she called after me with a wide grin.

Yes, I did know the area, and I told her so. I then made some comment about how surprising it is to see so many people in the streets on a Monday; whereupon she informed me that it was not at all a Monday, but rather was a Friday.

Clever girl! This I did not know!

"Well," I said, "if this is Friday, then we have a great evening planned! Come to our party tonight. You will be an honored guest. Only… you'll have to wear different shoes." I looked down at her feet.

She was wearing some fashionable heels that resembled hatched turtles scampering around.

"You don't like my shoes?" she asked, startled, pressing a surprised hand to her flourishing breasts. "They are Cavalli shoes!"

"They look like hatched turtles who are scampering around."

...And so the conversation went on, as riverside prattles often do. Finally we said farewell until tonight, and bid and happy goodbye, kissing cheeks. And did she have a name? Yes, she was named Chryseis. Of all names to be called!

"Goodbye, Chryseis!"

"Goodbye!"

We kissed cheeks a second time and off I went, cantering with pleasure. What a glorious time of day! I had no clue what time of day it was, but I knew it was a glorious time. A season of victory was on the horizon. Being so muddled with lack of sleep, I didn't know which season we were in, nor which was approaching, but I knew it would be one of victory. And if the god who shoots arrows sends plague in the coming days, or on this evening's feast, I will take the beautiful Chryseis on a sturdy ship; or better, up a mountain to where great beasts roam, and I will offer her to a monk. We will burn goat's fat and chant the hymns of sacrifice, and I will accept no payment for my happy work.

10th Soliloquy

Summer came as summers do, summer came, sweet summer dew. Burnt by the sun of the first clear hot mornings... afternoons we gathered and sang—pastoral songs with sweet pastis; wine, that ancient man's release. I was called away some nights, and on some days, for sensual adventures...

Chryseis had been among the most innocent of all amorous affairs. We met once more in the gilded monumental night, and walked with the golden assemblies of lights behind us, along the Champs Elysées. We would come to make love in the apartment of one of her friends. Later, wandering back to where I would sleep the rest of the night, I passed through the Place de la Concorde. I was joyful, as was my custom. Rounding the Obelisk of Luxor, with my back to the Crillon, my front to the Seine, and the vast space of the Concorde unfurling around me—as would appear the quiet lip of a hurricane to a star gliding over the shelf of the earth—it occurred to me that I was walking alone now. Not just alone as usual but more alone than I'd ever been. Cast out into the world, I was responsible to no one and to nothing. Abandoned to the fiery beauty of this world, I lived in my mind the life of a heroic god throwing spears from his ship at the silvery moon, rounding the cape of the ocean stream, all the while, on this earth—such a prospering platform—I was encased in glass littered with eternal lights.

My body was hard and strong. I was expanding with each continental step I took. Never before had I ruled such a heroic life! Though I was alone, no longer with a woman—I had Chryseis no more to kiss. Her soft lips to taste no more in the sweet and fragrant midnight air. I had her not, no!—but I had the stars swarming above me!

...I kissed those stars over the Place de la Concorde. I crossed the bridge over and again, kissing the stars and drinking the night, singing the river that flowed on beneath me. I kissed the stars and I watched them drop their needles of light over the city. Needles of light, fell through the night, to prick the skin of the Seine—that holy River Seine!

The next the morning found me tearing myself joyously out of bed with a great yearning to work. After all, what was important to me if not work? Nothing could equal it. Still, in the heat of summer, in the French capital where bodies are light-clad and well-shaped, where women's dewy lips utter longings on first meetings, in a place where friends toss spirited wine along their teeth at joyful symposiums held each and every hour, I felt it necessary to be among the people—*in the polis,* if you will. That is why, when Daphné called on me, bidding me come see her new apartment at the Place Vendôme, I quickly threw my affairs in a leather travel satchel and walked downstairs to cross the river.

Heat swooped around us like starlings tangled in the pleasures of mating in flight. I had come to the crest of the stairs and walked into Daphné's and found her in her new bathroom, applying dabs of sweet honey-cream to her pale white cheeks. The apartment was wide and clean, boxes around ready to be unpacked—neat stores of decorations ready to be placed around. Near the bath were stacked hefty crates of beauty elixirs: lotions and oils, face potions, ointments for the hair.

"Innocent Daphné?" I inquired, cupping her in my hands, "Who helped you bring these hefty crates in here?" I lifted her to where the bed was supposed to be and laid her down. We undressed and began our starlings' flight, clean in the brightness of day. Her thighs were white as split ivory in the afternoon light; and they beaded with crystalline sweat and trembled with her heaving breasts, her gorgeous moans, her childish gasps. She cried like a naïve young girl, as she did that first time she made love to a human being. It was us, one year ago, on the other side of the city. I brought her to a spacious room in Montparnasse. She said she had never slept with a man before. I thought I'd heard her wrong.

"Young girl!" I said back then, "So charming are your clothes arranged. How would they be in disorder?" Thus, I proceeded to undress her—casting gentle garments amid the glasses on the table. Then, I entered inside her, strong and firm, and when she broke and bled, no longer intact, I realized what I had done. She said to me then that silly phrase, *"Maintenant, je suis une femme!"* and I knew then what a child I had found. I almost felt sorry for my ruthless seduction, but in the end I didn't feel the least bit sorry. My intentions were true. I laughed and invited her to meet me again and again; and I enjoyed several glorious months with my little virgin Daphné, always once a week—always on a Sunday.

Daphné and I had met just days before that time in Montparnasse, at a luncheon on the grass on an island in the Bois de Boulogne. I was in a large group of a dozen or so friends and strangers, drinking iced wine and eating gentle bread. Someone in my group, a gushing fawn, was telling the rest of us how a certain kind of grape, which she was now eating, tasted just like those grapes she ate when she was a little girl. All the while she was piling seeds on the blanket and giving them names. As I found such stories about childhood to be vulgar and in poor taste, I decided to leave the group and take a solitary walk through the gardens and woods in the heat of the day.

I crossed the spots of sun, burnishing the green lawns, and traversed the cool shadows shed by leafy bowers. Then, I came to a lake; rather, a pond. There by the pond was a girl dressed in all white, dipping a silk net into the clouded water. She was trying to catch the silver minnows swimming in the pond. Yet every time she dipped the silk mesh of her net into the water to swipe at them, the fish scattered, and she would gasp and exclaim: "Stupid fish!" and then say, "Oh!" and sigh, and wait till they gathered again near the edge in their school so she could try again—only to repeat the failure.

I approached the white-gowned girl, my eyes fixed on where her summer flesh met the hem of her cotton summer wear. I scanned her with the stealth of a hunter-beast who, in a mere glance, can tell where the meaty parts are on the limbs of prey and sees whether or not it is worth the chase. I admired her round fleshy breasts. Ripe like August fruit pressed against the seam of a carefully sewed robe. Her legs, calves pressed to thighs where she kneeled on the edge of the pond to dip her net in the water. Her knees were bare, as she had pulled up her white robe to ensure no grass stains would splotch her knees. She looked at me with the widest eyes possible when she saw me approach, as a baby rabbit looks upon a lean hound who has found it tramping in the grass. I laughed at her tiny silk net and told her she would be lucky to catch a pond snail with such a net. She frowned and said she knew. I then told her—not in words, mind you, but in the clever look that manhood bestows on one lucky enough to overcome boyhood—that she should start to run and I would chase her.

"Go on through the woods, little girl!" I called, "*Vas-y, petite fille !* …I will give you a head start!"

Thus she dropped her net and started off. She ran and I pursued her. Her sandaled feet kicked up tiny pebbles. My sandaled feet tore up limbs and stones. She looked behind her with fright as I pursued her across planted berms and fertile lanes, through the thinly planted woods. And then, when I finally overcame her and leapt upon her shoulders, she laughed and fell down in a clump on the grass. I fell upon her and kissed her neck. I took her lips to mine and she gave them willingly and easily, and no longer was I a predator, but just a soft child of a summer garden. And her hands coursed my limbs the way the wind courses the sturdy limbs of trees. That was all one year ago.

Now, in her new apartment near the Place Vendôme, we have been making love in the daytime on a little quilt spread over the floor. Afterwards, heaped-up tired in a hot sweat, Daphné fell asleep against me, but I was not tired, and the heat was so stifling. I wanted to go to the window so as to open it to let in a draft. Slowly, to keep her from waking, I pried sweet clinging Daphné from my body and slithered off the quilt until I could stand and go to the window. Once the window was open, I looked outside to see what kind of view could be had from Daphné's new place. 'Perhaps I can see the Colonne in the center of the square,' I thought. From the window, I noticed there was a thin railing in full sunlight. Looking to the left, I saw some metal steps that led from the railing to the summit of the roof. I could hear people up there talking, laughing. It seemed a merry afternoon party was underway on Daphné's rooftop. I peered up and saw a man sitting at a banquet table on the roof. He was dressed in a bright yellow suit, and had a violin case on his lap and looked as though he were about to play. Leaving the window, I went back by the quilt to find my clothes. I then returned to the window and, dressed more or less, I stepped out the window and onto the railing. Then thinking that any violin playing might wake sleeping Daphné, I closed the window behind me, careful not to latch it. I then started up the welded stairs to reach the summit of the roof.

All the people were happy and laughing at the banquet table set up on this place. They greeted me warmly as a welcome stranger and bid me sit down so as to share with their food and games.

"Nagel was just about to play us something on the violin," the well-dressed people said, pointing to their friend in the bright yellow suit. He laughed and told the other guests that he would love to play the violin if he could, but he didn't know how; and anyhow, there was no violin in the case. He said he just used the case to carry his dirty laundry. We laughed at Nagel's wit, as he opened the case that housed no dirty laundry, but a well-carved fiddle. He then played a cheering song. His fingers skipped over the strings like stones skip over water. After he finished and had set the violin down, we set about eating the mighty bread and lavish plates to stay our appetites. There were tender gourds filled with sweet relishes glazed in spicy creams. There were waxed beans spotted with the dust of charred red peppers. There were bubbling brebis creams, fragrant cheeses of all sorts, flakey breads spread with lemon zests and salty olive pastes, and the broiled skins of sweet zucchinis and violet aubergines. This, and there was plenty of cool wine to drink.

After we stayed desire for food and drink I felt full from everything, from the merry songs, and the pleasure of making new friends, and so I said farewell to the rooftop symposium.

"So long!" I called, "Perhaps will come another day!"

"We hope so! It's been a pleasure!"

One of the ladies at the table said she was getting married in a month, and asked me to attend the service. Another, an older gentleman, asked me to join him on his stately yacht should I be near the Mediterranean that season. I shook all the men's hands and kissed the ladies and hurried back down the stairs to the railing to return to Daphné's apartment.

Pushing Daphné's window open, I entered quietly into the apartment. I closed and latched the window behind me, as was my custom when entering through strange windows from rooftop railings. I surveyed the pretty body of Daphné, which was still sleeping gently as a child does, her soft hair flung about. Ridding myself of clothing, I climbed nude onto the quilt and wrapped the tender girl in my mighty arms. Daphné was sweating from the heat of the afternoon and her skin was white and moist and tasted sugary on my lips—lips that sucked on her small shoulder as I fell asleep.

"What is that boiling sound?"

"Aleksandre, you're awake!"

"Was I asleep?" I sat up on the quilt of the floor and rubbed my eyes. I looked to the kitchenette where Daphné was tending a stove. Red flames were leaping around a Bialetti pot.

"I'm making coffee, do you want some?"

"Good girl, yes!"

"And something to eat? I have yoghurt."

"Yoghurt? But I'll tell you fair Daphné, I couldn't eat a thing. I'm stuffed! While you were sleeping, I attended a banquet out on your rooftop. I had an excellent meal…" And I begun to tell her all about the plates of cheeses and the iced wine, and the man in the yellow suit who played the violin; and I didn't leave out a word but told all and even said to Daphné that should we be in Cannes or Saint Tropez, the two of us, we could take a ride on a stately yacht. And after I'd finished my story, and all was said, Daphné tossed back her head and laughed hysterically.

"Dear child, what are you laughing at?"

"At you!"

"Why so?"

"You couldn't have gone outside on my roof while I was sleeping! It is shut tight and wrapped with this chain and bolt." And saying this, she abandoned the stove and walked over to the window to demonstrate her speech and I saw that what she was saying was true. The window was sealed, keeping in all of the heat, the free-flowing wind outside could only be imagined. "…You see, Aleksandre, it's locked up! . . . and the key for the lock is hidden in my closet. And anyway you couldn't have gone outside because you fell asleep before me. We made love and then you had a happy smile and said that I wore you out more than anyone has with what you called my 'large magnificent lips,' and then you rolled over and fell asleep!"

"I see it is true! But why do you keep that chain around your window?"

"Because I've only lived here a week, and there's a strange man who lives next door. I've only seen him a couple of times. Each time I look out of that window, I look left and see him peeking right. What perverted eyes! His is the window just next to mine. I was afraid he would come in through my window one day and steal me, so I bought this chain and shut up the window and hid the key in the closet…" Daphné paused and kissed my chin… "But now you are here and I do not feel afraid, and I'll give you the key and you can go open the window." So she spoke as she came from the tidy closet with a slender key in her hand, and bid me unchain the lock. I took from the latch the hefty chain and opened the shutters to look outside. I expected to right-away see such a wild place as was displayed in my memory, but outside there was no sloping path up to a rooftop feast, there was no man in a yellow suit with a violin. There was just a thin metal railing near a steep climb to nothing. A high peek of nothing! Below, the streets buzzed with afternoon traffic. To the left, I saw the neighbor's window where a strange head tufted with oily black hair was poking out, eyes peering right.

"Your neighbor is interested in us," I said to the sweet girl who sat naked and voluptuous on a quilt on the floor. "How does one know what is merely a dream?"

11th Soliloquy

The "Midsummer" Soliloquy

For this potent soliloquy to flood the imagination, the heroic *flâneur* must return again to those gamey streets where the scents of ideas first arrived in passing, like wisps of steam from métropolitain vents, or breaths from untouchable clouds. On certain fertile days, I live the life of a dozen men as I wander the quarters of the city. Here, my ancestry is endless. I parade like a bronze-armored king, a swift-footed prince, ruling over time in silver-tapped heels. I am a ruthless despot with the black eyes of a hunting hound. Mine are the streets and the feasts in the doorways. I stop and I stoop to taste the flesh and the skin, the silk-straps and panty-strings of the sweet daughters of the earth, these girls of the city, you rosy-limbed creatures sprung from heaven-shaped thighs.

Coursing the rue Saint-Guillaume and the rue Perronet, I live the life of Baudelaire in a moment's time. Here, no relics of bordels adorn the streets, nor fallen shawls from wrinkled hags. In the evenings, a pleasant sun casts itself in broad yellow-grey beams, falling in painted strokes on mammoth forms. The sun sets and I see tenebrous baudelairean forms trembling in the shadows behind cellar grates. Here there is no end to my power. I can write an epic on a strand of hair. I can devour a head of perfumed braids the way a tiger eats a rabbit. Heed my words!, I care not whether my glory will endure to be retold to generations of coming men yet unborn. My *kleos* already reaches to heaven when my eyes gaze upwards. Here I live a hundred centuries in a dozen footsteps' girth.

As we, who are living, take pleasure in hearing of our occupations on this, our mortal earth, I will sing now a fragrant song; one which I'll call, 'The Midsummer Soliloquy'…

It was a time two days after my love with Daphné was spent on her voluptuous quilt in her high-born room at the Place Vendôme. The summer was at its zenith in the wealthy epoch in which I lived. I was richly dressed in linen, unshaven, of a manly age, handsome of face, a body chiseled and made strong by summer sport. With purpose I walked along the lamp-lit arcades and crumbling tchotchke brocantes on the rue de Rivoli. The day had been hot and heaven's fierce eye cooked the city like bread in a stone oven. Now was evening and a dry warmth puffed in bursts like steam from old machines. I shuffled past broken-backed Parisian laborers and weary foreign travelers snapping photographs…

Scenes of the city: A man was curing warts in the arcade. He stood on a box, beating a ladle against his cardboard medical diagram, dabbing ointments on curious passers-by. A similar inventor was selling the 'eyeglasses-to-end-all-eyeglasses.' This merchant leapt from crate to crate, gasping in exalted joy, singing the virtues of his holy lenses. One merely had to wear a kilo of coiled springs and transparent plates strapped to the forehead to see all there was to see in this world. A perch was set-up where a one-euro monkey was signing postcards for tourists. An old cocktail lounge near Galignani's English bookseller had its doors wide open. It pilfered smoke from the silent clients inside, and tried to resurrect the Can-Can. All of this reminded me of a similar scene from a time long ago…

It was the old century.

I had drifted down to a foreign seaport. There, I rented a small room over a brick marketplace that looked like this very arcade in summertime, with the hot breaths of air puffing through the brocante stands and the vents in the bricks. I was of a youngish age, no more than a boy. I had come from wayfaring and had met a friendly swindler named Felix. Felix had been working on a fishing boat offshore and was docked for the summer and the two of us lived upstairs and earned money selling opium out of our room. The room was cheap and rundown but comfortable, with two mattresses on the floor, one against each wall, and a table made of planks in the center of the carpet that was always covered with pads of sketching paper, wine bottles, pipes, and ashtrays. Felix had come ashore at the end of spring with two kilos of black tar opium that he'd bought from his ship captain. He was turning a handsome profit. I paid into the share and joyously threw myself into the work—though joy is a hindrance advisable to be abandoned in such a business. Cold-handed Felix enjoyed counting profits more than feasting in revelry, and so was meant for the trade. He and I would come to part ways that autumn, as men are made for different lives; still that summer he was a loyal friend and we laughed many a pleasant night away, until came rushing the gold and bluish beams of dawn.

Summer nights we would work and play the lyre and the mandolin. We drank sweet rum and sang and made love to eager girls. A steady stream of young female university students and tourists kept the business going in the pensions near the harbor. They would stray to drink coffee and wine in the marketplace in their laughing groups; and we would catch them by their naïve hands and lead them upstairs, funneling them into our well-worn room the way recalcitrant housecats are cornered and funneled back inside the house with slow side-steps and focused eyes. We relished those girls with their wheat-fed breasts, little Pollyannas raised in northern towns with their powdered thighs, legs flavored sugary-vanilla and rubbed with the scents of inexpensive middle-class perfumes....

Other times we met and made love to the low-born castaway girls of the city—black-stockinged bartendresses and blousy tramps employed to work in drinking dens, or at the hat-check counters in strip clubs.

There were shyer girls too, also itinerants, those who moved from city to city looking for a new way of life or a job on the stage. They worked pushing breakfast trays in the morning cafés, so they'd leave for work while Felix and I were still sleeping; sometimes they would return the next evening, sometimes we would never see or hear from them ever again. So many girls to tell about on that long-lost summer, adolescent gypsies with crazy eyes and dark secrets. That was the life around the marketplace. The air from the harbor nearby was salty and humid.

Downstairs in the market, night had fallen. I paced back and forth in front of the sod crates, where flourished tender poppies in the summer night air. I sniffed their scarlet blooms and hefty milking pods. It was on a night that we were to sell five grams of the 'black smoke' to an old vagabond who claimed to live on a barge in the harbor. He was a strange, disheveled figure with a pockmarked face, and we didn't trust him to come up to our room where we usually did business, so Felix went upstairs alone to weigh out the product and package it. We planned to exchange the money down at the wharf. Now, while I was downstairs pacing back and forth, waiting for Felix, I noticed some patrolmen had shown up. They were milling around the brocante stands casting me suspicious looks every other moment. A cold flush went up the rind of my back, a sick feeling jabbed my gut. I was more than a little paranoid. I hadn't yet visited a jail cell in this part of the country and I wanted to remain anonymous here. I thought to cancel plans and made a few steps towards the closed door that led to the narrow stairs that went up to our room. I needed to signal to Felix, for as soon as he appeared on the street with the product, that gang of patrolmen would surely fling themselves upon us. Where was the customer hiding? I peered around the corner and saw the shady vagabond smoking a rolled cigarette quietly by a street leading down to the river.

"Where's your barge?" I whispered to him when I reached the shadows.

He pointed down the road and continued puffing.

"Do you want some tobacco?"

I nodded and took a pinch and began to roll it.

"There are police over there." The worry in my stomach was growing worse.

"They're not looking at us," said the vagabond, "They're here for something else."

How does he know what they are here for? And what is that *tap-tapple-tap*, I heard footsteps coming around the corner. It was Felix, he was shuffling fast. I motioned for the vagabond to follow us and met pace with Felix. The three of us headed off in the direction of the harbor.

There were even more patrolman down by the docks. They surveyed us carefully as we stepped across the planks, passing the roped up boats. A new policeman seemed to appear with every turn. My paranoia was now paramount.

"This way. My barge is over here."

"No, we're not going there," we told the vagabond. "Let's just sit on the edge of the docks a minute."

"Look at the moon!" I said aloud as I sat myself down, letting my legs dangle over the black waters, "One would say it is swollen. It is like a green apple, that moon!"

"It is just a moon," said the shrew-faced vagabond.

Who was this character?, I wondered. Just another dirty bum living on a garbage-boat in the harbor? A creature like this would be cooperating with the police. Five grams costs no great sum, but where has he scored the money to buy it? Look at the way he was dressed! I scanned over my shoulder. People could be seen coming down the docks—shades with flapping holsters. I thought to nudge Felix and suggest we stop the deal and cut-out, but in the end we went through with it. I grabbed the old bills from the vagabond's grimy hand while we three sat down on the docks with our legs hanging over. If anyone approaches, I thought, I'm going to leap in the harbor and swim beneath the boards, straight back to the sand. Felix handed the vagabond the opium wrapped up in brown paper and the vagabond slipped his dirty finger in to take a piece to taste it and tucked the rest of the package into his jacket. He mumbled some parting words and we nodded as we stood up and walked away, off down the docks past the patrolmen. I didn't look to see if they were watching us but listened to hear for their footsteps, should they start a pursuit. I was a great runner on foot, then as now. Aye, no man could outrun me on two legs. So fast was I in the footrace, that I almost yearned for the chance to prove my speed against pursuing police; but happy was my stomach that we were not pursued. I was flushed with relief as we quietly left the docks in direction of the marketplace. Felix and I had a good stack of cash now, and we went quickly up to the room to count it and put it away. That night, we invited two short, dark-haired Swedish girls, one from Stockholm, the other from Göteborg, to come up to our room. We had met them eating in a café the same evening. All of us smoked opium and drank together; we sang and played the mandolin, and I made love to the taller of the two. Such a fragrant recollection!

That was all years ago, long before I had traveled to Paris, back in the days when I swindled fools and drifted around—an airy youth in canvas traveling trousers; brown ramblin' boots, they lasted long, made of African leather. These days, I would stroll in summer linens, stitched by Europe's finest tailors—the greatest couturiers of Paris and Milan fashioned my evening suits. A famous English shoemaker sent me these shoes: c.i.f. London . . . Aye, these were empirical times!

Yes, now was a more handsome age. The plentiful money adorning my pockets was crisp from the treasury, not brown and crumpled as sorry bills gets from passing through the soiled hands of vagabonding harbor-rats and opium peddlers. Now it was night in Paris and I was walking in fine clothes beneath an ivory-laced portico knowing all luxuries were mine. "Great life!" I cried, "How you lay yourself before me like an ardent lover!"

As I lined the gates of the palace of the Louvre, I was startled by a sudden gust of very cool wind that caught up in the overhead trees and swooshed upon my face. So strange was it, in this month of summer, that I stopped momentarily thinking about all that might arrive at this private midsummer feast in the gardens of the Louvre whereto I was headed, and focused on the qualities of the autumnal odors that had accompanied such a untimely breeze. My eyes watched the way the leaves in the trees overhead were flapping moistly on dark branches, and my memory cast back to a time a few cold autumns before…

Oh memory, speak of the beautiful Anne, with whom I spent one amorous night in blistery autumn…

Autumn, that wild season when rural men rack orchard trees with sticks and weep with the desire to kiss faraway Demeter's supple breasts, to set lips to her travel-swollen eyes. They seek goddesses, but I desired only Anne. The two of us had planned to meet after twilight in the Jardin du Luxembourg. She had just performed onstage for the first time at the Comedie Française, and I had watched the performance and when we met hours later in the gardens, she was still wearing the red silk costume feathers in her hair. It was cold, so she also wore a coat. She looked so beautiful with her pale face and those red feathers in her auburn hair and her elegant well-cut peacoat of black wool. How slow we walked, our eyes fastened to each other's. Weaving between the sodden mounds in Autumn rain, we sought no umbrella, nor did we brush the moist leaves that clung to the wool of our shoulders. With wet fingers, we coursed each other's blue-veined wrists splotched dark with night—glory to the season of Autumn!

"I will leave France as soon as I get the money from my brother," she told me after we had kissed on the stones in the damp and misty park. "I can accomplish greater things as an actress in Italy." Certainly, she is living there now—in Rome, or Napoli.

I would write her a letter, I thought. 'To Anne…' I would begin, with her perfect neck and the good-smelling small of her back. Such prose I would draft beneath this fine portico. I would sing in the letter of the perfect love we had made in the blue of little-morning in that apartment overlooking the shady-lanes of the Luxembourg Gardens. The balcony was near to us and the door was open, and we could hear the birds and the sounds of automobiles beginning the day. She had cried and her aching voice reached to the low shelf of clouds in the coal-stained sky. Such love I would remind her of in this poetic letter! I would hurl such a letter by post. I would let it flutter over the rooftops of Florence, and wind down near the Tyrrhenian Sea.

So happy was I to be dreaming of Anne. It was all spoiled, however, when I came close to the entrance of the palace that was nearest the Jardin du Carrousel where the soirée was to be held. I was stopped by two young minettes who eagerly wanted my services. They were short chubby parisiennes, who had otherwise pretty faces in the French fashion: soft and sciurine cheeks, squirrel-like girls with beaked noses. They hovered in clouds of familiar Lolita Lempicka perfume—I admit there were nights I'd slept in such fumes, embracing girls of tender age, flavors of ivy and adolescent anis, sweet sugar pouring from unbundled hair. These particular girls were dressed like they'd come in from the middle-class suburbs for the occasion. Their outfits seemed chosen and fitted with great effort: black satin, cotton-weave dresses brushing against thick pale ankles, dropping into tall block-heeled safety shoes—clumsy middle-class heels that clopped awkwardly as their wearers saw me approaching the velvet ropes. The girls ran up to me with their dangling handbags…

"S'il vous plait, monsieur! Can you help us get into this party?" The doormen smirked at me, I noticed from the corner of my eye. They appeared very amused. "Take us into the party?" the young girls pleaded.

"I'm not going to any party. I'm just having dinner with a friend." With that, I walked past the minettes and greeted the men guarding the door. One was the familiar Josiah—a stately black African with limbs of steel.

"*Comment vas-tu, Aleksandre!* You're coming to the party?"

"I didn't know it was a party," I told Josiah, clasping his hand, "I thought it was a dinner." With that I passed the velvet ropes and entered into the hall.

In the anteroom, people were trading coats for tickets. I passed into a large salon where I saw the guests had assembled. Men and ladies drank aperitifs and chatted. I immediately spotted a girl whom I knew intimately. She was the bronze-limbed Aurélie, beautiful dark-haired girl of twenty-two. We had spent a week together making love back in the spring and then she had left to travel to Polynesia with her family and I hadn't seen her since. She quickly clung to me and kissed me and I smelled that familiar scent and tasted that familiar flavor of her lips and I could feel by the way she embraced me that she wanted to take things from where they left off and that it was desired that I remain with her, faithful by her side throughout the evening and perhaps the next morning. I still, however, needed to find my friend Giovanni whom I had come to see. I was told he was in a private salon playing drafts with the host of the party. I took a glass of champagne from a servant and went down the hall.

"Mon cher ami!" Giovanni stood from the gaming table to embrace me. The other players remained seated.

"Bon soir, mon vieux!"

Amusing story about my friend: Giovanni, marchese di Roccaverdina, hailing from Rome. He was the grandson of the last Romanov Princess. She had gone into exile after the revolution and her son married a French woman and moved to Italy. Giovanni was exceptionally short, blond and strong, with the heavy chest of Ajax. Upon his jacket dangled medals. His hair was carefully combed. He drank cognac through glistening teeth. Giovanni and I had traveled together, once upon a time. For two weeks we shared the springs at Baden-Baden. Now we met only rarely, at the occasional Parisian soirée. We took pleasure in drink when together, and when drunk, Giovanni would brag to all present that he had once had the pleasure of going to bed with one of my women after our trip to Germany. He praised her amorous games and detailed her flesh as the cards were dealt.

"Such stories!" I would laugh and throw my head back. "Let me remind you, my dear Giovanni, that I once lived for a month in a hotel in St. Petersburg with one of your own women: pale Polinichka. She draped herself across me under lavish sheets in our fine room on the Nevsky Prospekt. For a week she bled and for a month she swooned. I remember I had lied to her. I told the dear fawn that I would marry her. She was a baroness if I recall. Nobel but frail. Oh, those were heroic times!"

"I believe it! I believe it!" the other gentleman in the room would laugh.

"Maybe so! Maybe so!" Giovanni would howl in happy words. We sporting men would all then swallow a long snifter of brandy and continue at our cards.

Now was a new night. We were in a lavish rococo salon overlooking the dark Jardin du Carrousel. I had just joined the table where Giovanni was playing drafts with the son of the patron of the feast. The patron's son was a dwarf named Marcel de Puispeu, and he had the pallor of a split potato. His features were fine and his eyes were narrow, crowding close to a small beak of a nose. His hair was dry and fluffed in the modern fashion popular among *fin-de-race minets* from Passy or Neuilly-sur-Seine. The two played drafts and Marcel laughed with a shrill voice whenever he moved a piece. I sat myself at the gaming table and was introduced to Marcel and I politely thanked him for the feast— after all he was the host and his father was the sponsor.

"Do you know my lineage?" Marcel chimed at me.

"No."

"I am a descendent of the Countess Dembowska. Do you know who she was? She was the unrequited beloved of the great writer Stendhal. He loved her but she was too good for him and refused him. Such is my lineage . . . too good for Stendhal!"

As the youth told his bragging tales, my thoughts drifted to Stendhal's *Scenes from a Parisian Salon*. A vivid image came to my mind of the young Octave gazing on the mountains of the Morea while taking a mixture of opium and digitalis, to end his life for love, the way so many characters had done and would continue to do. Giovanni stirred me from my imagination with an anxious voice...

"Did you see Sarah when you arrived?"

"Poor Giovanni's in love!" Marcel laughed with joy, "He's a romantic!"

"I didn't see her," I told him, "but I didn't look at all the guests. I came straight in to see you."

"I would say she's in Mykonos, playing on the beach," chirped Marcel, "It is the season. I'll soon be there myself with my beautiful fiancée, Lara. Do you know her?" He turned to me with curled lips, "Lara de Causans. She is my fiancée"

"She's my second-cousin," said Giovanni.

Just then some unknown person at the game table blurted out: "I've never been to Mykonos!" This young man remained nameless for the entire evening.

"You're lucky your girl is here tonight." Giovanni bowed his head sorrowfully, lamenting his missing Sarah.

I pitied my great friend Giovanni at this moment. I thought to myself, 'Nowhere is there a romantic monogamist like Giovanni. Like any man, he brags from time to time about nocturnal conquests; yet at heart, he wants to love one woman simply and purely.' I recalled that time he saved a girl's life on the coast of Malta. She was accidentally drowning and Giovanni dived in and saved her. And because he had saved her life, he thought romantic love with her would be the most suitable thing, for then the circumstances of his having saved her would make the union more strong and profound and their relationship would have nothing banal in its foundations. And he tried to love her romantically, although she was a feeble creature of only sixteen years, cross-eyed, with a cleft-lip and waxy hair. She was ugly but he sat at her bedside while she was recovering and he tried to love her but in the end he couldn't. Then he met her older sister who was quite pretty and had no cleft-lip. Giovanni then fell in love with the sister, thinking that marrying the sister of the girl whose life he'd saved would also be immensely poetic, but in the end the sister went mad and was sent to work on a farm for mad-people in Bucharest. Such was his luck at times!

"The thing about women," Marcel piped out, "is that they are everywhere. There are flocks of them out in the hall right now. Take a few. Serve yourself! Ah, you are too romantic, Giovanni! You will ruin your life with such romance!"

"Marcel, you are right. I will go out after this game and find the most beautiful girl in the place and dance with her and take her away." Giovanni swelled his chest at this idea and smiled.

"Oh no! That would be impossible! For the most beautiful girl here is my sweet fiancée, Lara, and she is going away with me, tonight!"

"Well," said Giovanni, "if you are leaving this party tonight with the most beautiful girl, I'm going to another party on another side of town. There, I might find a wife..."

"A wife?" coughed some older gentleman who was seated in an armchair by the game table, who up until now had spoken not a word. "Best to keep out of that mess! Bachelorhood is the best, young men. I tell you, quitting a relationship is like quitting smoking. Not long after you do it, you will be surprised to find yourself walking one day down a sun-washed street with the sudden realization that you have no constraints on your person, and you will tremble with euphoria! Monogamy is just the thing for surrendering to another person your power to decide if and when you are happy."

"Completely wrong!" chirped the dwarf, "Monogamy is fine when it is with the most beautiful girl at the party. Your philosophies have not had eyes to set on my love, beautiful Lara de Causans. Of course, monogamy is sour if you put your faith in one like Mademoiselle Sarah, on the other hand. Do that, Giovanni and you will ruin your life! . . . It is funny," Marcel added then after a moment of pause, turning to me specifically, "We all here try desperately to ruin our lives, and I am the only one who fails at it. I fail miserably!" With this he placed a losing piece on the draft board.

"Yes, but you are learning," I smirked. "Giovanni will steal your king."

"Thank you, Aleksandre!" smiled pleasant Giovanni. "You're a good friend."

"So where do you come from?" Marcel asked me, feigning a voice of interest.

"The desert," I lied.

"Really!" Marcel then began to tell of his father's collection of old classic automobiles, swords and motorcycles. He had invested millions in these treasures, I was told, and glad of such news. Now the game was over and Giovanni asked me to go out to the terrace with him.

Out on the terrace, lanterns were lit and summer gnats swarmed around their flames. The stones stairs led down to the immaculate gardens of the Louvre. One saw handsome couples strolling between the prim hedges. The moon shone like a thick silver coin.

"I have been in Rome," Giovanni chimed gaily, "Opening a new hotel. You'll have to come see it. The money went quick though, I don't know how I'm going to manage until it gets off the ground." Then Giovanni's tone turned grim. "Please Aleksandre, do me a service. If Sarah comes tonight. Will you ask her how she feels about me? But be discreet."

"I am your faithful and discreet friend," I replied and sipped my cognac. We felt the warm summer air on our faces as our eyes surveyed the garden. From the nearby terrace, separated from ours by a hedge, ladies voices could be heard giggling. They were interrupted by cello strings, and then the ladies clapped and began to hurry in to dance.

"Let's go inside."

Back in the gaming room, the young plain-faced Marcel de Puispeu was still at the drafts. He had begun a new game with the nameless man, and was eagerly stacking money on the table. Giovanni walked up and set a hand on his shoulder.

"Come, Marcel, the ladies want to dance."

"Ladies always want to dance," replied Marcel, keeping his narrow eyes on the table. Giovanni and I left the room and walked through the main hall. There the cello sounds and sensual hums of violins were wrapping themselves around each other the way a young girl wraps hair into braids. The dancing had begun. I went to the table to take a glass of champagne. An old society lady heavy in pearls greeted me and said the party would move out to the gardens after some dancing. Apparently tables were laid in the Jardin du Carrousel and a feast of magnificent means was to be unveiled at the striking of midnight, delights never before enjoyed in the capital. I was glad of that and crossed the gilded hall to find Aurélie for a dance.

"Hello my pretty one," I said to her and clasped her bronze-colored hand.

"Hello my pretty, where did you go?"

"We were gambling," I replied. And the two of us danced.

"What a small tummy you have," I said after we'd stopped, caressing her waist as one caresses a jewel on a ring. "You know Aurélie, I am going to package this tummy in a postal box and tape it with strapping-tape. And I will mail it off to the high-peaked Alps. And after those mountain people have enjoyed your little belly for a month, having fed it with the cheeses of mountain ewes to make it plump and full, I will come like a robber with a mask in the night and steal it for myself."

"It is making noises, my tummy. All there is in it is a cup of chocolate and the white of an egg." As she was saying this, I was working hard to devour other parts of her body, with fine discreet nibbles as one should try to use when amongst others in high-society. Just then the music was interrupted by the chiming of a spoon on crystal. The old patron wanted to make an announcement.

"Messieurs, Dames…" the patron began, "It is my pleasure to introduce you all to a man of high esteem." All the guests looked around to see whom the patron was referring to. All eyes settled then when the patron spread his arms to welcome in an old man with wild white hair and a German nose.

"This is the celebrated scientist and inventor, Doctor Hermann Schliemann," said the patron, and everyone clapped. We didn't know why we were clapping but it was a pleasure to do so and soon we were relieved to hear an explanation about Doctor Schliemann's work. It seems he had invented a method of placing a series of lenses that allows one's vision to magnify seven thousand times as it spirals any which way, so that far-off objects hidden by walls can be seen in monumental form. A drop of water dispelling from the faucet in the maid's water-closet, for example, would be seen as a tidal wave by someone who places an eye to a lens in, say, the garden. Or a flea than jumps onto the sofa in the library would be seen as a leaping lion to someone peering the lens in the garage. Sound too was magnified, though how this was done wasn't revealed.

"What is the reason for such an invention?" asked the guests.

It was explained...

A little girl, Marie, who is very young and so tucked in to bed now, lives across from this palace with her father, the Grand Duke So-and-so. Marie loves fireworks in the garden. She loves their bright flashes of light that fill the eyes and their loud pops of sound, like thunder. She would always ask her daddy, "I want to watch the fireworks in the garden tonight!" Whereupon he would usually have to respond, "No, my little Marie. I'm afraid it is not possible. For tonight is not..." *La Fête de la Bastille,* for example; "nor is it any other date on which fireworks are ignited." And Marie would cry and cry.

There came a day when the Grand Duke was visiting with a friend, who happened to be this scientist and inventor, Hermann Schliemann. Schliemann overheard the Duke's quarrels with his little girl and got the bright idea to invent this machine. "This way," said Doctor Schliemann when he first unveiled the device to the Duke, "when your daughter wants fireworks, she can sit in the dining room and press her eyes to the lens, and you can go up on the roof and stand in a certain place and strike a match, and that match's light and sound will be magnified seven-thousand times, so that it will appear as an intense powder blast. It will pop and roar like cannons firing. It will be greater than any fireworks show on earth, your simple striking of the match. This way your little girl can have a fireworks show every night!"

"What a fine thing!" chimed Aurélie with laughter, clapping her hands as the other guests did. I took her wrist and stroked it and put my lips to her blushing mouth and kissed her well, caressing her bronze-tinted cheeks. We were told the celebrated scientist would demonstrate his invention, but that it would take some time to set up the lenses. People began to talk amongst themselves. The music started up once again and we all danced. I twirled Aurélie around many times and she seemed never to tire from such acrobatics and I didn't either. Finally her girl friends came up to tell her some giggling news and I went to help myself to some thankful champagne.

As Aurélie was occupied with her friends and Giovanni was talking to the brother of the evening's patron, who was the uncle of his missing beloved, Sarah, I decided to drink a private glass while entertaining private thoughts, walking around the palace rooms. Downstairs there was a door that led out to the gardens and, as the air outside felt fresh and clean, I exited the palace for the dark yard.

It was a place across the way from the area where cotton-clothed tables were set out on wide lawns in anticipation of the midnight feast. Separated by a hedge, where I stood in the garden was secluded, though large. There were no tables here attended to by servants laying spoons. There was but an empty patch of dark-stemmed grass whose points were tipped by the light of the moon. Such are the patches of midsummer grass that nymphs and naiads so cherish; though I saw no sparkling stream nor fountain's plume. But on the edge of the patch, appealing trees with leafy bowers, dark underneath, also silver-capped, grew from random crests on the graceful hilly lawn.

It was then I heard a quiet feminine voice inquiring of herself in the night. Just as I circled around a tree in search of the source of that voice, a treacherous cloud covered the moon and the whole garden was cast into darkness. I looked up at the midnight sky and watched as the wind pulled the cloud gently across the shiny surface of the moon, removing it like a marriage veil, and brightness again fluttered in my eyes.

When I looked back down at the silver-coated garden, I saw coming around the tree a young woman in a white dress carrying a white rose on a long stem. She wore jeweled sandals and wore her dark hair back in ribbons, streams of it fell down over her ivory-white face. One forearm was pressed against her full, well-formed breasts; so round, like summer fruit, my eyes fell on the shadows made by that dress. The flimsy petals of her rose pressed languidly against the side of her nose as she paced slowly around the midsummer-night tree. Apparently deep in introspection, she occasionally muttered undiscoverable words aloud in a light womanly voice. I then dashed upon her place…

As a way of making play, I smiled widely and said to the girl:

"Mademoiselle, your rose is wilted."

I expected her thoughtful countenance to return my playful words with a smile or a laugh, but instead, the girl looked up at me with solemn eyes. She then looked down at the rose, then back at me. She held the flower out, saying softly in a flat tone, with no joy in her voice...

"Here, you can have it." And handed it to me.

How beautiful she was!, this lady, strolling on a moonlit night by herself in a quiet garden. Not even a night bird danced in the trees. Not even a leaf fell when the noiseless wind blew. Even the swollen moon, of all things, was silent. Looking at her, I entertained a thought that was so peculiar, so out of character for me, that I still cannot believe it was I who thought it. Looking at her, I told myself, 'If I were to ever sleep beside this girl, and take every naked curve of her body in the palms of my hands as my groin ventures to the nest of her womb, then I would need no more from this life and would be able to die right then and there, with no regrets, in pure happiness; for no better thing could come in the future after such lovemaking. Let me lie upon her on a holy night and then I can die in ecstasy, wanting nothing more, et cetera...' Such were my thoughts and so strange that it was I who thought them!

"You have a lot of confidence giving me this single rose," I smiled to her, as I accepted the gift, "No woman has ever tried to win my favor with fewer than a dozen roses at a time. I have rich expectations." To this she finally grinned.

"As do I." She circled around me, as I crept slowly around the tree. The rose, I took and, breaking its long stem, I slipped it in my linen jacket to make a buttonhole.

"I wear a wilted flower nicer than you," I teased, "If it blooms again, I'll give it back, for a healthy rose would look fairer on you than on me."

"I don't want it back."

I looked at the rose in my buttonhole and wondered what had inspired me to claim it wilted. It was in fine shape—full, with tender white petals, slightly blushing, like the cheeks of dancing winter maidens.

"Why are you alone in this garden?"

"My date wanted me to dance with him in the hall, but I wanted to come out here alone."

"I can see why. This is a much more beautiful place to dance. The moon has been your date these last few moments, no doubt, and the sweet streamers of wind have been your violin strings, weaving in and around you, around the branches of these trees; while the limbs of the trees are the arms of your lover whom you have not found, but who comes behind you in surprise while you are dreaming and mumbling aloud, and..." with that, I stole across the path to the tree close to the girl and brushed my palm against her bare arm. "...he touches you softly." It was an innocent gesture, but the caress of my hand on her arm was felt by us both and the feeling resonated throughout our bodies.

She turned to me... "Who are you here with?"

"No one."

"No one?"

"Yes, you see, I am an outlaw who has come alone on this night, silently through the shadows. I am a skillful thief who often trespasses on summer nights into palace gardens to steal noble ladies who wear white dresses and carry white roses. The rich fathers of Europe fear me and dread my arrival at their estates. Many a European beauty is under lock-and-key in honor of my celebrated exploits. Have you not heard of me?"

To this she smiled and her pupils dilated, filling with her tiger-brown eyes with watery black. She dashed away then, and I came around the tree, we met up on the other side. Her breast heaved in her dress the way the bosom of a wounded partridge heaves when it has fallen on a trail in the woods and struggles for life, its blood seeping from where it has been shot, soaking the dark soil. I stood near her and the wind pressed the sleeve of my jacket against her wrist. I watched her eyes for a moment and then let my gaze fall down to her tender lips.

"If you have come here to steal me," she warned, "I'd better alert my protector. His wealthy father has a large collection of guns and swords. I don't know if he would be so afraid..."

Guns and swords? ...and motorcycles, too? It couldn't be!

"I'm with Marcel. Do you know him?"

"Marcel?" It appeared her cavalier at this feast was the feast's host himself—that prissy dwarf with whom I'd gambled with Giovanni in the gaming room. He was not even a man, but just a boy.

"No, I can't say I know your Marcel . . . Or wait . . . I did meet him, I think. Wasn't he the one playing drafts with us a little while ago? Yes, that was the one! My good friend Giovanni stole his king."

"And now you want to steal his queen," she smiled, the clever girl.

"My desire is beyond belief, dear girl. I shall steal you at any cost." And with that, she was mine. I drew forth and felt the first touch of her willing lips on mine, and then drawing away so as to taunt, but not for too long, so as to fade the feeling of the touch, I came back again and pressed my lips hard to hers and felt her fresh lips and tongue against mine. My right hand stroked the nape of her neck and my left held very firmly her small waist, the gentle bone of her hip. We lapped each other's mouths like thirsty animals coming to drink at the edge of a stream; like nymphs and naïads splashing water with playful hands in a wading spring, so our tongues splashed one another's happy mouths. We ended the embrace and gripped each other tight. After a moment, we fell into joyful private introspection and walked arm-in-arm along the grassy knolls, between the garden trees.

"So you are here with Giovanni?" she asked me.

"Yes, Giovanni . . . Your cousin."

"How do you know he is my cousin?"

"This is a palace full of cousins."

We walked a little while. I maneuvered her far from the hedge. Beyond guests were beginning to leave the palace to sit at the banquet tables.

"Still, you know who I am?"

"Lara de Causans."

"You are right. So it seems I have a reputation at your gambling table."

"I believe your reputation travels beyond there, my fair Lara."

"Oh?"

"Your name courses the servants' lips and floods the imaginations of tired children as they drift into dreams in far-away cities."

"Charming! So can I know who you are?"

"A thief in the night."

Just then, a white-jacketed servant exited the palace doors to the secluded garden where we were and approached us two. Lara quickly dropped my hands and I let her free herself for the moment.

"What is it?" she asked the servant with suspicion.

"For Monsieur," said the servant, handing me an envelope. He bowed and took leave. Lara watched with great interest as I tore the envelope. I suspected it to be a note from my host, the dwarf. 'He has noted my disappearance as well as the disappearance of his lady of the evening. People were wondering and he felt dishonored, and, relishing as he does his father's gun collection, he decided to challenge me to a duel. A formal request sealed in an envelope and delivered by a servant. A bold lad, he is! . . . I hope his tiny frame deceives one and he is a good enough shot to tuck me in bed like a proper Pushkin. He had better be a master marksman, or else I will blast the fool into his family's tomb at Père Lachaise!'

So were my thoughts as I grew heated in spirits, hoping for such a chance to scrap with the boy. I tore the envelope open and unfolded the card inside. It was penned in neat cursive and read...

My Dear Aleksandre,

Because I am your friend and trust you, I will not get angry or suspect there is more to this than what appears on the surface. I am not a jealous person and I know that you have very good reasons for doing what you do, and that if I don't understand some of your actions, I should better just smile and realize that the motivations for such actions are veiled from me. I say this not because I enjoy being wounded, but because I enjoy your sensual friendship so much that I can overlook your quirks that sometimes drive me mad.

While you were helping yourself to champagne and I was talking to my girl friends, the scientist was setting up his lenses for a demonstration. When he was done, he allowed us all to take a peek. I was in line right behind my girl friends and was eager to look to see what was making them blush so much as they dried their moist hands on the hems of their dresses. Well! You can imagine how I felt when I looked and saw a giant image before me of you kissing another girl with unbelievable passion! Those lenses really are capable of a great deal! That scientist really deserves all the attention he gets. One could see you and this girl were outside in the garden someplace, and so much you were magnified! I could see the texture of your lips and the beads of saliva string like bridges between you as you mashed your mouths together. There was sound too! I don't know how sound comes through lenses, but this scientist thought of everything. I could hear her passionate gasps and your groans. I thought I was hearing a wolf eat hapless prey in the wilderness. Your little whispers between kisses were as a lion's roaring in a jungle. The kisses themselves were giant waves crashing on a beach. The girl's gasps were the cries of feral birds! Never had I seen such passion, except for that time back in spring when it was you and I who engaged in such games. I just hope that you are happy with how things have turned out. I won't go out into the gardens yet but am waiting for you to leave for if I see you with this girl I might not be so nice and tactful as I was behind the scientist's lenses. Good night, Aleksandre. I am happy to remain always,

Your special friend,
Aurélie

'How poetic she is!' I thought, reading that letter. So they all had seen us through that clever lens! Guests and host alike had seen me with the beautiful Lara, prize of the host of the banquet. And his father, the royal sponsor of the event, the old man who had paid for the chocolate I tasted on his son's girlfriend's lips, who had supplied the champagne that ignited in me the desire to go out in the garden where I'd found my prey, walking around with his son's flower in her hand—he too had surely seen our amorous exchange!

"My flower!" I exclaimed to Lara as I noticed my buttonhole had fallen out, while I tucked the note from Aurélie in my jacket pocket.

"You don't need that flower," she said, and then following curiously with a question, "What was the letter all about? . . . What do you mean *which* letter? The letter you just tucked in your pocket!"

Just then, someone interrupted us by calling Lara's name from across the hedge by the tables. It was Marcel, the dwarf.

'Now I get my duel!' I rejoiced, 'Just like Pushkin!' But before I could turn to address the hedge, Lara had taken my hand firmly and was leading me off in the other direction. "Come," she said, "this way leads out to the street."

"I'll hail a taxi."

"I have a Vespa," she told me, "But I only have one helmet."

We stood out front near the rue de Rivoli, in front of a slender cream-colored Vespa.

"I will drive. I don't need a helmet." I was feeling very drunk and merry.

"No, let's take a taxi," she begged, "I already had an accident once. If we crashed and you died because you weren't wearing a helmet, it would be my fault and I would be messed-up forever." Her slender hand tugged at my shoulder as she nagged about the helmet, but I didn't care. I wanted to ride the motorscooter and not sit in some slow-rolling taxi-cab. All the while, as she muttered praises of prudent behavior and spoke sharply against dangerous bare-headed escapades, I strapped the helmet to her pretty head and kissed the mouth that sat between the ear-guards and placed the pretty girl on the back of the Vespa, then ignited the engine with me on the front, and we were off... soaring at reckless speed through the winding Parisian streets.

Lights flew by our cruising vessel as Lara gripped tightly my waist. The alcohol bubbled in my tingling windswept head as we rode along. Lara's chin pressed hard to my shoulder, we soared past the Place de la Concorde, up the Champs-Elysées, around the Arc de Triomphe. I thought of my friend Giovanni with the stolen king, as I sailed along with my stolen queen. Such a beautiful sensation pressed against me. She soon urged me to slow with tight gripping hands and crooned into my ear questions of where I thought we were driving to.

"I know where we are going," I said, and increased the speed.

"No, go slow. You can drive my Vespa but only if I get to choose where to go."

So be it, girl! I sped up again and flew on her directions down the Avenue Victor Hugo towards the great midnight abyss of the Bois de Boulogne, I felt her beautiful arms taking support around my waist and her breasts pressed against my back and that sudden and most bizarre thought came once again into my head: a thought whose nature was so foreign to those of the musings that tend to flock about the gallery of my mind; yet the spirit of the champagne and this girl wrapped around me and the romance of the wind exhaling warmly on my mouth as we sped down the avenue made me think once again that… 'If the night shall permit me to sleep with this girl, to feel her naked skin unbound and wet, lying wildly beneath my grip, I shall wish to die then and cease to breathe. As I pass into the chaos of the dead, I will reflect that my life was the happiest and most fulfilling a mortal or a god can live. Let me make love to this woman and die in the cradle of her hips.' …Such was the eccentric thought tramping across the rummy surface of my mind!

Soon we came to a château. There was a garden cottage adjoining the Jardin de Bagatelle. We parked the Vespa and royal Lara led me down a dark path into her stone palace and we lit a lamp and kissed. On a dry bed I draped her body and unclothed her and she appeared before me naked and wild, just as she had been in my vision on the avenue. I knew now she would give herself to me fully. I pulled the last strap from her clothes and slid her panties down her slender thighs and felt the hot wetness seep across the surface of her skin while I went deep inside and listened to the sounds escape her mouth.

I have a memory of being a tender child once, so many years ago. I was a quiet observer alone in the world. It was daytime, in autumn, and I was walking down the leaf-littered road near the house where I lived. The moist air smelled of the sprouting mushrooms and the thick moss on the trees. The sky was dark with heavy clouds. I stood so small in comparison to the sturdy oaks and the high-leafed maples, and I heard from over the tops of the trees a loud thundering sound in a long stream that had no beginning or end. The sky erupted with this furious shaking noise and I thought at first it was an airplane, though I knew it wasn't. It was too loud to be an airplane; and unlike thunder, it poured into the center of the sky from every direction. Was it the voice of God, or Nature, or was it the celestial guts of the world? . . . incomprehensible! For many moments that stormless sky rumbled over my head and I watched and listened without moving. I was a fragile child in awe of this life that was new to me. Just as it was then, that rumbling sound, loud and long; so was the rumbling sound now, many years later, streaming from the wet and moist open mouth of the beautiful Lara de Causans as I made love to her. With her neck bent far backwards, her throat trembling, her hair was a nest of flames on the pillow.

After we lay sweaty and beaten, a heap of beautiful flesh. I draped myself across her and laughed with delight, for now my thoughts had not changed. Although the lovemaking was finished, there was not that shudder of emptiness that often follows sexual climax, that sober and hollow regret. Now, just as before, I was triumphant. I knew I would greet Apollo's arrow of man's sudden death with a joyful and satisfied heart, should one fly and pierce my breast. My life had been one glorious moment after another culminating in this intense realization of perfection. I swam in dreamless sleep and when I woke up I felt sweet Lara wrapped around me.

It was early morning when she roused me the second time. She wanted to stay in the bed in her little château and sleep with me all the day, but she couldn't, she said. She had a family brunch that she was late for and so she had to leave. I was groggy. I knew I'd only slept an hour or two. Lara took a pen as we got dressed and scrawled the address on a scrap of paper of where I could find her again, should I want to find her again. I stuffed the paper scrap in the pocket of my wrinkled trousers and buttoned last night's wrinkled shirt and yawned. Out in the garden I kissed her casually on the corner of her mouth and watched her speed off on her Vespa. I then walked off through the Bois de Boulogne in search of a café where I could take a coffee. The crisp morning sun fell on my head and my hair grew towards it as do flowers.

In a café in the sixteenth arrondissement, a cripple was at the brass counter plunking burnished coins with smoky fingers aside a frothy-green glass of *perroquet*. One could see a patch of blue sky through the window and the gate of a sunny garden outside, leading into a park. I ordered a coffee and took the newspaper from the bar and began to read. I was too distracted by all my joyful recollections to concentrate on the paper. I drank another coffee and then reached in my pocket to find some coins to pay the bill. Among some cash, I found again that scrap of paper with an address written on it of some discreet bureau or other where I could go meet Lara again, should I wish to. Another scrap would lead me to the gentle Aurélie. All these scraps of paper dangling in my clothes! The sun beamed into the café and fell warm upon my cheek. I took the newspaper in my hand again and leafed through the pages. 'I could just throw these scraps away!' ...Such were my thoughts, tired as I was. Folly was seated atop the pillars of thought in my head, pillars constructed from my midsummer adventures, and a happy lack of sleep. A joy to be awake and alive, I needed nothing. I could just throw those scraps away and go talk to the birds in the park.

12th Soliloquy

The peak of the wild season came when Saint Tommaso, Defiler of
Cities, came tramping with his leather sack to sprinkle joy and happy
debauchery on all the capitals of Europe, much in the same way the
fabled founder of the world was supposed to have come sprinkling
gorgeous seeds and lush chunks of land for the new people to grow their
fruit and tend their homes. It is said that this seed-sewing went on until
the ancient wanderer arrived in Greece and had nothing left in his sack
but sand and rocks, and so laid the place with dust and waste. This is
why the country of Greece resembles an old dusty coin. Likewise, did
Saint Tommaso feel himself a dusty sand-scatterer when he arrived in
Paris, disheveled, with a dripping nose and worn-out clothes. But this
was not because his plentiful sack of joy and debauchery was empty,
rather because he had been up for days in Saint Tropez, spending time in
merry ways, and now it was Sunday and time to rest.

    I myself had just spent a week of sensual folly in a large palace of
an apartment on the Place de l'Étoile, belonging to the elderly Marquise
de S—. The marquise was still beautiful for her two and fifty years, and
by the time the week was through, she had succeeded in depriving me of
no luxury, and had bestowed upon me every earthly delight. Disheveled
from pleasure, I stopped in Saint Germain first, before going to the café
in Beaubourg where Tommaso and I had agreed to meet, so that I could

challenge myself to a footrace as well as change into fresh clothes—for nothing degrades the spirit of a man more than the absence of daily sport, or fine clothing—both clean and well-fitting.

Under the door of the room to which I held key, I found two letters, sealed. One was from Nadja, the other from youthful Pénélope. I hastened to read the letter from Pénélope and ran inside and opened it by the window where I could read it with the sun on my face. In her letter, Pénélope wrote that she was in Paris and wanted to see me—or '*stay* with me,' rather—but she couldn't find me, and so she was leaving and going up to her father's place in Norway. "I knocked on your door every day for a whole week!" she complained in her note, "and you never answered! . . . Oh well! Too bad we didn't meet up, we could have had fun together, etc. Oh well, bye! *Je t'embrasse fort!*" signed, "Your Pénélope."

A rush of sorrow swept through my body. "A whole week she was here!" These words flew out in a heavy wind, smothering the ceiling as my head tossed back and the note tumbled to the floor in anguish, "...While I was eating cultured cheese with ancient spores, drinking sacred wine and devouring an agèd marquise, my dear sweet, young, innocent Pénélope was knocking on my door, wishing to come in to stay with me!"

I smashed my head against the wall... "Devil take my fate!" My words turned to thoughts once I'd thrown myself on the bed near the window... 'Oh well, I'll find a heroic end to this composition that is my life sooner or later. I could try to go find her in Norway. I wonder where in Norway she is? On her father's island? In Oslo? For all I know, she's in goddamned Cape Town! No use, I'm going to be late to meet old Tommaso if I don't make my sport, clean myself, and hurry on my way....'

Once I had lapped five times the perimeter of the Jardin du Luxembourg, coursing at a speed so fast that no automobile could match it, neither any lean steed or wildcat; only the high gods on Olympus could hope to attain such speed; once my muscles were toned and bathed and wrapped in beautifully tailored clothes, pressed by the three maids who toil in a basement on the rue de Seine, I left the quarter and headed off to Beaubourg to meet Tommaso. Relics of the fair Pénélope lingered in my mind, but I knew that perfect love was not to be attained in this lifetime, no matter how gorgeously life continued to lend itself to me. I had a heroic life, empty of great love, yet all the more heroic for that emptiness. Anyway, I would meet new women that night as I descended on Paris with my old friend Tommaso. Their sweet erotic company would lull the absence of my fair Pénélope.

The sun hissed with foul breath when, in Beaubourg, I arrived. Beaubourg: that spoiled quarter—singular wasteland which one hastens to overpass as soon as one has entered it. I was seated in a patch of sun with an iced pastis, wishing for sleep to overtake me; for the night before, pleasures—all but the pleasures of sleep—were offered to set the crown on our week-long feast. On our last night, the beautiful marquise invited two jittery runway models to compete in our celebration games, and we tested them to display their amorous skills.

Waiting at the café, I lazily watched some pigeons pecking at the shoes of a woman who was seated next to me while I dropped eyelashes into the palm of my hand. Then came Saint Tommaso, Blue-Eyed Spoiler of Cities…

He came from over the hill, prancing like the piper in a merry tromp. While the sun dropped down between two buildings, resembling a coin dropping through a slot, the sun's light lit his hair from behind and those savage locks flung wildly like the streamers on a war-chariot. His hair glowed like the golden helmet of Athena. I imagined his tapping cane to be the great trident of Poseidon, spreading the seas, wrecking ships and basking in the smoke of sacrifice that men burn for him on far Ethiope's shore. His leather sack, puffed-up and sealed, I envisioned to be carrying the whisping winds of Aeolus. Wide was his grin, and loud was his happy roar as he approached the café stand…

"Wake up! What are you doing in this stinking café?"

We clasped shoulders and greeted each other the way close-tied brothers do after a long separation. Tommaso flopped on a chair and ordered a pastis and we talked a while…

"It's good to be in Paris! I have to meet my fair-headed Chloé later in the week, but these next few days are reserved for pleasure. Let's call the 'Spook' for some tonics… *Après, on va chercher des michtonneuses!"* Tommaso roared of laughter, then quietly murmured… "What have you been doing lately?"

"What have I been doing? Aye, friend, these are heroic times! I've been drifting through the quarters of the cities, drifting through the cities of Europe. I went to the Sahara no so long ago. Many adventures. Many women, and feasts of every sort. There are some girls who want to come with us tonight…"

"Ah, tonight… that's something I wanted to ask you about. But, which girls are they? Come on, let's walk…"

Down the road a ways… "Wait, *sale type !* I have something more potent than pastis. Let's sniff some of these…" Fumbling with the latch on his sack, Tommaso looked at me with his elated smile and bleary eyes, and proposed we inhale some elixirs he'd bought upon his arrival in Paris. He pulled from his leather sack not what I thought would be its proper contents, (the mighty winds of Aeolus), but something not too dissimilar: two tall and slender vials containing gases, corked and sealed—vials purchased from a brothel on the rue Saint Denis. The labels of the stupefying gases were rubbed-off and could not be read.

"Sniff this!" We placed the bottles to our noses, inhaled them, and instantly our bodies were charged with laughter…

"You, my friend," Tommaso laughed, ruffling my head with his shaking hand, "You are cut in the shape of a hyena! Do you realize this?!"

"You are one to talk," I cried, "with the head of a pickled lamb!"

…So we roared as we drank these gasses with our hearty noses. We lapped them up the way dears lap cool, fresh water when they come to a still stream in a forest clearing. Large were our eyes as our wet noses drank those swirling winds. One would say we were ancient heroes quaffing Helen's sweet vial of nepenthe to forget all woes. And as we quaffed, we danced around. And as danced, we laughed and sang!

Once the gases had been properly tasted, once the winds had unclouded our eyes, Tommaso returned the corks to the vials and we settled back on a bench down along the quai to where we had wandered, far from where we'd begun.

"I want to drink a pastis," said Tommaso, "Let's find a café."

As we sat on a terrace, drinking anis, Tommaso proposed his plan for that night. He had been asked by a friend—some old lady from Venice who kept peacocks in her house and imagined herself to be the widowed mistress of Lord Byron—if he would assist a foreign traveler who was visiting Paris on business. He was a count and friend of hers living in Dubai. He and his valet had arrived in the capital the same morning and they needed someone to escort them from a certain office on the Grands Boulevards to the Hôtel Intercontinental that evening, as they didn't know the city and were carrying quite a lot of loose cash and were afraid of robbers. After the Intercontinental, Tommaso explained, the count would happily pay for champagne and entertainment in the velvet salon at Mathis Bar, so as to make the chore worth our while.

"Can't their hotel just send a car for them?"

"No," Tommaso shook his head, "A car would scare them. They are doing some shady business and a car would make them very paranoid. I hear they are very little men and very paranoid. The woman said they needed strong, trustworthy types to help them transport this cash. You and I are trustworthy types, I told her, or strong at least."

"I don't want to waste an evening."

"Bah, help me out here!"

"Only for one hour, Tommaso. I don't mind a trip to the Intercontinental, then a walk to Mathis Bar for champagne, but I don't want to spend the entire evening with little men from Dubai."

"Alright, it'll only take an hour."

Two hours before midnight, the count and his valet appeared from a passage near the métro Bonne Nouvelle. The count was short and jaundiced and resembled a wine cork. He wore pitch-black glasses. Behind him stood his valet in a floppy hat—also a short man. The valet had wide gaps in his teeth and hiccupped violently. "We are very much enjoying Paris," said the count over and over.

"What's in there?" Tommaso asked, eyeing a calfskin briefcase that was being handed to him by the floppy-hatted valet.

"Ten-zousand euros in cash."

"All right. But listen. I need a drink first before we walk to any hotel. Let's go to Mathis now. We'll go to the hotel after."

Hearing this, the yellow-faced aristocrat turned his dark glasses towards the wide eyes of his hiccupping valet, who was walking behind him, limping to keep up.

"Oh, no!" the two men chimed in unison… "First the hotel! First the hotel!"

"All right, we'll first go to the hotel."

And so we began to travel on foot.

As well-built ships careen over the slick surface of the sea when the wind is good and the night is clear for sailing, so did our legs move swift down the far-sweeping boulevards. Tommaso held the calfskin case full of money, while I walked unhindered. The tiny valet carried a bag that equaled him in size, which he said contained the men's shirts and dainties.

When we came to a passage near the rue Vivienne, I noticed Tommaso was having trouble with his leather sack. He first fixed the strap over his shoulder, then he looked at me with cunning eyes. He then began fiddling with the latch.

"What's wrong with your bag?"

"Oh, nothing," he whispered, "Just that I have this pastis in my head and I'm trying to keep up with this case in my hand and I'm worried the strap will break on my sack and I'll lose my possessions." The sack had indeed opened slightly and a leaf of paper had already fluttered out onto the pavement. All the while, the count continued forward, blindly swinging his head, while his valet limped along beside him.

"Come into this passage," Tommaso signaled.

I followed him as he walked astray on the rue Vivienne.

"Can you hold my cane and the briefcase while I fix the sack?" Tommaso handed me Poseidon's trident and the calfskin case of money. I took the case and the lofty cane while Tommaso, Blue-Eyed Defiler of Cities, opened his sack and dug inside with crafty hands and a look of intrigue in his eyes. I looked ahead to see if the valet and the count had noticed that we'd stopped.

Before I could make heads or tails of the situation, Tommaso tapped my shoulder… "I just have to make sure that the corks are in tight." As he said this, he retrieved the vials containing the winds we had breathed earlier that day. "I was starting to get worried that the corks would fall out, you see, lugging that hefty case around!"

"Did anything fall out?"

"I'm not sure." Tommaso said this slyly as he nudged the corks in the vials; apparently pushing them in farther, though one wondered now his true intentions. Then, with a swoop like the upflight of starlings, that sight that takes men's thoughts away from the activities of the day letting them take pleasure in the promise of springtime and the greatness of our natural world… so came the swoop of winds as not *one*, but *two* corks dislodged from those happy bottles!

Whoosh!, came the winds to get us, sweeping us upward. Chuttering, we flitted. We looked below ourselves, fluttering, and saw the distant rue Vivienne becoming farther and more obscured. Our laughing alone blew us a full métro station away! Tommaso's cane danced in my hand as our eyes swirled. I marveled at how the aristocrat and his limping valet were little spots now, way off in the distance, resembling pin pricks on the ragged skin of the city.

We traveled far on those gusts, laughing and seething with reckless joy. All the while, we told wild stories, shouting through the air.

The mighty winds soon thinned out and began to lower us back to the holy ground. Like the toy-thing a famished child plays with on a sidewalk while his mother is busy in the nearby kitchen preparing flavorful treats to eat—the child tosses the forgotten toy aside when she calls him in, saying the snacks are ready to eat—so did the wind then toss us aside, casting us into the doorway of some little café where music was playing and girls were dancing in little skirts. They asked us who we were and we told them we were iguanas who had come from Mexico and the girls laughed. All the while, waves of delight flew around me as the winds started up again... *Woosh!*, out of nowhere, we were thrown again into the sky...

I came to lose Tommaso then completely as my vision grew dark and colors of light swirled in violent counter-clockwise directions. When my eyes steadied themselves, I realized those pins of light were the stars and I was washed up against some curb in a clean part of town that had been hosed down by salty currents of sea. No they weren't either the stars. There are no stars in Paris, and we were obviously still in Paris. I could see the columns of the Louvre. And the pins of light were the streetlamps standing tall around me where I woke after the deluge. Then I felt a head pressed against the hard bone on my stomach. I looked down and saw Saint Tommaso, Defiler of Women and Cities. His stout body flopped against me.

"*Sale type!*" he cried, clutching his head, "Those were *some* winds that carried us away!"

I picked myself up and looked around me. So did he.

"I'm afraid we lost our companions," we said to each other, looking left and right. It's true, the aristocrat and his floppy valet were nowhere in sight. Now it was just Tommaso and myself, standing outside 'Chandelles'—the famous libertine den on the rue Thérèse, not far from the Louvre. We looked at each other with eyes that said... "How unfortunate!"

I saw then that Tommaso's cane had not been lost. It was propped up in a doorway. Further inspection of our surroundings proved that we had neither lost the aristocrat's calfskin briefcase that had been entrusted to our care for safe transport to the Hôtel Intercontinental.

"Clever Tommaso!" I cried, and clasped his shoulders, rejoicing in knowing such a treasure had not been stolen by the robber-winds. He opened the case before my eyes right then and I saw that there were many stacks of bills: roughly ten-thousand euros, all in sweet-smelling cash. To our luck that case had been blown in the same direction as us, while the aristocrat and his valet were blown completely elsewhere.

"What good fortune that such a thing as this should happen by fluke and not by design!"

"Some fluke!"

"I think your old lady friend in Venice is going to be worried," I told Tommaso as I sat petting the stacks of money with my happy hand, "That we should be now alone, two great friends, with no burdens and a new-found fortune…"

"Was that design? Of course not! No, that was a fluke!" Such were the flukes that befell one when in the company of Saint Tommaso, Blue-Eyed Defiler of Cities, and Captor of their Women.

I brushed off my good clothes, only a little the damp from the voyage, only a little wrinkled from being thrashed by winds, Tommaso shut the calfskin case and tucked it under his arm. We heard the empty vials clink in the pocket of his tailored coat, and he shook his head with sorrowful regret.

"We will find other winds," I said as a way to console him.

"I hope so, *sale type.* Anyway, there's nothing to do now but to go to Chandelles." With that, we lurched into the doorway of the famous libertine den.

13ᵗʰ Soliloquy

"The Chandellesque"

Inside Chandelles: singular Parisian den of sensual pleasures, from which no man departs without having tasted the joys of erotic folly and corporeal discovery.

The doorman greeted us with a friendly handshake. A freckled hat-check girl took our wrinkled jackets and we gave her our scuffed shoes which she tucked into cubbyholes; an usher then led us to baths downstairs where cakes of frothy soap, made in the finest fragrance parlors of Paris, were rubbed on us by tender maids. Lime and olive oil was applied to soothe the blows our bodies took when those robber-winds stole us from our companions and thrashed us about the city, dropping us down like orphans, alone but for a briefcase filled with many thousands of euros in splendid cash. I laughed at the thought of that little deception while the feminine hands labored on every part of my body.

After the girl who bathed me was finished, and my nude and bronzed body was scented and dried, I sat wrapped in a flowing towel on the edge of a velvet sofa near a plate of chocolate and grapes, which I picked at, nourishing myself. It looked as though Tommaso had gone. The baths were empty, no sounds echoed in the halls.

I then heard a soft humming coming from the corner. I looked up and saw a woman seated on a stool, mending stockings. She was voluptuous, wearing only a silk slip, with dark, straight hair tied-back, a soft, pale face. She sang quietly as her needle dove through the fabric of her stockings:

On fait périr nos cafards
Le bourdon du désespoir,
A pétri toute ma vie
Le bourdon du désespoir,
Des angoisses les plus noires.

"What a pretty scene," I issued aloud, devouring my chocolates, surveying the heaving breast of this voluptuous stocking-mender, with her dark hair and her face like a spilled puddle of cream. Her neck, one would say a slender champagne flute; and those sweet-colored thighs, trembling beneath the shadow of thread draped across them. I recalled then, when I was just a day-dreaming lad in a far-away land, this is how I imagined these fabled Parisian women, busy at their toilette, mending old stockings in perfumed boudoirs. It was such a pretty scene, all of this, that I momentarily forgot how I had come to be here, that I had arrived with Tommaso who was off somewhere, who knows where, gone with ten thousand euros in splendid cash, (perhaps he was already in Ibiza, for all I knew!), and that a freckled hat-check girl was in possession of my shoes.

Just then I heard a man clearing his throat. I turned from the stocking-mender to see Tommaso entering my private salon. He was clean and bathed and was dressed again in his rumpled clothes. With him was the man whom Parisian Society knew as 'Bearded Mahir.' He was the patron of Chandelles, an elegantly-fashioned and notorious

Turkish rake. Tommaso held out the open briefcase for the curious eyes of Mahir to rummage through.

"Donne-moi ! Donne-moi !" demanded Mahir.

Tommaso cleared his throat again and sealed the agreement, handing over to Mahir four hefty stacks of cash, all banded tight. He then closed the briefcase and motioned to me to where I sat on the sofa with grape seeds spilling from my teeth. Mahir too motioned towards me and watched as Tommaso nodded his head and then invited me to join them in the next room. Mahir signaled to the woman mending her stockings across from me; and she, seeing this signal, took a hopeful appearance and made as if to set her needlework aside to join us too, but Tommaso shook his head no, and the woman saw this rejection and sunk down deflated in her seat.

Once the *patron* had tucked away the honors he'd received in flourishing cash by my generous friend, the two of us were ushered into a large salon reserved only for those who were considered kings among libertines in Parisian Society. It was here that the arrows of Eros were to be fashioned and flung. To tell of what I saw in this stately room:

Forty nymphs were lying on the floor, all nude and pink of flesh. Many were very young, in the first blooms of youth; small girls with braids and soft, tiny hips. Those who were not young were agèd, mature in years, their womanly legs tached like bruised bananas, with chests made tender from child-bearing. Their chests had the seasons of passion drawn across them, their over-ripe nipples were dark and stood high on white breasts as they themselves lay on arched backs, yawning in the afternoon. Near these women, the young, pink infantine girls played on their tight and supple skin, rolling on the floor across the beams of sun that spilled through windows of burnished glass.

In all corners, servants laid bowls for my companion and myself to eat from: there were sugared oranges of mandarin, sweet figs of Bombay, dusted plums from violet oriental shores. Caring nothing for tree-sprouting things, preferring the fruit of basking nymphs instead, we walked towards the center of the room to where two tall and slender female attendants unclothed us. One tried to help Tommaso with his cash-filled briefcase…

"Non, je la garderai," he insisted.

"Ne t'inquiète pas !" chirped Mahir, who fluttered over from nowhere and snatched the case in his quick-flying hands. Forthwith he disappeared behind an unseen wall, never to appear again.

Now it was just Tommaso and myself in the den with our two attendants and a handful of servants all set to task. Many were piling incense resins in bowls of burning charcoals to scent the room. Others were fanning the bowls with palm leaves and peacock plumes, sending perfumed smoke fluttering up the walls. All this was a delight, but the real novelty were these insatiable nymphs! . . . forty in all, sweet maids of all colors of hair and eyes—sexual women of noble years, along with naked and wet coquines in the first blooms of youth. Forty nymphs in all, all rolling on the floor with dusted feet and milky hands, crooning with pleasure, gushing with coquetry and cries of ecstasy. After their croons, they would lean on their elbows; they would perch idly, yawning in the afternoon.

"Venez à nous !" cried the forty nymphs.

We fell upon them in their flesh and they wrapped their legs around us like great white tangles of seaweed, the kind that wrap around boats trolling the shallow coves of sea-girthed islands, their captains seeking a sandy place to dock while they look on in amazement at the shore, at the strangely-decorated birds, the multi-colored trees, unfamiliar fruit hanging from sun-bleached limbs.

The limbs of forty nymphs reached up and welcomed us upon their heaving bodies. After I tasted the navel of one, pressed my mouth to the lips of another and held in my palms the mound of wetness that frothed from her groin, I felt four little hands wrap around my forehead in a playful way. Two tender children with wreathes of wildflowers—crowns on their golden heads —leaped upon me the way soft-furred pups leap on the full-grown coyote who is their father and master, the pups yearning to play. Like a savage wolf, I turned on the two young girls and dove inside them, ravishing them in the groin, devouring their breasts; they yelped in beautiful ecstasy.

All the while Saint Tommaso, Defiler of Cities, was far-off rolling on the ribcages of two agèd and devil-eyed women who had succeeded in bringing him into their private orgy, I had taken it upon myself to fall upon a young girl who was small and nude, save for a diamond star on a golden chain around her neck. We began to fondle each other. As she kissed me, she told me she had dreamt of me before: it was a year ago, back on her homestead far in the frozen Siberian tundra. She grew up there with her family until the ripe age of fifteen when she ran away to travel and live the life of a gypsy in Europe. She'd dreamt of me then, "…and now finally I'm meeting you for real!" she sighed with pleasure as she chewed on my jawbone. Her eyes were wide as glaciers, with pupils that spilled watery black like the liquid resin that drips from scored poppy pods. Her lips were hot and red as coals on a winter hearth. She informed me that she was deaf in her left ear, so I had to turn her head to the other side to whisper my cantations of seduction while I made love to her tiny body.

After I'd conquered that winter beauty, I crept away on all fours and paraded around the room like a hooded lion, stopping only to stand upright in each corner, taking the form of an ancient *herma*: that phallic guardian of man's territory. Only the beard I lacked, as my face was properly shaved. Sweet incense smoke billowed around me from the copper bowls placed near founts on marble stands. I spied Tommaso not far off, lying on his back in a slick of white fluid. Around him, five or so nymphs had gathered to knead his naked limbs and pay homage to them. Like Nausicaa's maids who gathered on the beach to wring the water out of the bridal laundry, so resembled these nymphs who gathered to knead Tommaso's limbs. This water that escaped was creamy and white and it ran like a white carpet under his body, like the gluey trail of a garden slug. Saint Tommaso rolled in his slick, laughing with pleasure, crying aloud, extolling the *état mineral* he'd attained.

After making these observations on the outskirts, I returned to the flocks and found three new nymphs I'd yet to touch. They were basking in the center of the room, arching their backs on the floor, stretching their beautiful bodies and humming melodious songs. Around them, sat baskets with burning candles. The candlelight was cast on the walls and leapt to the windows that dimmed with the advancement of evening. In the darkness, I approached the three and laid my hunter's hand on the small and firm breast of the one who had the longest hair and the straightest limbs. Her legs split gently as I touched her and I stroked her stomach and seized the wet blooms of skin between her frothy legs. When I charged inside her, her melodious song turned into slow, soundless, airy breathing, like the wind that caresses the sails of a boat careening over the smooth sea, so did her breath caress me. The two other girls nearby continued their singing, calling me they way naïads, or winged bird-women on rocky islands call to the homesick sailor as he passes on his swift ship. But I heeded them not. I was happy to remain with my long-haired beauty who cried with ecstasy as I ransacked her womb. I dove inside her and her girlish teeth bit her tender lips and she inhaled and shuddered, throwing her head back to offer me the most vulnerable portion of her neck. With her climax, she clenched her womb and pushed me away, though wanting more; she was unable to receive the great pleasure I gave her again and again and needed to rest. I called the two other serpentine girls who were curled around the baskets to come over to me. They slithered dutifully and wrapped their beautiful arms around my neck and I pressed my tongue to their fiery limbs. I drank their waters and swam in their groins that were like nests in the woods: fleshy and sour in their humanness; sweet and firm in their goddesslike beauty. Firm as marble—deathless and ageless.

After I had tasted the flesh of forty nymphs, I lay on my back and pulled the limb of a nearby sleeping girl on top of me, to cover me and serve as a blanket and I let dreamless sleep overtake me.

When I awoke, what must have been many hours later, I stood and shook the sleep from my hair. Rubbing my eyes, I began to muse on the price of ewe's milk cheese in Paraguay. My thoughts then wandered to that time back in Budapest, when, while composing an opera, I accidentally deciphered the ancient script 'Linear A.' Realizing the effect such a discovery would have on the world, and more importantly, on my art and the direction of my career, which I did not want to alter, I ran out of my hotel and threw the evidence of my discovery in the Danube. 'Linear A' sank to the bottom. I left Hungary a few weeks later with a finished opera and a heart at ease. Now I was waking up in Paris, at Chandelles...

I looked around and saw forty sleeping nymphs.

Forty nymphs, still like sleeping stones. The sex had dried on their naked skin, from where we had laid, lit by the morning light falling from high-up windows.

I searched around for my clothes, and for friend. I found my trousers draped over a copper kettle in the corner of the room. There was a rolled-up note jutting out of the belt loop. I pulled it out, unrolled the paper and read these words, written in the Tommaso style...

SALUT CHIEN, JE ME SENS PAS TRÈS BIEN.

ALORS, JE SUIS RENTRÉ CHEZ MOI.

AMUSE-TOI.

Shrugging my shoulders, I dressed to leave, and crept out of the room where we'd had our orgy—quietly, so as not to disturb the naked sleeping nymphs; though now that it was morning, it seemed that they were no longer human females, but were now mere marble statues, or moreover, just images stained on my eyes like relics of a dream—like the traces smoke leaves on walls after it has traveled up them and fled for the sky through vents in the ceiling. They now were only as alive as the molted skins shed by snakes that blow with the wind down dusty roads. I imagined if I were to caress one of their naked shoulders, my hand would turn to water and pass over it as a stream passes over a stone in a brook. Alright, enough imagery! Time to button my shirt and go upstairs to find my shoes.

"Did you have fun?" asked the freckled hatcheck girl. She was awake in her booth, reading a feminine magazine behind the velvet curtain. I gave her my ticket and she brought me my shoes, smiling rosily.

"You sure are bright for someone who hasn't slept!"

I clasped her hand. She had a thin bracelet on and I slipped my finger between its chains and her wrist and brought the wrist up to my mouth to kiss it.

"Monsieur—" she began to laugh.

"*Chut !*" I cut her off as she spoke, as she was about to utter my rightful surname, bestowed on me at birth. I pressed a finger to her lips. She laughed again, snapping her teeth at my finger.

"Do you know how many stories go around about you in this city!"

I told her I did.

"How do you get away with the things you do with all these girls?"

"I don't know." I was getting weary from standing still and wanted to leave and walk through the city.

"Aleksandre, I think you're the biggest rake in all of Paris!"

"Probably."

"You are *too much* of a rake!"

"Really? That's a funny thing for the hatcheck girl at a libertine den to say."

The freckled girl laughed at this and we kissed on the lips as do brothers and sisters and I left and walked out and down the rue Thérèse.

I thought to return then to a room to which I held key, to work a little, or sleep off a few more hours. But after the night I'd passed, I desired to see a close friend, if only for a cup of coffee and a short discussion. Tommaso had fallen ill and would need a day to recover, as was usual for him after a night of such folly; whereas I kept strong with diet and daily sport of the kind all men should strive to excel in, so long as they are of firm body and not brittle of bone. I had the strength of a boxer after this night; though I suffered from soul-sickness, having suffered an orgy with ageless women whom, though goddesslike in appearance, I would never know closely enough to join with, to be made myself ageless, deathless, repelling the injury of years to my mortal skin.

Later, walking through the Marais, I was much more gay in spirit, singing:

Glad ol' whiskey can't be beat,
I won't have to dodge every cop I meet.
Da la dee da!...
I want nine men goin' to the graveyard,
Only eight men comin' back.
Da la dee da!

I stopped and bought some roasted cashews from a vendor, paid him two euros, and continued on my way. I wanted to rouse Tommaso for coffee and so walked on towards his home, eating the cashews all along, wondering aloud…

"Why *'Rest in Peace?'* Why that phrase? That's the most ridiculous phrase I've ever heard! You die, and they say *'Rest in Peace!'* …Why would one need to 'rest' when they're dead?! I spent thousands of years of world history resting. While Agamemnon was leading his ships to Troy, I was resting. While Ovid was seducing women at the chariot races, I was resting. While Jeanne d'Arc was hallucinating, I was resting. I wait until airplanes are scuttling across the sky to burst out onto the scene, and I'm only going to be here for a short while, so when I die, I certainly won't need to rest again! Not while more adventures of the same kind are going on…"

I reached the rue Perche and dialed the code to open the gate. A slim elevator took me up to the third floor where Tommaso's apartment was. There I found another one of Tommaso's notes taped to the door, written in debauched French…

"Sale type…" it began, and went on to say that my friend was in bad shape, he'd vomited blood, his stomach was hurting, etc. For these

and other reasons he'd decided to leave Paris immediately and return to Milan. He was sorry. The whole time he'd been walking home from Chandelles, he said in the note, the grim figure of Death was prancing alongside with him with her leash around his neck and her hand tapping his shoulder, her boney fingers snatching at his belly.

"Well at least he had Death walking with him on his way home," I said, clasping my hands, letting the note and an empty cashew wrapper fall to the floor in despair. "That's already something! I walked here alone—*dans le néant, si tu veux*—eating salted nuts, prancing in the void!" ...So tired I'd become again, my thoughts were starting to percolate my head.

Later, in front of Châtelet, I passed an old woman who looked into my eyes with tremendous lust. 'It is my disheveled hair,' I thought, 'or the smell of animal mating fluids on my skin.' Her hungry glance made the bristles on my spine rise and stiffen with delight. I decided to charm the old woman and threw her glance back at her with my own look of erotic desire. I held my wolfish gaze until her eyes cast downwards, as though she were a blushing young girl of seventeen. Timidly, the old woman yanked her shawl over her withered breast, clutched her parcel, and passed me on the narrow sidewalk.

Trees were shaking their leaves, and the bouquinistes were setting up their carts of used trade-books, antique photographs, tchotchkes and copper trinkets along the Seine. 'It must be fairly early,' I thought. Then, 'why do I feel gloomy this morning? Not gloomy, but pensive. Some men consider themselves rare for having slept with forty women in a lifetime. I slept with forty women in one night—this last night past!'

There was a sign on a shop along the quai that announced it was Veal Week in the quarter. Veal Week?? ...I wondered what that meant.

I began mumbling phrases aloud, such as... "It is a strange life I live," and, "I should go to the pharmacie to buy some codeine and paracetemol..." I searched in my pocket to see if the usual roll of crisp currency was pressed into the seam, as I never carry cards, only a roll of cash in the front pocket. '...This whole experience I'm living, this sequence of poetic days and erotic nights, this Parisian *Chandellesque,* where nymphs litter the streets and naïads grow in the branches of the trees that line the boulevard. Maybe the hatcheck girl was right, I am too much of a rake.

'...And so what of it? Am I to move to Normandy? To hell with the hatcheck girl! The life of a Parisian rake is the life to have! . . . "No, I don't want a beautiful woman this afternoon, thank you. I want to get some work done. I'll let you know if I change my mind." ... "Later," you ask? "Yes, maybe later..." The rake puts his hat on and leaves the desk where he's been writing at eleven o'clock at night to tramp down the sidewalks under smoking lanterns. He ventures up a road and into a dark haunt, a place known only to those who take pleasure seriously. There, where girls' flesh is worn like scarves around the neck. Now, it is daytime and it's getting hard to keep walking. The sun is pecking at my nose. The skin on my face feels loose—as if it has slipped off the bones. If I press my chin and push, I'm sure the skin will slide over to the back of my neck... I'm at the end here!

'...No, I'm not at the end. I'm in the middle. If you look, friend, you'll see we are right in the middle of it all. Right in the middle! . . . In the middle of the road of our life... *Nel mezzo del cammin di nostra vita...* I came to find the right road lost... *mi ritrovai per una selva oscura, ché la diritta via era smarrita...*

'...You know what the problem was with Dante? Yes, the problem with Dante is that he was a coward! . . . Hey, what is this here?!'...

I planted my feet on the sidewalk before a familiar sight on the quai de la Mégisserie, across the street from the Seine. Behind me, the rows of potted plants and flower bulbs sat on rusted nursery stands; and to the right were the bustling *animaleries* with their crates of hopping rabbits, live birds, and other critters ready to be sold. And here in front of me, among the old wooden and windowed façades of the buildings, was one vision from my past in plain view, and another one, hidden, but there to be seen.

It was an old brocante called 'The Bone Shop.' I knew it in earlier times. It was here that I'd met August and his friend Pavel, long ago. Here, we'd spent some evenings together drinking and telling stories up in the loft above the shop where the two slept and bided their time when they weren't working downstairs. I'd forgotten about this place. Now the windows were dark and covered in a film of dust, so I could not see in; yet on the door, there was a simple sign pinned-up that read: CLOSED FOR THE MORNING. BACK AT MIDDAY.

A look at my watch: coming on eleven. Good news! "I will return at noon to pay them a visit. They will be happy to see an old friend. We will drink coffee and talk of seasons past...."

I thought of Pavel and August. Pavel, that young Russian vagabond, handsome and strong, with a brave soul set on a life of adventure. He too, like I, bound himself only to the road of hazard the way a high-soaring falcon, having nothing else to attach itself to, binds its wings to the chains of the eternal skyway. Then there was bald-headed August who knew nothing of travel, having never left Paris city-limits. His ambitions were few but his virtues were many. He loved people and delighted in hearing wild stories told. His mother had opened the Bone Shop during the Second World War to sell fortunes to credulous people, along with tarot cards, animal skeletons, loose semi-precious stones, silver and copper in many forms, dyes and powders, crushed insects legs and wings to make magic potions, as well as healing herbs. She performed mystic curiosities and became a well-known *clairvoyante* in her time. People gathered in the Bone Shop at night to ask her to read their palms and grant them passionate love and eternal life. When she herself died of old age and a weak heart, August took over the shop. He, however, performed no rites, having little interest in the occult. He simply sold the jewels and silver lockets and other curiosities to denizens of the quarter and tourists alike. When he met the young Pavel, the two became great friends and the one offered the other a place to live in exchange for work. The loft upstairs where they slept was very small: having only a medium-sized bed for August, a tiny cot for Pavel, as well as a table and four chairs.

I recalled how I'd decided to compose my *Vermian Opera* for those two friends. It was on that long-ago autumn night when I'd just come back from Denmark. I came at a late hour to the Bone Shop and they invited me upstairs to their loft and we drank whiskey together. Then, happy and drunk, I made up the idea for the opera on the spot and spent over an hour telling them the narrative. They were to be the main characters. It would involve songs of travel, tales of friendship, hymns of growing up and leaving home, exploring the world, heroic adventures. There would be an odyssey, too. There would be no heroine, no monumental love affair, but there would be an odyssey! All this, I'd told them but I never wrote it. Living my Parisian *Chandellesque* of intoxicated orgies, I'd let season slip into season. Now I was back at the Bone Shop, yet the only thing written about its heroes came not from me but from them: a few words on a sign to say that they'd be in the shop at midday. That was the document of their lives. Much time had passed and my monumental opera—destined to be my own life's greatest work—was still just an idea. All the forty nymphs of flesh I'd tasted the night before had been unfamiliar flesh—beautiful flesh, yet strangers' flesh, still to remain strange and now far away. Nothing familiar remained. It was morning, I was tired, with no festivals in sight. Nothing that night to come. And I yearned right then for something I could keep and carry with me on this drifter's road to which I was bound. A manuscript with my *Vermian Opera* dashed in ink on hundreds of glorious pages, or a just one single word, a phrase, uttered by a beloved girl who would not fade in the morning like a flake of soot from a wisp of candle smoke, yet a girl whom I could love and continue to…

"Love!" I cried, clasping my hands. "That is the sensation that is missing! Love! If I can experience falling in love, I can put a heroine into my opera. I can make it a monumental tragedy. Pyramus and Thisbe, Troilus and Cressida, Tristan and Isolte. Stories of that kind are written by composers who know what love is. I, the greatest seducer in all of Paris—perhaps the greatest seducer of our time, in all of Europe—have gone so long without knowing a woman whom I've yearned to see in the afternoon light. I've forgotten what love is. I haven't known love since that spring when I penned my last and only great tragedy: *The Twilight Tragedy*, oh so many twilights ago. I would be incapable of writing another like it now, so distanced I am from love: that holiest and most pitiable of human conditions. If only I had a sweet youthful Cordelia to long for and to occupy my thoughts . . . (Johannes' Cordelia, not Lear's.)

. . . I need a woman worthy of idolatry to bring me to a new level of passion…"

'Oh, muse Pénélope,' I called inwardly, brooding on bygone times—this was no invocation, but simple brooding. 'Where are you now as I wander the earth? We promised we would reunite! Oh, how people love to give promises. We promise in the morning and then forget in the noon. In the evening we remember our promises and laugh to ourselves as we eat hearty meals. Then in the night, we sleep and give it no more thought. What nonsense! Yet, how capricious we are, us human beings. How silly we are tramping around in mortal flesh. It's laughable, really. I could use some coffee! Yes, coffee! Ethiopian coffee. Coffee harvested on golden Afric's shore, on high tropical mountains. I will procure this at Madeleine, at the luxury market stalls. Then I will return to offer it as a gift to my old friends, August and Pavel. I'd better buy them some twelve-year-old scotch as well. They had such bad whiskey the last time I visited…'

This idea made pleasure leap in my heart, and with swift steps, I started off towards the Madeleine.

14th Soliloquy

No man ever walked with as much purpose down the rue Saint-Honoré as I that morning when, glad of heart, I made my way towards the Place de la Madeleine to trade crisp European banknotes for a kilo of roasted coffee harvested on misty African cliffs, and a bottle of malt whiskey cured in the damp, heathered fields of the Scottish highlands, so as to offer a gift to two long-ago friends, August and Pavel, denizens of the Bone Shop—located across the river from the guillotines of the Conciergerie.

Soaring across the Place Colette, I turned my head to the sky and a light passed through a cloud and burst in my eyes. As a flash bulb from an old-fashioned camera, set on a handsome tripod to forever capture the portraits of well-bred babes who pose like porcelain dolls on polished chairs, bursts with a flash pouring crackling white light over creamy faces, so did the sun burst into my eyes that day washing my body with clean heat as I crept along the city streets. The spring air soothing me, my eyes refocused and I found myself instantly beneath the massive columns of the great church at Madeleine. A hot day! Weary from sensual prances with nymphs and sleepless nights, I was. Nevertheless, I was strong of spirit, and glad to be alive!

The smell of pistachios hung in the air on the north side of the square where the luxury market stalls were set up. 'I'll have to remember this glove-maker,' I thought, walking past the vendors, swinging an imaginary cane. 'Gloves like that would make a nice gift for a young blushing victim…

'What is that?!'

Just then came the smell of a warm body, the odor of a perfumed beauty walking in full sunlight ahead of me. Her pretty little bottom was making haste up the sidewalk. So lovely was that little bottom; small and firm, like a young plum. And they way her hips dripped with sexuality as she walked. Could one imagine a more delightful bottom? . . . neat and firm, yet soft and supple enough to sway in that beloved feminine way. Lost was I in the beauty of this female form, so much so, that it took me many moments to realize that the girl I was chasing was dressed as a blue-collar laborer!

So, I thought, she's a poor working class girl. Not a high-born maid. I decided to leave her alone and just continue on my way to find the coffee and whiskey. Better get back the Bone Shop as soon as possible. I spied the girl again from head to shoe—laboring shoes with dusty soles—yet the hands that swung by her sides were not the hands of a working-class girl. They were small hands, and appeared smooth, delicate, even aristocratic—although surely the girl was a sign-painter, wearing such splotched coveralls… 'Yet that is not paint on her backside!' No, it seemed she was dusted in white patisserie flour. 'A *boulangère?*' I asked myself, '…A professional dough-wrangler? A salt-toothed bread-monger? . . . Impossible!' With such a firm and neat derrière she couldn't have possibly been a *boulangère*. Looking at the girl filled me with such desire, despite her almost boyish resemblance, being dressed in housepainter clothes. The more her hips switched back and forth, making that bottom dance as only the female animal can dance, the more hungry I became, until I could feel my canines dripping with sugary saliva. I began to play a fantasy in my mind: I was the nude and muscle-bound Apollo chasing the innocent Daphné, pale of limbs and sweet of hips, on up a trail in the wilderness—'As soon as I get close enough, I will leap on her and spread her legs apart and devour her as she moans wildly, licking now my wrists as they press against her cheeks, now the smooth stones on the trail that rest like pillows beneath her chin . . . she lies in bed and drifts to sleep with me, my happy seeds swimming in her happy womb.

'Those hips are so distracting, Lord! How could I have ever lived joyous upon this earth, never having touched this beautiful laboring girl?' I needed to look at something else. 'Look at the columns of the church in the Place de la Madeleine. No avail! I'm still thinking of the girl. Anyway, that looks nothing like a church.'

Two little blonde weaves of hair danced on her smooth neck as she walked in front of me, brushing the white patisserie flour from her shoulders down over the cotton of her coveralls. My disobedient eyes skipped back again to those lovely little forms: her waist and that perfected-shaped bottom bouncing back and forth. Finally she looked back. Obviously having heard my footsteps which were no doubt loud and uncommon of rhythm, being in such a strange hurry as I was, though distracted by the sight of her beautiful backside, the laboring girl finally looked back...

It was when she turned around, that I realized this glorified being whom I thought I'd never known nor touched in my life was a girl I knew! That illustrious bottom, and where it joins with the waist, things which I'd thought only other, lesser, men had had the joy of caressing—a thought which caused me great pain—belonged to a body I'd once known quite intimately. It was the fair Sibylle de V—!

Sibylle was a tall blonde of great beauty, whom I'd slept with twice in her apartment on the Place de la Madeleine. She was a sweet blue-blooded aristocrat and her perfect body I'd tasted in its entirety, when purely naked and wet with the joys of love, we entwined ourselves in her rose-colored room. As she turned and recognized me, I cried to her...

"Good girl, what have you?!"

"Aleksandre, it's you!"

Smiling with delight, she ran up to me.

"Sibylle, Have you fallen into desperate times? You are dressed like a laboring girl! Have you become a housepainter? No, you have become a *boulangère,* I see! You are all coated in patisserie flour. And there is flour in your hair too! Have you been forced to slave on industrial projects, straining your fair eyes and scuffing your tender skin? Good God! Is your father not around to give you some money to help you make ends meet? Here, I'll lend you some…" As I spoke, I reached in my pocket to feel for some of those good European banknotes that were pressed to the seam.

"Nonsense, Aleksandre… So good it is to see you! A funny coincidence . . . You look cute, huh!" Sibylle pressed her pair of flour-coated lips to my tender cheek, and then went on talking… "What, these clothes, you ask? No, heavens! I haven't become any kind of *boulangère!* I'm just moving out of my apartment. These are moving clothes! I'm carrying things down to the truck to put them into storage. The flour is because some spilled on my head when I was in the kitchen trying to get the pots down off the high shelf. I can't reach that high! Too bad you weren't there. I was on my tip-toes on the highest stool trying to get those stupid pots! There are still a few boxes. I have to load them in this truck parked over here. Today's my last day in Paris. Tomorrow at this time I'll be alone in Buenos Aires. Can you imagine? Buenos Aires! I'm going to live there for three months. If I like it there, I'll stay. You have to come visit me. South America of all places! What are you doing at Madeleine?!"

"I'm buying a kilo of tea leaves to send to a friend in Russia," I had no reason to twist the truth, yet I did so anyhow without intention, and doing so, I immediately felt the pleasure one gets when fabricating creative tales. All the while I spoke, I had my hands clasped to the girl's tender shoulders dusted in white patisserie flour and was feeling the noontime sun on my face. 'Why, I wonder, did I stop sleeping with such a young, yellow-haired beauty as this sweet fawn standing before me?'

"Tea leaves to send to Russia? What a strange idea! Don't they have tea in Russia?! Which way are you walking?"

"This way, let's…"

"Wait, Aleksandre! . . . Your arms are so strong, you know this?"

"Yes, yes…"

"So can you help me with a couple of boxes? And there are still a few things on the shelves, and you are so incredibly tall, you can reach higher than anyone else in Paris! Please bring your strong arms up to my apartment to help me with a couple of boxes. Please!"

To this, I leaned down to kiss her; and she dodged me, the clever girl.

"And you," I replied, smiling, "your eyes are the clearest and sweetest eyes in all of Paris. Won't you please use them to look at me more? . . . And your lips are the most beautiful I have ever seen. Won't you bring your beautiful lips close and use them to kiss me? Please bring those sweet lips to mine and kiss me.…" And kiss me she did, with a kiss so deep and pretty that we yearned to let others follow it; and still more after that until kisses of all kinds were tumbling over one another, while our wet mouths nourished themselves. All of this—her mouth and her beautiful body in my hands—brought me such pleasure, that I agreed just afterwards to help her finish moving the last few boxes out of her apartment on the Place de la Madeleine so she could go to Buenos Aires.

Up a swift flight of stairs, my feet followed the little flour-girl into an apartment that I'd seen before, on two autumn nights, decorated rose and cream, with clothes on the floor, photographs on the walls, and furniture everywhere. Now it was empty: just a parquet underfoot and plaster putty on the walls.

"It's bare, huh! I spent two days boxing everything and cleaning up the place. There are just three more boxes. But they're big!"

I walked past her into the bedroom where the bed sat, empty of sheets, only the wooden frame and the mattress remained. A cardboard box sat beside it.

"Familiar bed," I sighed happily, pulling sweet Sibylle on top of me as I flopped down on the mattress. We kissed for a while, and when tired of doing so, we stood and brushed each other off.

"We once had fun on this bed, do you remember?"

Yes, I did remember. I remembered clearly that night when we first were alone together. Leaving her girl-friend at a café terrace, we walked down the rue de Sèze past the closed dress boutiques and turned into the great Place de la Madeleine. It was a mild and cloudless night, following an evening of black-skied showers, the kind of autumn night that fills city-dwellers' hearts with poetry and gives songs to those who wander alone. I, however, in the company of my ribbon-haired beauty, goddess-like in form, needed no poetry and no songs. Let the abandoned shepherds in lonesome landscapes far away stir their hearts with poetry and songs.

"I like tonight," Sibylle had said to me then, quietly, nestling her chin into my sleeve as we walked past the church. She looked up and pressed my hand tight against hers. I felt the cuff of her peacoat brush its wool against my hand. I looked up to see if I'd need to open the umbrella again, but all the clouds appeared to have gone. "It's strange, the Madeleine. It doesn't look like a church at all."

"It looks like a courthouse!"

"Or like the temple of Athena, built on the high Acropolis."

"Are you sure it's a church?"

"I'm sure of nothing. I'm sure of nothing but the holiness of your beauty… Come, My Love…." All the while we exchanged pleasant words, I plotted how I was to get Sibylle alone in a room where I could seduce her with kisses and convince her ample clothing to tumble recklessly from her pink thighs and gather in sleepy piles at her tender feet—those feet I'd never seen, though I'd imagined them to be tender.

"Where should we go?"

'I have the keys to a room on the Avenue Marceau,' I thought to myself, 'It is near *Le Baron*. I will suggest that we finish the evening at Baron. She said she likes that nightclub. On the way to Baron I will tell her I have to stop in at my place to get some money and change my shoes. I don't want to dance in these shoes, I will say. She will come up with me and I will put the right music on, pour the right kind of wine, and if the young child is deserving, I will pluck her a well-fashioned song on a rosewood guitar. After, we may go to Baron or else finish the night in our private nest of dreams.'

"We'll go to Baron and take a drink, and dance," I said.

"What an idea! Can we walk there from here!"

"Yes, we can!"

"But I'm wearing heels. Can we stop at my apartment so I can get some shoes to walk in? I don't want to walk there in heels."

"But where is your apartment?"

"It's right here… Oh, you don't listen to me! I told you I lived at Madeleine. My apartment is right on the *place*."

"I thought you still lived with your parents at Versailles."

"I told you they sent me to Paris so that they could live in peace and so I could study in peace. Oh! You weren't listening when I told you about me when we were with Julia tonight!"

"Dear girl, if ever I would not listen to you, it could be only because I had slipped into a dream after being cast into a fantasy while sleeping on the oceans of your eyes, those starry seas passing beneath the moonlit bridge of your nose. So, should I fall into a reverie when your sweet voice leaves the perfection of your lips." So saying, I pressed my mouth to her mouth. I kissed her hot neck in the darkness and felt steam rise from her scented skin.

"The moonlit bridge of my nose?" she laughed, "You're adorable, huh! Come up to my place with me for two seconds so I can get some shoes to walk to Baron in."

What a lovable girl! Not only had she taken me at my word when I'd uttered so tediously that final romantic plea—a plea which I was feared she would suspect as being insincere nonsense—but my sweet fawn was even inviting me to her bed without any insistence of my own! Now we wouldn't have to go to the nightclub, nor would I have to court her through the avenues of the city, late as it was. She gripped tightly my hand as she opened the large gate and led me upstairs to her room.

It was a room like so many girls' I'd seen, decorated in rose and cream. I accepted her offer of a glass of wine and looked out of her window, out onto the courtyard. It was a small courtyard and the neighbor's window across the way wasn't far off. I took the wine and after we drank we kissed and fumbled with bra-clasps and panty-strings. We lit oil lamps and heavenly candles with high, leaping flames. I seized then her pink body like the stem of a slender poppy, her skin like the pelt of slender prey, and wrapped it around my arms, sturdy as banister stairs, and I climbed up her, much like a fierce ram climbs a mountain slope to chase a plump hare. Tender were her thighs. Sweet were her cries. Light, her feminine groans.

I remembered then the strange part about that autumn night, the first time I slept with Sibylle: As I was prancing on her in the throes of love-making, giving her my hard, sun-baked flesh, letting her soft, white serpentine limbs slither wet around me; while we tore at each other with passion the way men and women do once the years have aged them enough to allow them those sensual pleasures which are veiled from the very young and of which children never dream, I cast my gaze up as Sibylle lay beneath me, receiving my body, moaning and pressing her fingernails to the skin on my spine; and I saw across the room and through the window and across the tiny courtyard, into the next window. There was a little girl watching us make love. She must have been six or seven, just a child. With two dark colored braids, her face a silhouette so I could not see clearly her expression; though she was close enough—as the courtyard was small and the distance between her parents' window and ours was not great—so that I could tell she was looking right at us and with great interest, she leaned on the windowsill, seemingly hanging on our every passionate breath. I thought then to mention it to Sibylle, to climb off of her naked body and cover my groin and go to the window to close the curtain. Then I thought the better of it. 'Why not let the child witness this passionate scene?' I thought, 'It matters nothing to me. Let this be her initiation into the confused and senseless world of the adult human being. She will be a different child after tonight. I, on the other hand, will not be a different man. Tomorrow I will wake after having slept as usual. I will wash myself as usual, and go about my way, leaving Sibylle behind. I will work and take pleasure in the day....'"

Such were my thoughts which I reflected on as I made love to this woman, while a young child observed our passionate mating ritual from across the courtyard.

"Yes," I sighed, thinking back to that time, "We had fun on this bed." Whereas now I stood in daylight, standing, embracing Sibylle while she in her laboring clothes allowed the patisserie flour to splotch my finely-tailored black cotton shirt. "Sibylle, why don't I carry the bed down to the truck and save the boxes for after? The boxes are easier to lift. We should do the hardest part first."

"The bed? Thank goodness we don't have to move that bed! The bed isn't mine. It belongs to the apartment. Try and move it! It's rooted to the ground..."

"Good, we will leave the bed then."

Outside, Sibylle and I put the last of the boxes in the truck parked on the Place de la Madeleine and we kissed a loving goodbye. She said she would send me her address in Argentina once she figured it out. We went back upstairs to take a final inspection of the apartment—the rooms were completely empty except for the bed, its mattress and wooden frame. "I'm going to the airport right away," she told me. And could I do her a favor?

"What kind of favor?"

"I have to give the key back to the landlady at five this evening, but I won't be here at five. Can you come back to give it to her? She said she'd be here between five and six to take the key.

I thought for a moment. It was after midday, late as it was.

"But what would you have done if you hadn't met me by chance here on the sidewalk? *How* would you have given the key back?"

"But I *did* meet you by chance!" she smiled, the clever girl. And so, by means of her logical charm, she convinced me to do her this favor. I took the slender key from her slender hand and put it in my well-spun pocket. Then, helping her to latch the truck door, I watched her hired-driver speed away to put her boxes in storage. I kissed the fair Sibylle a final time, knowing I might never see her again; or that if I did, that it wouldn't be like it was this time or the last time. Seasons change ardent lovers, years distract us, and new friends pull us along our reckless path. "So long, my dear! No, don't make any promises! We will be changed by life and other things. Let it be so!"

She didn't hear me calling these final words, for she was gone. And I, wishing to confide my soul in someone over coffee, having not slept properly for a long time—a bout of madness whirling in my head— went about my way, off to the luxury market stalls, to buy some gifts to bring back to some friends.

PLATE 02 – La Madeleine

"It was a mild and cloudless night, following an evening of black-skied showers, the kind of autumn night that fills city-dwellers' hearts with poetry and gives songs to those who wander alone."

15th Soliloquy

"Pavel's Confession"

The cobblers and the *joailliers* were making their din, the rosewater dealers were dabbing their wares on the arms of passers-by in the luxury market stalls where I had employed a coffee vendor to shovel a hearty kilo of beans into a paper sheath. "Nothing grown on the spoiled blue mountainside of Jamaica," I warned him, "better to give me the finest peaberry picked in the far-off Pacific, on the steamy slopes of Polynesia's volcanic lands." Forthwith after, I engaged a distiller to furnish me with a half-liter of cognac. "No scotch for my friends after all. Better to keep to the grape at this hour in the early-afternoon. Give me some good eau-de-vie—*Fins Bois!* Mashed grain shall only be used for farewells and other lamentations; whereas Water-of-Life is what reunites friends and brothers torn apart by time." So saying, I paid two handsome bills, took my roll of change and clothed my eyes in dark glasses to step out into the sun...

Those scenes in the marketplace were just memories as my sturdy feet wandered back to the Bone Shop beneath the burning sun. The paper parcel packed with coffee and cognac, bundled tight, sat in my underarm. On my brow, sweat pricked my skin like a sprig of hungry nettles. I thought to call off this adventure right then and there and go to sleep in Saint Germain. There was no sense in continuing with these nettles spitting their cocktails of poisons into my body and this wild pack of imaginary lapdogs yapping and chewing at my ears. No, I would not find a bed to sleep off my troubles. Later, after a run in the park—that joyous activity that tones the muscles and inspirits the mind—I would sleep yet again, waking not at night, but late in the golden morning. Once refreshed and alive, I would pack up quickly all I could muster in a single suitcase and move to Alexandria.

"In Egypt I can work without these locusts of Parisian Society feeding on my mental crops. Aye, what are you saying?... Have you lost your mind?!"

When I returned, the door to the Bone Shop was unlocked and the "Back at Midday" sign had been taken down. I turned the knob and entered. Beside a solitary lamp in the dim room was the face of Pavel. He looked as though frozen in time. Beside his hands that held a long copper letter-opener—a tool that resembled a sturdy dagger, sharp and foreboding—and a polishing rag, sat a vodka glass and a small flask. The stone figure came to life when he saw his guest and rose up, dropping the rag and the copper dagger.

"Dmitry!" he hailed to me, using that old-fashioned name. It had been a while since anyone had called me that. Clasping shoulders, the two of us embraced to show respect for the passage of time and the seasons that flee.

"Dear Pavel, so good it is to see you! I brought rations . . . Here, things for you and August: coffee and cognac." So saying, I unwrapped the parcel on the desk. I then borrowed Pavel's polishing rag to uncork the cognac. "I see you've already started drinking this morning, eh! Do you have an extra glass? No, we can share one. Here... It's too early for me to drink." I poured the cognac into the empty vodka glass. Pavel took a swallow and placed his hand on my cheek...

"Thank you, Dmitry. But look at you! It's been over a year now since we've seen each other. Did you go back to Belgrade?"

'Belgrade?' I wondered, 'Of all places!' I reminded myself then that I'd better to keep my story straight with whatever I told Pavel last time...

"Yes, yes, Belgrade. I was in Belgrade all winter. Family affairs. Then I went to Rome. Got a lot of work done there. And you, what have you been doing? What is that?"

"What?"

"Nothing, you just had a feather or something on your chin. Now it's off. So, Pavel, how are you?"

"Me, you ask? I'm better than ever, friend. I'm in love with a girl. We're getting married... But look at you!" Pavel clasped my biceps, "You're in good form. You've been blessed beyond measure. A handsome devil. I'd say you outshine even the gods in beauty of face and nobleness of stature. I'd liken you to Zeus or Ares; or the hero, Agamemnon, or strong-legged Achilles."

"Oh, the flattery, my young friend, you make me smile. While you, yourself, know well what it means to possess godlike beauty. I hope it will never fade. I would liken you to the immortal youths: Apollo or Adonis; or to the hero Patroklos, or swift-footed Antílokhos. Only the immortals sung about in stories can match your glory."

Thus we two men continued our flattering speeches, finding joy in our meeting, for flattery is a pleasure when men are alone and without women. Just as it is likewise a pleasure to war with one another in good sport, fighting either with fists or sarcastic jests, in the boxing ring, or on the wrestling floor. For some time we continued to compare one another to the deathless ones and the heroes of antiquity; though none mentioned the sacred son of Laertes, and we both knew why; for neither wanted to raise awareness to that other heroic virtue—namely that of ruse and word-craft—which would soon be employed fervently by us both with intention to destroy the other. We carefully disguised our intentions in our interaction that afternoon...

"May I have some more cognac?"

"The bottle is for you."

"I've already been drinking since early this morning. I'm happy. That's why the 'closed' sign was up on the door. I was drinking vodka upstairs while writing a letter to . . . well, to an old friend in Russia, and I didn't want to be disturbed. Now I'm polishing this stuff to sell. It's sharp, this letter-opener, eh? It could slice a hand off—or a head! I've been rubbing it on an oil stone. It's very sharp, etc."

"Good, that's all very good, Pavel. But where is August? I thought he never left the shop."

"Oh, August! Yes, he's in Montparnasse today and tonight. His uncle died this yesterday and he went to go close the matter, to seal his uncle's apartment—Hic!—Did I just hiccup? Yes, I've drunk a bit! Can you imagine? You go and die and leave behind all you ever did or attempted to do in this life, and then someone comes the next day to 'seal your apartment' and 'close the matter' in one day and a night. That's how it was phrased! August went to go *seal* his dead uncle's apartment in Montparnasse. He'll be back tomorrow and that will be the end of it! We were just talking about you the other day, wondering when you'd be coming back to visit us, and if you ever finished writing your epic about us... 'The Vermian Opera,' it was to be called, remember? You said you were going to write that epic about us, remember? It was to be called, *The Vermian Opera*. Oh, I could never forget a title like that!"

"Yes," I sighed, pressing my damp forehead into my open palms, "*The Vermian Opera*." I took a nearby chair to seat myself and support my weary body. Locks of hair fell over my hands and I felt the moistness on my crown. Pavel set his glass of cognac on one of the display cases in the shop and approached me. "No, Pavel," I continued, "I didn't finish writing it yet... but I will. I have it all in my head, you see. I've been busy working on other projects... ballets, mostly. As well as a picaresque romance about a mysterious traveler who seduces noblewomen and makes off with their fortunes—it's a sort of an instruction manual. But I will put holy song to page very soon and complete my ode to you and August, very soon, don't worry!"

"Yes, you have to," cried Pavel, wringing his hands, "For otherwise, no one will remember me in the generations to come. August and I will be forgotten. Our lives will seep into the forgetful soil just as the black ash of summer fires seeps into the ground when the rains of autumn begin. You must sing our names like the ancient bard sang of the heroes so that we can live forever. You must!"

"What time is it?"

I peered to the window of the Bone Shop that was covered in a film of dust and tried to gauge the hour by the quality of light.

"One o'clock or so, I think."

"I'm afraid I'm feeling strange, Pavel. But you, you are a little drunk, so you can't... No, no thank you, I cannot drink that now. I don't know when the last time I slept was. I'm feeling flushed. I know I slept last night, at least for a moment. I slept in a nest of forty nymphs, each one's fragrant sex blushing like spring petals between her legs as she inhaled the winds of sleep. All were naked, piled up, their breasts and groins rubbing against me. That's a fine memory, eh? But it didn't amount to a long and peaceful sleep. When was the last time I slept a long and peaceful sleep? It must have been months. I'm going to faint I think, I'd better leave and go sleep. I'll go to Montmartre now. When August is back, will you please..."

"You need to drink coffee!" cried Pavel, "You brought this coffee. I'll make some!" Pavel scurried about and returned with a sheath of Polynesian beans.

"I'm afraid my judgment is not good. I feel that I'm capable of some rash mistake."

"What do you mean? You aren't happy?"

"On the contrary! My life is a jug of wine, filled to the brim yet tilted to spill with constant pleasure... These are heroic times, my dear Pavel Ivanovich. I've never thought this kind of happiness was attainable. Joy spills from my body like milk from a ladle. The world is a vast savannah where I am free to run wild like the first man on lush Eden's fields, all around me Eve and her sisters are dancing and delighting in the existence of flesh. Great it is to be alive! It's just that..."

"Just what?!"

"It's just that I'm tired. I'm tired and I cannot sleep. I run too fast and I close my eyes at the approach of dawn only to open them a moment later and my body feels hollow, my skin like perforated leather. My bones jostle one another and my skin yearns to separate. Do I look like I am a hundred years old? No? Well, my judgment isn't good and I fear I will react the wrong way if something occurs... what is this?"

"It's your coffee! I'll have some too. Do you want milk? No? What's wrong with this kind of milk? It smells like good coffee. Where are you going?"

"Just over here to see if you have a spoon..."

On my way to the sink in the back of the dusty Bone Shop, I stopped when my eye took sight of a very old book sitting inside a glass display case. It had a leather spine and yellowed pages filled with an archaic, handwritten script. 'Strange book,' I thought. I wanted to take it out and study it, but first I wanted a sip of coffee but the sugar needed to be dissolved so I left to find a spoon at the sink.

Still at the sink, while stirring my coffee, I eyed some packets of dried herbs and powders arranged on a small shelf. I had to squint to read the names on the labels of the packets—so blurry was my vision on this day. 'GRECIAN FOXGLOVE' one of the packets was labeled. 'Grecian foxglove?' I smiled to myself. Or *Digitalis lanata*, as it is also known. A very powerful plant. I began to think of Stendhal. 'What a discovery!' A packet beside the digitalis was labeled 'CALAMUS ROOT' Having no use for the calamus, I picked up the packet of toxic digitalis and slipped it discreetly into my pocket. I then retook the coffee spoon...

The act of stirring my coffee put me in a kind of rhythmic trance in which I remained until I caught Pavel making mischief out of the corner of my eye. He was hunched over like a creeping thing, scuttling like a shadow across the floor. I watched him stealthily cross over to the glass case where the curious old book was on display, his shifty eyes darting back and forth. He was trying to see if I was aware of him but I pretended not to notice, feigning to be deeply concerned with my coffee's state of affairs. So I stirred my sugar; and glancing imperceptibly over to him, I watched him seize a dark-colored blanket from the floor and inch it carefully over the glass display case in an effort to cover it and conceal its contents. After he covered the case, he slithered away.

"You are keeping parakeets?" I perked up in a resonant voice that echoed in the somber room. I carried my coffee over to where Pavel stood by his desk. He was pretending now to be occupied with the buttons on his shirt. I set my cup down on the desk, placing it in top of the polishing rag so that the heat of the cup wouldn't damage the wood. "When did you get parakeets?"

"What do you mean, parakeets?"

"One would say it was a cage with a parakeet under that blanket. You covered him to shield him from light so he could sleep. You need to cover a parakeet's cage when it's time to sleep…."

Pavel's face flushed. He turned nervously to the display case. "No, that… a parakeet, you ask?… No, it is because there is an old manuscript in the display case, a four-hundred year old book. August asked me to keep it shielded from the light to protect the pages. I'd forgotten. It is a very old book!"

"Which book? I'd like to have a look!"

"Elizabethan manners… It is a book on manners… in English! It was printed in London. You wouldn't be interested though because…"

"Why wouldn't I be interested?"

"Or perhaps you would be interested!" Pavel smiled slyly, "Let me take it out so you can have a look." With calculating hands, Pavel inched back the blanket only enough so that he could slide open one side of the display case and reach his hands in to feel among the contents. A moment later, he pulled the weathered book out of the case, draped the blanket back down so it covered completely the side of the case. Then, and only then, did he turn his back to the case. He set the book on the desk and began to leaf through the pages.

"It covers everything from greeting a king properly to how to hold your hat so that people don't thinking you're begging alms. August might not be happy about the book being exposed to light like this. I'd better put it back...."

"Yet it's so dark in here," I replied. All the while I was thinking: 'Pavel's mistake was to remove the book from the display case and then to *cover the case back up* with the blanket, claiming the book as the one object in there necessary to conceal and protect from light. This makes me curious about the rest of the contents. Why did he put the blanket back? Why must the blanket remain on the case when the book is no longer in it?....' Taking the opportunity while Pavel's back was turned, I set my hand on the case and pushed the blanket away in a swift movement, as though out of clumsiness, as though a draft in the room had taken part in the act. Before Pavel could react—he still being hunched over the desk inspecting the book—I crouched to look at all the objects in the uncovered case. It was then that I saw it...

Next to the book were several fountain pens, some antique inkwells resting on the felt. Objects of no consequence. It was near to those pens, however, that an item was displayed whose site mangled the nerves in my stomach and sent me into a rage.

Inside the case was a lady's necklace: a chain of white gold, bearing a single pendant. The golden chain was woven of threads thin as gossamer. The pendant was a Russian winterberry encased in a drop of magnificent amber. "Pénélope's necklace!" I seethed. A foam of rage filled my head and chest. It was the necklace I had given to her long ago. No other necklace was there in this world to match this one. The pendant was obtained in Petersburg, the gold in Copenhagen. This gift I presented to Pénélope in Paris, long ago. She said she'd cherish it like nothing else. Now it was sitting for sale in a miserable brocante on the quai of the Seine. See the rage that seethed inside me...

"Pénélope's necklace!" I roared, and with delirious hands I grabbed the display case door and flung it open, wildly reaching inside, grappling about; I seized the necklace. Then, dropping it, I turned around and latched my mighty palms around the neck of Pavel Ivanovich.

"You!" I cried, "Either you are a thief... Or else..." As I furiously clenched Pavel's neck, I thought only of milking the life from it. "What have you done, scoundrel! Where is the girl?!" Bearing my teeth like a wolf, I searched in Pavel's frightened eyes, waiting for them to reveal to me the reason why he had my gift to Pénélope in his possession. In the shackles of my hands, Pavel hung limp and choked out some words, his eyes were swamped with fear. I watched terror grow in him as the veins on his wet forehead spun like cords around his hairline. Squeezing the skin on his nape, I heard the seams of his shirt tear. My fierce animal eyes looked into his as I waited for him to save himself. "Go on and speak!" I shouted, "Speak quick, you scoundrel. Speak if you want to save your life!" Just then his eyes that only a moment ago had been fearful, gained a sudden strength and turned to eyes of hate. Trembling beneath me, Pavel choked out these words...

"I bought it from her! That's why I have it. The necklace belongs to me!..."

"Liar!" I shouted; and fully aware that Pavel was under my subjugation, I loosened my grip slightly, though I kept hold of his tender throat. My mind raced, trying to imagine what had happened... "How did you... *buy* it?" I demanded, "Where is she?! What have you done to Pénélope?!" These questions flew out of my mouth like wasps leaving a hive, meanwhile horrible scenes involving Pavel and Pénélope flashed in my brain. Flushed with a sudden terrible fear, I pushed Pavel away...

My eyes twitched around the somber room. Returning my gaze to his face, I searched in the sallow pools of his eyes. Unbearable thoughts ravaged my imagination. I knew it was now too late to save his life. Nothing I could do at that point would be too rash. All I desired was to pierce his soft flesh with my mighty hands and tear with my teeth the arteries from his neck. Keeping a tight grip on his neck with one hand, I reached with the other to the desk where I retrieved the copper letter-opener, shaped like a sturdy dagger, which he had freshly sharpened for me on an oil stone. I grabbed the dagger and rose it before his eyes, ready to pierce his supple skin. Before I could press the dagger to his throat, he leapt to the ground to supplicate me.

On his knees, he assumed the position of the vanquished warrior: one arm, he wrapped around my knees, gripping them tight. The other arm he rose to hold my chin with his hand. This position forced his head to raise up, leaving his throat vulnerable. He stared hard into my eyes with frenzied desperation...

"Please don't do it, Dmitry... Spare me and I will tell you everything. You will see I am not a thief... Please let me go and we will talk. I will tell you the whole story...."

In response to his supplication, I clenched his wrist where he held my chin. With my hand that held the copper dagger, I thrust it down towards my suppliant's exposed neck so that the sharp blade was pressed against the veins and issued these words...

"I should spare you? Why should I spare, when you did not spare she who is for me the only thing worth sparing in this world? I told you to deny her no service, to offer her everything and deny no service. Was this your service to her and to me? To rob my poor girl? I'm afraid there's nothing you can say in this corrupted season. Perhaps if this had been an earlier day, if my mind weren't so mangled by the sight of you and this dank and dusty room, I would've spared your life and not cut your throat. But why should you be spared and my troubles be suffered? You think because you are like me? . . . You think because you too left your native country and everything behind to wander far and live the heroic life, braving the path that strangers brave, living always on the outskirts, that you persist in this in spite of your fear like me, you think you should necessarily come to a heroic end? Poor child! Maybe you will die a fool reaching for the sun! Why not?! Even to save all of the blood from spilling from your veins and preserve your life wouldn't be worth the troubles of even one night's headache weighing on my brow. I would do fine to dispose of you even to save myself the slightest discomfort. For I too will die like you, but I am better than you Pavel. I don't grieve for you at all...."

In the final croak that Pavel uttered beneath my feverish hand—a hand driven by a brain that knew nothing of sense this afternoon, so drunk was I from sleepless nights, weary from months of high living and charged with the madness of constantly dwelling in an artist's fiction—on the day I almost killed Pavel Ivanovich, he managed to express a few words that made me curious—at least enough to delay the happy journey of that blade to his tender throat…

"Pénélope is coming back. . . *achh*. . . for it!" he croaked. Then he blurted… "She left your necklace in my care! . . . *squawk!* . . . She is coming back for it! I'll tell you all!"

Hearing this, I dropped my copper blade on the ground and seized my suppliant by the collar to demand an explanation to this madness.

"What do you mean, she *left it with you*? When is she coming back? Tell me and if you lie to me one word, I will spill your blood all over this dirty floor!" So saying, I unhinged my captor and let him hobble beside me to a seat on a leather canapé by the blackened window. "…Sit and tell me all."

"Please!" Pavel begged to me, motioning towards the back of the room, "Let me get one thing that will prove to you that I did not steal the necklace from her…" He started for the back desk and I didn't stop him but watched carefully, always eyeing the copper letter-opener that was on the floor near the desk—'in case he should grab it and charge me,' I thought, while feeling around the shelves beside me for a new object . . . I found a metal bar of sorts which I planned to dash across his skull, should he try to collect the copper sword and charge me.

"I'm just getting a note I wrote to August," Pavel called from the back hall, by the sink, "I left the note in the box where we put the mail when it arrives, in case that . . . in case I would be out when he returned from his uncle's. I did not want August to find the necklace and sell it. Sometimes I leave this shop for two or three days at a time, you see. I didn't want August to sell the necklace. Pénélope left two other things of value in my care. She left a bracelet given to her by her maid Gulya, and some gold earrings given to her by Themia. They are in the display case as well."

Pavel retrieved the note he wanted to show me and returned to the canapé and sat down and pressed it on the table for me to see. I read these words…

August, please under no circumstances give anyone the jewelry that is in the far display case (the case below the picture of your mother wrapped in ivy). I will explain everything when I get back, but these items—a necklace with an amber berry, a gold bracelet and some earrings—they belong to Pénélope. Please do not allow anyone to buy them or take them. Only if Pénélope comes herself asking for them back—and to tell of the despair, should she do that!—only then should you surrender them and only to her. I hope it went well with your uncle's affairs. I'm sorry again that he is dead. See you soon, my friend. — Pavel.

After reading the note twice, during which time Pavel spread his drunken fingers on the paper and blurted 'You see!' again and again in a tearful voice, I started to believe that he was not a thief and that there was an even more disturbing reason why the necklace I gave to my virgin Pénélope was in his care. 'What trouble has she run into? She needed to flee from Paris even without her jewelry? Nonsense! She left it behind by accident...' Then the most horrible of ideas came into my head... 'If Pénélope left it by accident here in the Bone Shop, then she had to have taken it off her body. She would have had to of removed the necklace, the bracelet, as well as the earrings, then left without remembering to put them back on...' A sickness mounted in my gut... 'But why did she take them off at Pavel's place? Did Pavel seduce my virgin Pénélope?!' Such thoughts! 'If he's touched Pénélope, I will take that copper knife and castrate the fool!'

"Tell me why did she leave them here? Did she undress herself with you and then forget to dress again entirely? Tell me!" I grabbed Pavel's arms and clenched them and he trembled... "No, Dmitry! She took them off at the door and handed them to me. She handed them to me and said she would be back for them soon. There were tears in her eyes. Let me tell you the story... *Oh, there were tears in her eyes!*

"It all started weeks ago..." Pavel begin to recount, as soon as I'd refilled the cognac in his glass and watched him sink into his seat with a mixture of calmness and horror... "The first time Pénélope came to the Bone Shop, she was looking for you. She had received a letter. The shop was mentioned in the letter but you were nowhere to be found. August and I sat here on this same leather seat, entranced by the beauty of this new strange girl sitting across from us drinking her coffee—so wild was she! We told her that we knew her—or *about her*, rather—that you had described her to us, and that you had asked us to deprive her of no service; and since we were indebted to you, we would offer her whatever we could, despite our poverty.

"'But I don't need anything in the world!' she had said, '…Just to find Dmitry. Do you know where he is?' She was very loyal to you. It happened only very late and by accident that we kissed each other down here, while drinking wine and talking. I told you, you were nowhere to be found!… So I kissed her and she kissed me… hic!" Pavel excused himself for drunken noises while my stomach turned with jealous fury. "Go on!" I ordered, "Continue your story!"

"…So we kissed and then we began sleeping together."

"Sleeping together?!"

"She told me she had only slept with you before and no one else. August was sound asleep in his bed, I took her up to my little stuffed cot and laid her down and…" . . . 'I will kill him,' I thought all the while, 'Slaughter him on his filthy stuffed cot or on the floor of this dismal room, the damned Russian vagabond, dirty little worm… "Wait!" Pavel cried, seeing the anger flushing my face. "We talked about you constantly, she and I, and fondly, the way a young brother and sister talk fondly about an older sibling, the older brother who has left the confines of the home to brave the world and face all its inherent dangers. I loved you and she loved you and it was based on our love for you that our passion for one another grew. There was nothing treacherous about it, we kept waiting for you to come. But you never came!…

"I knew that this was the only woman I ever wanted touch and hold in my arms. I swore a devotion to her: I would live the rest of my life with her and devote myself to her happiness. She said she'd wanted *you* to swear such devotion to her once but you refused. That you were always busy traveling around, that you saw other women. She mentioned a time in Barcelona when she waited two weeks for you in a tiny pension while you were neither here nor there.   Later she learned you'd been tramping around Austria with some buxom blonde movie actress...."

"So I'm the one to blame for having let the bird grow bored and flutter off into some stranger's coop. But tell me about the necklace!"

"She would come late at night... We slept together a few times over the last couple weeks. Always late at night. She would come late and tap her fingernails lightly on the window." Pavel demonstrated tapping on the surface of a dusty table by his knees. "...like that. She would tap and I would climb down out of my cot and let her in—careful not to wake August—and she and I would go upstairs and make love on my cot.   After, we would lie together awake under the blankets whispering to each other. In the morning early she would wake before the rest of us and slip away. No trace of her would be left. August never knew...

"I saw her only once in the daytime. It was an overcast day, like so many we have in Paris. She came here in the afternoon and I left off work to go walk with her through the Tuileries. We talked about the white-colored statues we passed on the garden paths and we talked about the future. I said I wanted to marry her and take her to America..."

"America?" I interrupted, "Why *there* of all places?!" ...telling him that was absurd, etc.

"She said that neither of us had enough money to go to America or anywhere else. That we were doomed. She told me the story of how a man named Philippe, friend of the family, had gambled away her sister's fortune and how her father was very old now and was in poor health; and how since I didn't have a place of my own to live—squatting on a cot in August's Bone Shop, as I do—we wouldn't be able to marry..."

'So Philippe squandered Themia's money away!'

"'I'll figure out a way to buy tickets to America,' I told her. 'Once we are there, I will work in a store until we have enough money to buy our own store. I will work hard to provide for you and a family. We will have children and they will grow up in America and take over the store when I die'—hic!"

"Pavel, tell me about the necklace!"

"Yes! Then there was one night—exactly a week and three days ago—when Pénélope came at an early hour in the night. August was awake upstairs doing the accounting, adding figures together, and I was down here, on this same sofa, fixing some trinkets that had broken. Suddenly the tapping came at the window and I jumped up...

"'Pénélope!' I cried in a hush, as soon as I'd slipped outside to meet her, 'August isn't asleep yet,' I told her. 'It's okay,' she muttered through a veil of tears, 'I cannot stay. I have to leave tonight to see my father....' She pressed her damp hands to her tear-stained face and I opened the door to lead her inside.

"'It's Pénélope,' I told August, who'd heard the commotion and descended the stairs, 'Can you leave us to talk?' Without a word of reply, he took his hat and stepped out into the darkness.

"I remember the way she looked at me with a sudden look of horror before pressing her wet eyelids into her cupped hands to cry. Here, she sat. Just like you and I sit now, but then there was so much despair. She explained that her father was very ill and that he was probably going to die soon and that she needed to go north to see him. She wouldn't tell me where he was. I asked if he was in Norway or in Sweden, but she wouldn't give me that information. She only said that she needed to go north... 'To a city of coal and stone,' she said, 'on the coast of Leviathan's Sea.'"

"Curious!"

"'But why can't I come with you?' I asked. . . . 'Because I need to go alone, Pavel. But when I will come back for you, we will go to America together and get married.' . . . 'When will you come back, Pénélope?' . . . 'I'm not sure. Soon enough...' With that she stood, and said goodbye, pressing lidded eyes to the swollen knuckles on her hand.

"Ach! You will not come back!' I shouted after her, sick with rage and sorrow. She stopped by the door and listened, petrified. 'You are crying so much because you are leaving Paris for good. That is why! Why won't you tell me where you are going? Are you going to Oslo?

Why won't you tell me where your father is? Is your sister in Paris? Tell her to come see me. Is she really 'ruined' as you say she is? Tell me!...'

"'Stop!' Pénélope screamed, turning to me. Then a drop of silence. The darkness outside blew into the shop in a terrible gust as the door creaked open to let her thin body slip through. A final time, she ran back inside and pressed her salty mouth to my lips and declared her love for me... 'I will come back!' she promised. (This is where the necklace comes in.) When she kissed me this last time, she took off the necklace from around her neck. I recognized it as being yours. She had told me about it when she first started coming to the Bone Shop—back when we were casual about things. I was always jealous of that necklace. She continued to wear it even after our first passions were exchanged. It made me terribly jealous but I had to accept it. Now on the last night I saw her, she gave it to me with her promise, spoken through a blanket of tears, she took off the necklace, she took off also a bracelet given to her by Gulya, her maid, and some gold earrings which Themia gave her, and she handed these three items to me... 'These are the only possessions that mean anything to me,' she swore, pressing them into my palm, 'Keep them safe and I will be back for them and for you in three week's time. Then we will travel to America together and start our new life.' Pénélope gave a final painful look at my own face which was by now also crying, also filled with tears, and she stepped out into the darkness. Clutching her necklace—as well as her bracelet and the earrings—wet with tears and cold with despair, I stood in that doorway and listened in sorrow to the quick little sound of her feet as they shuffled up the quai and were gone.

"Now her jewelry sits in that glass case over there, waiting for her, as I sit in this miserable Bone Shop, also waiting for her. But do not grow angry, Dmitry! I deserve to be with her. You never gave yourself to her fully before; and still now, I believe, you wouldn't be able to give yourself to her completely, nor to any other woman. You have *many* women in your life. I have *only* Pénélope and need no other for as long as I live!"

Finishing his speech, Pavel sunk down deflated on the canapé. I sat up straight and, leaning forward, spoke... "Grief, Pavel! Your story has stirred sympathy in my chest." So much was sincere, as hearing

Pavel's confession put strange sentiments in my heart. It was true, I was once Pénélope's true and only love. But I shall accept that time and other things had come to change that. Considering what had been said to me, I felt a lightness come into my chest, and felt the crisis was coming to pass. Still, I wove my reply carefully. I wanted now to see Pénélope as soon as she returned in a week and a half's time, though I later concealed my reasons for this. All was weighing on me: the hope at seeing my youthful Pénélope again, the confusion from a lack of sleep, along with the potent sip of cognac I'd taken that afternoon. All of this pressed me with strong desire to play the benefactor. After Pavel had finished his confession and had dried his eyes, I reached into my well-sewn pocket and retrieved the slender key which Sibylle de V— had given me to return to her landlady that evening at five. I handed the key to Pavel and said...

"Please do me this favor, Pavel. Take this key and promise me one thing: I have an apartment in Paris sitting empty. It is a beautiful apartment on the Place de la Madeleine, I've owned it for many years and it's now empty as the family I rented it out to has recently moved back to Chile. Look, here is the key. Do me a favor and when Pénélope returns from her father's sickbed to be with you, go with her to live in this apartment. I promise you it is a beautiful place: spacious and clean, it looks out on a quaint little courtyard. She will be happy there and you too. All I ask in return for this gift is that when she comes, and you two are properly moved in, that you write me and invite me to dine with you. We three will have a 'Last Supper' together and we'll toast to your life. After our feast, you will be free to do as you please—you can either take Pénélope and move to America, braving the grim uncertainties in a bitter world that await you there; or you can remain in Paris and marry Pénélope. Here you'll both live in comfort together and free of cares in the home I am providing for you at the Place de la Madeleine. Just one feast together is all I ask in return. Once Pénélope returns to Paris, you and she will prepare a feast for the three of us. We will dine and talk of life, settling matters. I give you my solemn oath... after this Last Supper, should you both remain in Paris, I will visit you two no longer, unless I am called on—nor will I attempt to contact Pénélope, unless it is by your wish, as well as by hers, that I do so. Here, take the key! It is a generous gift, you realize! Apartments at the Place de la Madeleine don't grow on plane trees in the Parc Monceau, you know! All I ask is that you make up your mind now and not a second longer...." So I spoke with feverish words, as the humidity dripped from my desperate brow.

After my speech, Pavel stirred strangely. He leapt from his seat and clasped my legs in humility. With squirming eyes, he gave me a look of fear that suddenly turned cold. He recoiled then and said calmly without emotion...

"No. I don't want your apartment, Dmitry. This condition that you made: that you see Pénélope again for a final feast, this will cost us too much. I fear she still loves you. I cannot let you see her. Take your key back and let me be alone. You shall never find her. When she returns to Paris, I will sneak away with her myself to America. There I will work and provide for her all by myself, without the help of another—as a man should do."

"Aye, good luck with that, Pavel. In America you will find yourselves among unsupportive company. Let me tell you! Maybe you will find a tiny hovel and put dinner on the table by working long hours as a clerk in some store, or as a laborer. If you are lucky, and you don't get consumed by drink or by greed, you may accumulate enough savings after a decade or so to buy a little grocery of your own in the squalid immigrant-quarters of Brooklyn or Queens. There you will slave and grow old, your spine sagging more and more with each day that passes; and at the end of your life with Pénélope you two will scrape together the seeds gathered in the corners of the walls, where the rats scurry and the termites nest, only to see they really don't amount to anything at all. Is that the heroic life you sought when you left your native Russia? Here, I am offering you a chance to prosper. To live a flourishing life in Paris. All you have to do in return is let me dine with you one evening and see Pénélope a final time."

"This forecast of our life in America is nonsense, Dmitry. Wherever I go, I will attain heroism, for myself and for Pénélope. It is asking too much, for you to see her again. You will ruin her. She told me the story of how you met. She was a very young girl, and was just a conquest for you. You wanted to conquer her the first day you met, and when you didn't, you became bitter and left in the night without saying goodbye. Later, despite her warnings, you came to see her again here in Paris, and then in the South of France. She was cautious, but you managed to seduce her, taking her virginity in a villa in Monte Carlo. She fell in love with you after that and you took her away, only to abandon her shortly after. A few more times you reappeared in her life, only to seduce and then abandon her again. Each time, she became more and more distraught. Only when she met me, the second man to come into her life, did she become truly happy. This she told me. I gave her love as well as devotion. I neither seduced her, nor did I abandon her. I gave myself to her purely, having desire for nothing else other than to see her happy. She did curse you! . . . still, I'm afraid that if you see her again, she will fall under your spell again and be ruined. I foresee that what will begin with a 'Last Supper,' as you call it, will end in tragedy. You do not love her, but only want to sacrifice her. I will not let you *crucify* Pénélope—hic! No, Dmitry. I refuse your offer. There is no generosity in your offer. Here... Take the key back... Take it!"

"Pavel, my friend..." Shaking my head, I spat remorseful vows, all the while pressing the key that had been thrust back into my hands back into my adversary's calloused palm. "Pavel, please hold the key for a moment. Yes, good . . . Now, what is all this nonsense about crucifying people? First of all, have I ever shown anything but generosity to you? Did I not, on the first occasion we met, offer my generosity to you and to August both? If you recall, I gave to you and asked nothing in return. So was I with Pénélope. Now, you must believe me, that if I need to see her again, it is not because I want to steal her from you, or ruin her. I just need to finish my hero's tale. My work depends on seeing Pénélope a final time. If only you knew... Oh, I'm weary of this! You're an ungrateful creature! Listen to how things really went between Pénélope and me and you will understand. This story you told confuses me. Surely Pénélope had had masked intentions when she told you about our relationship together. She told you this so that you would believe that she was vulnerable to me more than she was. For although we separated often, she knew that we did so out of necessity—for she and I could never be together. I was always pulled away by the needs of the wanderer, why she stayed faithfully behind—these are our opposing natures. But she did not become distraught. All the while she remained faithful, she pulled away from me with the needs of a woman, an enemy of time that slowly dries-up one's life. She knew she could not remain faithful long to a wanderer such as I am. If she ever was seduced by me, her suffering in my absence only weakened my powers of seduction, breaking any spell I may have first cast on her. She came to realize that she could find happiness only with one who could offer her devotion. Now she is in love with you, and if I see her again and the three of us are together, she will surely only fall deeper in love with you for she will see clearly the contrast between a faithful man such as you—one who can devote himself completely to one woman—and a capricious man like me: wayfaring and bound by no one, only fastened to the wandering road and the fleeting years that glide him along… Can you listen to me? Listen, while I tell the brief and accurate story of how Pénélope and I met and came to meet and know each other. It is a story filtered of all untruths that have been passed between lips made bitter by sorrows that by now surely have passed. Once you know my story, you will know I did not try to ruin her, nor will I ever. I ask only for the price of my words that you decide *immediately* if you will go to this apartment of mine on the Place de la Madeleine, and there live with Pénélope and receive me for a final feast so we may put an end to this matter once and for all."

16th Soliloquy

"Dmitry tells his own story…"

Seated on the burnished leather seat near the film-coated window in the Bone Shop that afternoon, I began to recount the following tale to the waiting ears of Pavel Ivanovich, with the belief that should the nobleness of my character and purity of my intentions shine through the simple recollections of long-ago misadventures, my subject might be compelled to accept the generosity of the gift I'd offered: an empty apartment at the Place de la Madeleine in Paris—a place whose occupancy its usual inhabitant (one Mademoiselle Sibylle de V—) would suspect naught as she goes trotting around the Southern Hemisphere with blonde locks trailing from her eager head—and also grant me an audience during a feast where bread would be snapped and wine would be drunk… (yes!, bread would be snapped and wine would be drunk!)… with our mutual beloved, the lovely and fated Miss Pénélope—singular heroine of gorgeous face and tender age.

"What's that, Pavel? No more cognac? No, please, I insist! Good. Yes, take a little more. I'll fill your glass. Now hear my tale, it all began like this…

The season was fair and few of cares...

I was still a very young man, though I was alone and traveling the world. I'd just received a commission to write my first opera and had come to Italy to relax and work peacefully, to get some sunshine and some summer sport.

It was only the third week of June, yet the air was scalding. I rented a villa for a dozen days near the town of S— and spent my mornings and afternoons at the lake, waterskiing and swimming. In the evenings I'd drive into town to dine by myself. After, I would stroll through the festive streets or go to the theater to see an opera. I slept well at night. The villa was outside of town, to the east. It had three spacious rooms and a colonnaded deck overlooking lush vineyards. It wasn't far to the lake. And it wasn't far into town. One could easily take a streetcar from the villa to the lake or to the town, and I sometimes did. Though I usually preferred to drive.

I hired a boat and a driver to pilot it while I waterskied first-thing everyday, staying in the best part of the lake where the private citizens skied—where there were almost no tourists on the beach or pleasure boats on the water. The lake wasn't large, and the air was dry and so hot that once the motorboat dove into its acceleration, and the triceps in your arms tensed and you were lifted up onto the surface of the water, the wind would dry you in an instant; and it felt as if you'd never gotten wet at all as you careened over the lake, ever faster, the edge of the ski slicing through the water like a hot blade cutting through ceramic—so clean and pristine the water beneath you, so creamy that sky, hot and blue above you.

It was early in the morning when we met. The final weekend of my sojourn in Italy. I woke as usual before sunrise so as to be among the first skiers on the lake. I could barely get out of bed, my muscles had seized-up, and I was worried I had injured myself and wouldn't be able to ski; but after taking my coffee on the deck, the cramps went away and I began to feel that exhilaration that comes in the morning in a warm climate, when one wakes early to bright weather and potent coffee.

I took the car and flew down the narrow roads, dressed in shorts and leather sandals. I recalled how on the same road the night before, when coming back from town wearing a white suit and tie after dinner with the red wine swirling in my head, feeling sad that I would soon be leaving Italy and returning to Paris, I'd seen some dear and raccoons crossing the road. Now, it was a beautiful clear morning and I wasn't sad any longer. I felt as strong as a god. Not a care in the world…

When I came to the dusty road where the first cafés were on the way into town, still some kilometers from the turn off to drive down to the lake, I stopped to put a few liters of fuel in the car. After I pumped the gas, I walked towards the little store to pay the attendant. A very pretty, rather young, girl was sitting by herself on the curb next to the store. She was dressed for the beach, with a towel wrapped around her waist and a little muslin shirt on top with thin straps that fell down off her small dark shoulders. She was busy looking at something on her leg. A bag and a shoebox sat on the ground beside her. As I approached, I watched a station attendant pass by and address her in Italian; she responded disinterestedly in English without looking up at him, and then mumbled something to herself in French. I found this curious, though none-too-original. Her legs were very long, and slender too, as one often finds on the beauties native of Catalonia, of Valencia, of Mallorca. Eyebrows so light, as though brushed on with oil by soft bristles; and they stood guard over downcast eyes. Her tiny breasts sat taught in her loose muslin top, displaying youthful cleavage, soft as lime. The firm summits of her breasts pressed the outlines of fragrant nipples to thin fabric. 'How could they be fragrant?' I wondered; as I could not smell them, I saw the absurdity of this observation, 'Those are the orange trees in the nearby fields that are fragrant, their sweet and pungent oils drifting in the arid breeze. The trees are fragrant, not her nipples!' The girl slid her hand over her knee and pressed her sandaled foot to the cement as she picked up the shoebox and set it on her lap and began tapping the lid on the box.

'A very handsome young girl,' I thought to myself, 'Very pretty.' Yet most young girls are pretty. Prettiness is the attribute of the young girl. Few, however, are beautiful. Beauty is bestowed on a woman when she is grown, and then only rarely. Only given that she is favored by divine fortune, and then only after the long years have evaporated what was pretty before. Nature distributes the gift of prettiness to young girls as one distributes bonbons to children. So, prettiness is only as valuable as bonbons, though sweet as cicadas' songs. Yet *beauty*—that holy gift—Nature gives only to whom Nature loves. Rare as a lunar eclipse, it shall be coveted. When it is gone, its memory shall be coveted. Those same long years which give woman a gift divine, later will split her bones, furl her skin and arch her spine. Lament that it is so!

Yet, concerning this slender and suntanned child I met that day while filling the car with fuel on that dusty Italian road: even if she was too young to possess a woman's beauty, oh how she possessed Aphrodite's charms! Some mistakenly call Aphrodite the goddess of love and beauty, but Venus knows nor cares nothing for love and beauty. *Sexual passion* is her happy domain! And this tender, stainless girl had yet to be initiated into either love or beauty; but her gorgeous body in its first fertile youth was sly Aphrodite's fresh pubescent playground.

I calmly gazed at her, though I was possessed by sexual hunger. She noticed my gaze and returned it as naturally as I could have hoped for. We performed our roles with perfect biological precision—mine the masculine, hers the feminine—and we conducted our first flirtation:

My eyes drifted up her face with desire and settled on her eyes. She cast her glance up to meet mine, first defensively, as warm-blooded prey, ready to leap away. Her look seemed to say: 'What do you want from me? Why am I being cornered? Let me flee!'

Then the second stage came: when that woman's instinct is sparked within her, fueling her eyes with a sexual charge. This is how the female animal tests the male, to see if he's strong or to see if she can overpower him with her charms and drive him into submission. His strength is both what she wants and what she fears. 'Look at my face and my eyes, my body too. You will grow weak before me and fall like a coward!' At this point in a sexual interaction, I am reminded of Circe turning men to swine. Many weak men fall before her. Finally, that brave hero comes who defies her look and draws his sword. He is ready dash his sword across her chest. She immediately submits to him and is overcome by desire. She invites him to her bower so the two can perform the sexual act.

I didn't fail the test, but kept looking at the girl firmly and steadily; my eyes penetrating into the blacks of her own; her pupils dilated, leaking black watery ink into the surrounding brown sea. I thirsted to leap this instant on her and devour her. When she saw that the charms of her face and her seductive eyes would not intimidate me, she moved to the third stage of the flirtation: the point where the female surrenders to her desire for this new male and lets him take control. Her eyes fluttered while I held my stare, never looking away, never looking down. And she responded to this with a smile of pleasure. It crept up her face and lifted the corners of her lips. She beamed with pleasure, at his point I smiled at her too. And now, realizing that she had not defeated me and could not, and that I would be the one to take possession of her, the corners of her lips that had raised, now pulled down the corners of her eyes, the way a hand pulls a curtain over a window. Her eyelids fell into pure submission. She looked at the ground. She was mine for the taking. I looked then away and walked past her without a sound.

Inside the little store, I paid the attendant for the gas and thought of the girl outside. My body was filled with rapture. As though I'd caressed the thighs of the Spartan queen . . . My friend, do you realize how beautiful it is to be cast into this sensual world?, this social den of sexual beasts where we delight in preying on each other and being preyed on? That moment she and I first looked at each other contained an entire epic in verse. You laugh, Pavel! But you were not there. There was an entire life's romance written in the moment when our eyes flashed together. It contained Leander swimming the Hellespont and Hero splitting apart virgin thighs. That young girl sitting on the curb with a shoebox in her hands, I likened to the ancient Nausicaa washing laundry on the shore. I needed to write her into my work. She would be my muse, my Erato. I would treat her like Nausicaa and let her marry another younger than myself—some soft-faced Italian boy. I would vow to let her remain stainless like Artemis . . . 'Or maybe I will enjoy her sexually myself!' I thought at first. I would charm her, seduce her, and milk the sweet youth from her body. Then I would put her into my work and read of her again and again, season after season, carrying her ageless company into my weary, agèd years. 'It is still very early,' I told myself, 'She's already been swimming today. Her hair is wet and tangled. She is in such disorder. It must be getting late...'

I stepped outside from the store and the sun burned pleasantly on the back of my neck. I walked to my car. There, by the car, the girl was standing. She was holding her bag and her shoebox, poised on her toes so that the heels of her feet cast dark shadows on the backs of her sandals—this latter detail, though minute, etched itself firmly in my memory and I still visualize it perfectly today.

"*Monsieur ? Vous m'emmenez vers la ville un petit peu ?*"

Why had she accosted me in French?, I wondered, when my car had Italian plates. Ah! I recalled I had a copy of *Paris Match* sitting on the front seat in plain view (the top was down). She must've had seen this.

"*Ça vous derange, monsieur ?*" (She'd again addressed me with the polite *vous*—and in a Parisian accent. And as she wasn't yet a woman, but merely a teenager, I thought to respond with '*tu*' but I used the formal '*vous*' instead, so as not to encourage her to act childishly. I told her that I would take her towards town a ways.)

She threw her bag on the seat in the back and set her shoebox by her feet. I turned the ignition, pulled out of the station, and started down the autoroute. She took her towel off from around her waist. She did this in a most carefree way, as if now that she was in the car, she didn't need to wear the towel to cover herself. She pushed the towel into her bag on the backseat. Her legs were bare and her thighs were naked. Only the area between her legs was covered with her bikini bottoms, as well as her backside too. I glanced between her small thighs and saw that the patch of fabric covering her pubic mound was humid, and the color shown dark in a moist triangle spot beginning where it appeared from within her thighs and ending halfway up to the elastic that clung to her little abdomen.

"It's a nice car," she said, "*Une très jolie bagnole.*"

"*Elle est efficace.*"

"'It took you long enough to put gas in it!"

"Listen girl," I told her, "as long as you're in my car, please try to hide your Parisian accent. I'm supposed to be in Italy for a couple more days yet."

"Oh, you're not Italian?"

"No."

"You're not French though."

"Not either."

"'What are you?' she asked, not being able to restrain laughter.

"Good question."

"Is your Italian as good as your French?"

"Not even close."

"Well, then you should be grateful that you have a young girl who speaks French in the car to keep you company."

"I'll trade you in for an Italian girl if we pass one up the road . . . Like I was saying, I'm supposed to be in Italy for a couple more days."

"You wouldn't trade me in," she frowned.

"I wouldn't?"

"No, you wouldn't trade me in. I'm a good find."

A pretty find, I thought, a very pretty find. The girl scratched the skin on her taut belly with her painted nails. Her little bellybutton was speckled with large grains of freshwater sand, as though she'd just come from the lake.

"You've been swimming?" I asked.

"No, I'm going swimming though. Later today. Now, I'm going shopping in town. Can you drive me to the piazza in the center of town?"

"No."

"No?!"

"No. It's getting late in the morning. I want to waterski while the water is still calm. It will get rough soon."

"But the lake is by the town. There is a beach by the town where a lot of people waterski. It will take you only two minutes to drive there after you drop me off in the piazza."

"Yes, but that is the north side of the lake. Everybody goes there and it's not good for skiing. The water's choppy and there are too many boats. I'm going to the south side where the water's smooth."

The young girl looked silently ahead and fidgeted with her sack as though she were looking for what to say next.

"I'll drop you at the streetcar station where I turn off to drive south, and you can take the streetcar into town."

"A streetcar?! You're going to make me take a streetcar?!"

Her look of haughty contempt gave way to a casual smile after she blew with pouted lips the strands of hair from her forehead. She asked me why I preferred skiing to shopping. After all, I could take her all the way into town and we could go shopping together. She didn't understand what was so great about waterskiing.

"It's a weird sport," she said.

I asked her what her favorite summer sport was. Her reply was something I'll always remember...

"Hunting."

"Hunting?!"

"Why are you laughing?"

"I wouldn't have thought that a girl like you would've ever shot a gun before!"

"But I don't shoot the gun when I go!"

"Well how do you hunt then?"

"I go with my father and watch him shoot the gun."

Oh, to hear such a thing! Can you imagine? How can one not be charmed by such an innocent response? I ask you that!

"But you're laughing at me again!"

"Yes, I'm laughing!" I told her, *"Parce que t'es trop mignonne!"* Such a rare and innocent girl. It wasn't the fact that she went with her old dad to watch him shoot game, but that this was her favorite summer sport!

"And your favorite *winter* sport?" I asked.

"*Winter* sport?"

"Do you know how to snow ski?"

"No, I don't know how to do that. In winter, hmm, I guess I like ride my bicycle along the Seine in the winter... Do you know Paris well?"

"Very well."

She and I continued to talk. We exchanged stories and names. She said her name was *Pénélope,* and that she preferred the English pronunciation; though she still pronounced it in the French manner, so that it rhymed with *antelope.* She said she was in Italy with some friends her own age, two other girls and a boy, as well as the boy's older brother, all from France. The five of them were sharing a small villa near my own. They'd been here a week already and were staying one more week. Pénélope had woken up early that morning and wanted to go shopping in town, while her friends wanted to sleep. She didn't want to take the car and leave them stranded at the villa, and anyway, she didn't know the first thing about driving a car, so she asked the old woman who came to water the lawns at the villa if she would drive her as far as the gas station.

As we flew up the autoroute, the wind was blowing fast over the windshield, but I could still smell Pénélope's sweet perfume. I knew the scent well. It was Christian Dior and came in a red glass bottle. Do you know this perfume, Pavel? It's enchanting. Many girls I've met and have gotten to know keep this red bottle on their bathroom sinks or on their nightstands beside their beds, while they keep the sweet scent on their napes and breasts. I've always enjoyed these girls and their Christian Dior. I brushed Pénélope's leg with full intent while we spoke, making sure to let it appear as an unconscious gesture, so that when I finally touched her again with evidence of passion, later on, it would not be the first time to make contact, and it would not seem too strange to her; she being so young, I didn't want to scare her, but to make everything seem natural. I behaved rakishly that day, I admit. I did want to seduce the young girl. But later in the night, everything changed. Still, I remember that day...

"What's in the shoebox?" I asked Pénélope. My eyes drifted to the floor of the car, I noticed there were holes punched in the box.

"A porcupine."

It'd been a gift from her friend's older brother. He was deeply in love with her, and so gave her a baby porcupine. She asked me what I thought of porcupines. I told her I didn't think much of them—at least I didn't think of them often.

The car raced along the road as the sun coughed fumes on us from the horizon. I came to the streetcar stop and pulled over to drop the girl off.

"So here I am then," she huffed in a bratty voice of disbelief, getting out of the car, "Fancy that! . . . Here I am standing at a streetcar stop . . . waiting for a streetcar!"

I smiled and said nothing.

"So you're leaving me at a streetcar stop?!"

"I'm going waterskiing, miss Pénélope."

"Okay, *salut!* . . . Bye-bye! . . . Bye then!"

She turned around and stomped precociously off, carrying her bag and her baby porcupine; while I turned the car around and drove south along the edge of the lake. I tried as hard as I could not to think of Pénélope, but to think instead of the skiing I would be doing soon.

Noon had stolen the morning, and there were already too many boats and many waves by the time I got out on the water. I skied well enough in spite of this, and felt in fine shape when I was finished for the day and paid the driver his wages and told him I'd see him first thing the next morning. After, I went and found a spot along the beach where there weren't too many rocks, where I could sunbathe. It was a private beach, though unregulated, where the rich foreigners (mostly Russians) owned summer houses along the lake and where the more attractive tourists came to swim. The place I found was between two coves and was full of coarse lake sand but no large rocks, and a few very beautiful women were already there, lying on towels to take sun. I rubbed oil on my limbs that were hard and strong and stretched out on the towel. I admired the way my veins pressed through my muscles after the intense sport. Some handsome groups of people passed me every now and again. Some went to splash in the water, however, for the most part this part of the lake was quiet.

I fell asleep in the sun on a towel, and it felt very good. When I awoke finally, it was to a sensation of something brushing my foot. I opened my eyes and squinted and felt the sun penetrating warmly in my eyes. I perched my head up and looked out over the water, then turned to see coming up from the edge of the lake, youthful Pénélope. She was wearing a bikini and had her hair tied back and she walked towards me with her hips swaying. There was another girl with her, and the two passed me. My eye settled on the bow where Pénélope's bikini bottom was tied around her waist, as it dangled low on her tiny hip. After she passed me, she turned back around, looked directly at me, and made her way to where I was lying. Now right next to me, she extended her leg and pressed her bare foot on my forearm. Her childish eyes laughed about this and her friend stopped and smiled and we said hello and began to talk.

Her friend was as plain as Pénélope was pretty. She was a short girl with narrow eyes, long pudgy hands, and thick legs; and she laughed at everything I said, whereas Pénélope laughed at nothing I said, but smiled a lot. She said they'd been shopping in town and had decided to go swimming. Her thick-legged friend admitted to me that Pénélope said that I'd mentioned the south side of the lake was better for swimming, with fewer tourists, and that's why they decided to come down here.

"I didn't say that!" Pénélope barked at her friend, "I said I wanted to try every beach on the lake while we were here! And that this side was supposed to be more chic!"

Hearing this, I couldn't help thinking what a child Pénélope was. She was such a child with those two neat little legs, that unblemished and girlish body, and the waves of hair crashing on the smooth and sandy rocks that were her tiny shoulders, gently set apart from a cradle of two delicate and firm, ripe and tiny breasts with upturned nipples. The fabric of her bikini like the wings of sparrows, upturned. Then, the slope of her stomach. Her small belly sloped and disappeared into the cinched elastic of her little bright bikini bottoms, sweet was the scent that poured from those bikini bottoms. 'Ô, youthful Pénélope!' I rejoiced inwardly, 'Slender Pénélope! So tall you are, way up there, while I squint in the sun from down here in the sand where I lie, and touch your tiny ankles with a straying finger. Hear how she laughs with nervous joy!, while I watch the sensual crease of fabric travel through the mound between her thighs.' Between her legs, that newly fertile mound appeared hot and ready to swell. Pénélope scratched her taut abdomen and pressed two fingers to the gloss on her mouth, while I admired her lush and ready lips...

True, at that moment I greatly desired this lovely and impossible child. Still, I wished she would leave me alone to sleep on my towel, and take her thick-legged, adolescent friend (named 'Fanny' from Nice or Cannes or somewhere) with her. I would have all the time to seduce Pénélope when I got back to Paris. For the seduction of a very young girl to work properly, a man needs to exhibit patience and complete indifference; he also needs to extract her from her peers, and I would get nowhere with thick-legged Fanny around.

I told the girls I would drive them back to their villa, and they were happy and went to get their towels and bags which had their clothes inside. I helped them pack the car.

"What happened to the porcupine in the shoebox?" I asked.

"I left him under a table."

"You left him under a table?!"

"Yes, in a café in town. I threw the shoebox away too."

"You did this on purpose?"

"Yes, on purpose . . . Why do you ask?"

"*Why* do I ask?? . . . But *why* did you leave him under a table?!"

"He was kind of gross!"

This explanation struck me as rather cute and quite vulgar. Pénélope and I had been speaking in French, and the word she used wasn't *gross* but rather: *dégueulasse*, which is less childish than the English *gross;* however, the way she phrased it in her vulgar teenage French... '*Ouais, bah... il était un peu dégueulasse, quand même !*' made her sound like those childish American girls when they say something is *gross*.

I turned the wheel of the car and flew quickly down the autoroute with Pénélope beside me and thick-legged Fanny in the backseat. When we came to their villa, Fanny ran inside meet her other friends and Pénélope stopped to say a lengthy goodbye. When she went to kiss my cheeks—twice in the Parisian fashion—I surprised her by taking her chin in my hand and pressing my lips to her neck. She laughed and squirmed at this and pulled away and I called her a baby.

"I'm not a baby! When are you leaving Italy?"

"Tomorrow's my last night."

"We should meet before you go."

"I'm skiing all day tomorrow."

"Well at night then."

For my last evening in Italy, I'd planned to eat at the best restaurant in town, with the terrace in the piazza, and then see an opera alone. A certain wealthy older woman whom I'd once been nice to in Rome—bestowing on her all sorts of masculine affections—knew all the theatres in Italy. She was a well-known patroness, and she wrote to tell me she'd reserved the best box at the opera for me for my last night and I could go with whom I pleased. I had planned to give the other ticket to the concierge to sell, but now that I'd met Pénélope, I told her she could come with me. First, though, we would eat dinner in the piazza together.

"*D'accord, avec plaisir !*" she chimed, bouncing on her toes. "We will spend tomorrow evening together then!"

She seemed very happy and continued to talk while asking me where I was going after tomorrow. She seemed surprised that I was going to Paris, although I'd mentioned it that very morning in the car. She'd acknowledged it in the car and even went as far as to say that we should meet up when she was back in Paris, '...so as to know each other in two different countries!' ...whereupon she'd taken a pen out of her beach bag and wrote her sister's address down on a scrap of paper and told me to come find her there. She didn't live in Paris, she said. Her older sister, Themia, did, and she was staying with her. Themia, as you might know, was born of a first marriage. They are half-sisters . . . Did Pénélope tell you all this? . . . No? . . . Anyhow, the girls' father (a Frenchman) was living a hermit's life on an island off the coast of Norway. He'd built a rustic house there to wile his remaining years away with his second wife (Pénélope's mother) who had grown-up in Oslo—though she had no Norwegian blood. Pénélope is half-Greek, half-French—though you must certainly know this! ...Anyway, when his second wife died, he continued living alone on his island. Pénélope stayed with him when she wasn't in school in Paris. While in school, she lived with her older sister in a nice, large apartment on the Avenue Foche. Her sister, however, would soon be giving up the apartment, and everything else she had in Paris. Her husband left her their summer house in the Balearic Islands, and she was considering going to live there all months of the year—except for a few weeks here and there which she would spend in Norway with her father. He was then already very old and his health was declining rapidly, so she wanted to spend more time with him and make sure he was being taken care of. Themia had been married once to a wealthy Stockholm banker, and when he died of illness at the young age of forty-three, he left her with their apartment in Paris, a house in Spain, as well as a modest fortune that might see her through ten, or so, years in Paris, or many more if she were to invest wisely or move somewhere cheaper. Anyway, life in the capital no longer interested her the way it used to. The sunshine and her father were all that were important to her now. She had nothing left in Paris and so was planning to leave to be with her family and find the sun. Once she gave up the apartment on Avenue Foche, Pénélope explained, she would either move to Spain or to Norway, but she wasn't going to stay in France.

"And it will be hard for me because I don't speak Spanish or Norwegian," Pénélope said, "But they have English-language schools in both those places. It's too bad they don't have French schools."

"Or you could stay in Paris, by yourself. You're old enough. Rent a *chambre de bonne* and live alone."

"Yes, that would be best," she smiled, "I should do that." A moment later she added... "So you have my address in Paris. Very well. But first we'll see each other tomorrow!... What time?... Okay, eight o'clock at the restaurant in the piazza. Okay, perfect... What?... Yes, I'll be dressed for the theatre! I can't wait. Oh, what are we seeing?... Who?... Pushkin?... No, I can't say I know him... *The Stone Guest*, it's called?... Very well then... Until tomorrow then... Goodbye!" She kissed me hard on the cheek and skipped off to her villa to meet with her friends who could be heard making noise out by the pool. I sighed and climbed in the car and drove up the gravel road to my own villa.

The next evening, I was freshly dressed in a linen summer suit. I went early to the restaurant in the piazza and made reservations, and then strolled through the streets until I came to the theatre. Inside, I checked to see that there was indeed a box saved for me. The best seats in the house were reserved for me under the name....

(At this point in my story, I almost slipped and told Pavel that I'd presented a 'forged' passport to retrieve tickets reserved under the name "Dmitry Marcovik," and winced with the realization that I would blow everything with that detail, as that was the name he knew me by! To Pavel, I was Dmitry Marcovik! Dmitry was the name I always assumed when traveling in Italy, and often elsewhere—especially in those younger days—I couldn't tell him "Dmitry" was a fake!... I caught myself and continued...)

...The best seats in the house were reserved for me under the name of Signora di Castiglioni, my Roman patroness. I took the envelope of tickets and tucked it into my pocket. After leaving the theatre, I headed back to the piazza to meet Pénélope.

I seated myself at the restaurant terrace in the piazza and ordered a Campari and soda, and began to relax. The bitter pomegranate liqueur tasted fresh and the alcohol lightened my thoughts. After the second or third glass, the waiter came to my table to tell me someone had called for me...

"*Signore, un messaggio per lei...*" the waiter said, handing me a note. It was from Pénélope. She'd called the restaurant to warn me that she was late getting back from the beach and would meet me directly at the theatre. She said not to wait for her but that she would come find her seat and would try to arrive as soon as possible to not miss too much of the performance. The message also said that she wanted me to come to a party with her and her friends after the theatre that was happening down at the beach. There was to be music, dancing, bonfires, etc., and that it would start at around midnight and that she really wanted to see me there—although she would first see me at the theatre.

"Damn her," I muttered to myself. I folded the note and tucked it in my pocket. I reminded myself how risky it is to try to plan an evening with a girl of that age. After finishing my Campari, I paid the tab and left to walk to the theatre to see Pushkin's *The Stone Guest*. I left Pénélope's ticket for her at the concierge in the lobby—though I had a hunch she would never show up to claim it—and went to my seat. It was a good production and I was sorry that I had to watch it alone. Sure enough, Pénélope never came. And after the show I went to the concierge and asked if anyone had come to claim the ticket.

"Yes, Signore," said the concierge, "your friend came half-way through the play and asked to be seated but we couldn't allow it. You see she was dressed for the beach and not at all proper for the theatre, and we couldn't allow her in!"

"You idiot!" I roared, ready to reach over and to grab the concierge's collar and shake him up, "If she wasn't dressed enough to enter your theatre, you should have come and found me and asked me to come down so I could deal with the matter!"

"Signore, we tried! But when we went to go find you to tell you your friend was here but couldn't enter the theatre, she just stormed off. She ran out in the street and we chased after her but she was gone!"

Annoyed, I left the theatre and walked out towards where the car was parked. A few minutes later, while walking through the streets that were lit-up and festive, I happened upon two women. They were with a man, all three were drunk and were yapping by the fountain in the piazza. They called to me and we started talking. One of the women was older and was quite good-looking. The younger one had large lips and was less beautiful, though both were so drunk and blousy in their loose clothing, and responded so well when I began my flirtatious talk, that I took an equal liking to them both. I suggested we all go to the bar to drink. Their escort was a courteous man, pleasant to talk to, and he told me that the better-looking woman was his fiancée. This bit of news didn't interest me. On the bar were little dishes which we could take on plates and eat from, in the Italian custom: pastas and cold salads. We ate messily as we got drunk on strong vodka mixed with San Pellegrino and bitters and I began to kiss the younger of the two women. Her lips were large and warm and very wet and she kissed sloppily and I held my hands around her waist and her waist was not as little as I wanted it to be. She heaved with pleasure as we kissed. All the while, the man and his fiancée were next to us at the bar drinking vodka and fondling each other. The time came when the man went to the bathroom to urinate and I began talking to his fiancée. While we talked, I touched her shoulders and arms and neck and then I began kissing her neck and then very sensually on the mouth. The younger girl made no protest and even began to pet us while we stood in embrace, and the woman I was kissing collapsed in pleasure and admitted to me that her fiancé was nice but that she didn't love him. I didn't care to hear such a drunken confession from a woman I had no desire to see in the light of day. Then I thought to take her away from her cuckolded fiancé and go with her to my villa and sleep with her, but in the end, although I was drunk and sloppy, I knew I wanted to sleep alone so as not to wake up on my last morning in Italy next to this woman's body, with her husky voice and her other imperfections. Drinking a final glass, I kissed the two women again each hard on the lips and when the man came back from the bathroom, I shook his hand and thanked him for the drinks he'd paid for, and wished him luck in life and left. Outside, the alcohol swished in my spinning head and I longed to get back to sleep in a soft bed.

Back at my villa, I pulled the car into the driveway. The sky was violet and the alcohol made the stars appear bright and more meaningful than usual. The yard was silent and I couldn't hear any noise coming from the neighboring villas and I assumed Pénélope and her friends were still at their party on the beach. I climbed up the stairs to the bedroom and set the alarm clock so I wouldn't oversleep and went to bed.

I was roused at about four in the morning by some commotion down in the yard. I was still quite drunk and my head spun with dizziness as I left the bed to go to the balcony and have a look. There, down on the gravel driveway, I saw three laughing girls running circles around my car. They were dressing it with ivy and other debris and they danced and giggled. They resembled three nymphs in the wilderness. Their laughter peeled out and hissed in the night. I left the balcony and ran downstairs to catch them. Two of the girls fled when they saw me approach from the porch of the villa. The third was Pénélope and she did not flee but smiled and laughed and ran to me. She held ivy and white orchids that shone in the moonlight in her hands, and I took her hand and she led me away to show me the decorations they had been putting on my car.

"It's a pretty garden for you!" she laughed, "Did you have fun? The theatre didn't work out, they wouldn't let me in! You didn't come to the party on the beach . . . I suppose you had a fun night by yourself. Oh, well, we had fun too!" She recounted some adventures at the lake where there had been, quote, 'millions of fires,' and lots of red wine to drink.

"Come inside with me," I said, and took her slender arms in my hands. She looked long into my eyes, I recall, I tried hard to keep my gaze steady. A few other words after, I don't remember what they were— I was drunk and very sloppy and I could still taste the lips and the skin of those blousy women with their tobacco smoke and vodka on my mouth from the bar back in town.

"No," Pénélope said, "I'm not coming in with you. I'm going back to sleep now." She turned to leave me, but stopped to plant a kiss on my wrist near my hand which still held her slender arm, and she said, "If you want to see me, you can come drink coffee with me at noon tomorrow."

"Impossible," I replied, and then I believe I told her simply, "I'm leaving first thing to go back to Paris. Come with me now to my villa. We'll drink coffee now together. The sun will be up in a couple hours. Look, the sky is getting pale!" But Pénélope said no again; and after refusing me, she turned and forced herself free from my hands and left, walking silently down the road—silent save for her feet that stirred the rustling gravel as she went on her way. I never saw her in Italy after that.

The next morning I woke early to the alarm. I felt fine, though a little the worse for drink. I had my coffee alone on the deck and packed my valises and went to pack the car. The morning showed the evidence of the last night's drunken frolic, when those tender nymphs had dressed my car. Then, in the moonlight, the orchid petals had resembled drops of silver mercury, the vines were youthful and eternal. Now, in the harsh morning light, those vines and flowers revealed themselves to be merely withered leaves and mortal petals browned—dead vegetation quickly drying in the sun. I winced with a shudder of depression at their sight, swept the mess off the hood with hasty hands, and cleared the debris from the seats. It was then I found a note fastened to the steering wheel. Snatching it quickly, I unfolded the paper and ready a short phrase scrawled in a girlish hand:

Monsieur Dmitry... If you intend to barge in on me when I'm back in Paris, you will certainly not find me among those happy to see you. - Pénélope.

"What a charming note!" I smiled with joy upon reading these words, "A perfect child trying to act like a lady. I really must write her into my work." The naïve style, and especially the use of the word *barge,* all of this filled me with tremendous pleasure (in despite of the note's unwelcome message). I tucked the paper in my pocket and continued in my preparations to leave Italy.

Back in Paris...

Summer was at its zenith. I'd again set to work laying pen to holy craft in the sweltering mansard I rented overlooking the summer square of the Palais Royal. The memory of Pénélope fueled my work. I knew she had to be back in the capital by then, staying with her sister on the Avenue Foche. For the health of my work I resisted all temptation to call on her. True, I admit, those two days I knew her in Italy she meant little more to me than 'seductive prey.' But now, after weeks spent under the hot zinc Parisian roof writing scores of music and poetic verse, she had come to be the most flourishing and fruitful of my muses. She'd become a sacred and important symbol of the feminine ideal. I needed to not spoil or ruin her until my work was finished.

Finally, in late-July, aware that she would soon leave Paris along with the rest of the city to go spend August on the coast, I decided I needed to find her at all costs. Perhaps she wouldn't be coming back to Paris after August. I needed to find her immediately to play out the rest of the story. The poetic form of my work and my life depended on it!

After breakfast one morning, I set off on foot for the Avenue Foche. On swift feet, I flew quickly past the Arc de Triomphe and stopped at the apartment house bearing the address written on the crumpled paper which I'd kept since Italy. Up spacious stairs I climbed and found the brass handle on the door with the last name of Themia's late husband.

They were home! . . . The two girls were out on their balcony. Pénélope lit-up instantly upon seeing me, beaming me a smile from over Themia's shoulder as the older sister looked expectantly at me a one does when a stranger stands in a private doorway. I stepped forward and Pénélope rushed to me and embraced me smiling; she then backed off blushing. As quickly as that fervent greeting came, it left and she looked at me blankly, listlessly, turning now to Themia who wondered who I was, now to the pitcher of cold iced tea brewing on the table on the far-off balcony terrace. When her eyes returned to me, the pleasure returned to her bright face. "Oh," she said with happy eyes, "So you have come after all!"

Long story short... I was invited to the terrace and we talked and Pénélope paraded me to her sister the way one shows off a souvenir brought back from one's last trip—suddenly pulled from a suitcase, I was a relic from Italy. "I'm happy you came—finally!" she said. I was happy too and told her so, and was flushed with the pleasure I knew I would feel, should I see her again. To my good fortune, Themia took an instant liking to me. She said I had elegant hands, and called me a 'ravishing beauty,' which sounded so strange as this is a phrase normally used to describe women, no? She asked me about the symphony I was writing. ...So when could she buy tickets for the first performance? ...And when would it be performed? ...Really? ...That soon?! And in Brussels, and in Krakow too?! You do say!' She poured on and on about Rachmaninov and Pushkin while Pénélope set the table for lunch. The three of us ate, and parted on the warmest of terms that day, and the next day I was invited to dine with them in Boulogne.

They became a family to me, those girls. Pénélope was like my little sister, while Themia was like our older sibling, our nurturing *protectrice*. No longer did I want to tarnish the youth of innocent Pénélope—just as I'd tarnished and destroyed innocent things in the past; yet for the pleasure of enjoying her perfect body alone I could have let all that is sacred go up in smoke. Still, my sentiments were pure. I wanted to know her forever, as a brother knows a sister, and see her walk through life unhindered, unblemished. One could say I had begun to *love* Pénélope. I even started calling her 'Sister.' And she called me 'Brother.' We laughed through the days and played as though it were springtime...

"Brother will come with us to Saint Tropez this August," Pénélope insisted to her sister Themia one day while the three of us were strolling together in the Tuileries Gardens. One could feel the heat scorching the city and preparations to leave town were underway by all sensible Parisians.

"Yes, we should go soon," said Themia, adjusting her hat, "We'll all three go together. Hopefully the sale on the apartment will go through while we're gone. It wouldn't bother me at all not to come back this city. Farewell, Paris! . . . You should come stay with us in Norway this winter, Dmitry.

"I thought we were spending winter in Mallorca!" said Pénélope to her sister in surprise, "Brother would certainly rather stay the winter with us in Mallorca than in Norway. You can do this, brother can't you? You said you can work from wherever you are." Saying this, Pénélope clasped my arm and urged me to run with her up ahead along the sun-blanched paths, through the trails of swooping trees.

A few weeks later, I received a letter from the girls. They were on the Côte d'Azur heading to Saint Tropez. The weather was gorgeous . . . And would I meet them there? Themia's part of the note said that she'd spent the week before in Greece and that she was dreaming of a life on a Greek Argolic island. There she would live the long days in a white-washed house on the crystal sea, basking in bountiful heat. She had her eyes on a property there but was waiting for her old father to agree to move with her before she would buy it. She couldn't leave him alone in Norway. After that part of the letter, she wrote that she missed me terribly.

A few days later, word came from Saint Tropez. The girls had rented a villa with a tiled roof and a grand colonnaded balcony over-arching the Mediterranean Sea—they described it as such: a palace built into a hillside, quite rocky, though spotted with lush patches of lavender and thyme. They invited me to come immediately and spend the rest of the summer with them. All of the comforts of paradise were there. Themia mentioned again how much she missed me, while Pénélope didn't say that she missed me, but that I should still come anyhow. Soon I descended on Saint Tropez, and arrived at the villa and saw that what they'd written of was just as they had described it, in all its splendor and all its glory.

Every morning, the hot sun would rise early, baking the stones on the terrace. The colonnades stood tall and old, like ancient heroes who'd been turned to pillars by mighty gods and made to stand guard over that historic sea...

Mediterranean... Middle of the Earth... *Mare nostrum...* Ah!

I would sit in the afternoons, when the scorching sun sent white flashes on the waves far below. Setting down my pen and my tablet, momentarily stopping work, I would look out over the sea and imagine heroes and gods running their errands. It was here that Heracles passed on his raft, flinging arrows at the sun. I would lose myself in daydreams until the servants would come with fresh pitchers of water and sprigs of icy grapes with sugary seeds and glassy skins. In the evening, cold cheeses and flatbreads were brought. There was always plenty of cool wine to drink.

Themia announced to Pénélope and myself one evening while the three of us were dining on the terrace that she would be going into Cannes for a week to visit some old childhood friends of hers. I assumed at first that Pénélope would go with her. As I didn't look forward to staying in the villa alone with the servants and Themia's Siamese cat, I planned to travel south alone to Spain. Then Themia told me that she had spoken to Pénélope about her plan earlier in the day and Pénélope had said that she didn't want to go to Cannes but wanted to stay with me in Saint Tropez. 'You're sure you don't want to come?' Themia asked her sister. 'Yes, I'm sure! I want to stay here with brother. There's nothing to do in boring Cannes, and I have no desire to see these friends of yours.' So it was settled.

Themia left by herself the next day while Pénélope and I were swimming at the beach. As soon as we came in, Pénélope disappeared and didn't reappear until dinner was served by the servants downstairs. That night, Pénélope wanted to come to my room to sit and read because she wanted company and the villa suddenly seemed very big and very empty. I let her read on the bed while I worked at the desk across the room. She was asleep on my bed by the time I finished working, and I quietly turned out the light and came to sleep on the same bed, but on the other side—letting her remain where she lay, bathed in the light of a fresh moon, glowing beyond the arch of the window. The glass shutters stayed open and there was no need for blankets, it being so warm at night.

I remember with great pleasure the moment when, that first night alone with Pénélope, I had woken up and lay sleepless in the humid room, thinking over the long path my life had led me. So many adventures I had had, wandering errantly this hospitable earth, meeting men and women of alien tongues, eating strange foods in strange rooms, among families born to far-off countries. So strange this life!

At once as these thoughts passed through my mind, I heard Pénélope stirring on the far-side of the bed. I fastened my eyes and remained still as I heard her rustle the covers and yawn, getting up from the bed. The bed creaked as she stepped down on the stone floor and an instant wave of sadness fell over me, lonely sadness, as I realized she had woken in the middle of the night, realizing she wasn't in her proper room, and was now going off to sleep in her own bed. Now I was going to finish the night in the empty room. I felt alone and suddenly very empty. Pénélope's bare feet made quiet slapping sounds as she crossed the floor. I then heard her in a nearby bathroom, turning the faucet. The water ran and it sounded as though she were drinking from a cup. She closed the faucet and the room became silent. One imagined that she was standing there thinking. Then, just as she had gone, I heard her come again. She was returning! Coming back to my dark bedroom, her naked feet slapped quietly on the stone floor—approaching the bed, she climbed back in, pulling the blanket over her and lying closer to me. My heart filled with joy as the loneliness vanished and I realized she would pass the night beside me after all. She yawned like a little child and stretched herself out, and then rolled close to me. Sound asleep we were, then stirring in the night, I felt her foot touch mine lightly. It felt good and I left it there and pressed my foot to hers as well and continued sleeping, feeling very good.

I worked all the next day and late into the night—taking a break only for a swim and for dinner. After we'd finished eating and the servant was clearing the table, Pénélope came again to my room to read. She wasn't as loquacious as usual and kept quiet while I sat at the desk by the dim lamp. I wasn't sure if she just didn't feel like speaking, or if she was trying hard not to speak so as to let me work. At last, she stopped the silence, when she got up to look out the window. Coursing an idle finger over the windowsill, she asked me if I liked Saint Tropez. I told her it was a fine place. She told me that the villa seemed very large to her, and very empty; and that the night before, when we'd slept in the same bed, she had felt safe and happy and that it was good to be near me, and she asked if she could sleep near me again this night. 'Because you are my big brother,' she said. I didn't tease her about this, but said simply that it would be a good idea if she slept near me again this night... 'But only because you are my sister,' I laughed.

Now this night, Pénélope slept a little closer to me, though she kept her back turned. She now wore only a nightshirt and panties. I felt a strange joy of the most sensual and unusual sort, picturing her there in the darkness, sleeping beside me in her night-shirt and underwear. Before turning away to roll over to the far-side of the bed, further from her, I pressed gently my legs to the backs of her naked thighs and she inhaled deeply. I felt my cheeks burn as she turned around and kissed me on the cheek.

"Goodnight, Brother," she whispered.

"Goodnight, Sister."

With that, she turned back around to her previous position, facing away from me, but our legs remained touching and I did not roll to the far-side of the bed but remained there, feeling her hot thighs on my knees and shins. Our legs remained pressed firmly together while she slept; then after a moment, her arm fell behind her in a seemingly natural and unconscious way, so that her tiny hand rested on my hip. I fell asleep deeply and woke late into the night to find her face was resting on my chest. I stroked her hair with my hand and she breathed deeply and turned in her sleep to face away from me, no longer touching me, she remained there the rest of the night.

The next day was scorching hot and muggy. All the fans were blowing and I kept myself cool by swimming in the pool between spurts of working. At night, the palm branches swept the humid stones on the patio of my room, and Pénélope reclined beneath them as she read the novel she had bought in town that day, while I sat inside with a pitcher of water and my writing-tablets, and my loose notes, working away. When it was time to sleep, Pénélope did not ask to sleep beside me, for we both now assumed that she would sleep in my bed. She stepped in from the patio deck with her long hair tousled and dark, and her lynx-eyes looking sexual. She was dressed in a shorter nightshirt than the night before, made of a light, thinner fabric; and she wore very small panties, the white hem on the upper-thigh was just visible when her wrist brushed her nightshirt momentarily up on her hip—she stretched out on my bed. The lamp was still burning on my desk when I turned to get ready to join her to sleep and she didn't hesitate to slip her panties off and throw them on the floor while the light was on and I was watching—whereas before she'd waited till the light was off and she was beneath the covers.

Once I'd turned off the lamp, and was myself lying down with only a thin sheet covering me, Pénélope eased her half-nude body into the bed and yawned a gentle yawn and kissed my cheek and the side of my nose, and then turned her back to me to sleep facing the patio door, which was open, letting in a faint salty breeze. She inched her body slowly beneath the sheet, backwards until her bottom was just barely touching my thighs and my groin. A vibration of pleasure coursed through my body as I experienced this sensation—I myself was wearing a pair of cotton underwear, yet my thighs were bare and her bottom too was bare and her hot skin touched my own and my groin stiffened and heat throbbed in my chest. Instead of moving away to distance myself from this young girl who'd become my sister, I pushed my groin firmly against the cheeks of her bottom. She reacted not by moving forward to distance herself from my touch, but rather back so that our two bodies were pressed tightly together. I inhaled deeply and moved my hand so that it rested on her thigh touching the naked skin that was warm but dry, although I felt the sweat beading lower on her leg from the heat. She responded to the touch by rocking her hip. She then turned her shoulders so that she faced me. Her eyes met mine a moment in the darkness and then she looked down. I looked at the gorgeous curve of her chin and her quiet cheek as she dipped her head low, her head of fragrant hair fell over my face. It was then that our four hands clasped together, holding the way children's hands hold, likewise as do the hands of ardent lovers cast into the throes of passion, likewise as do the hands of a young brother and sister when they are playing together in the yard, turning circles around the fresh garden lawn. Our lips fell together and we began to kiss.

It was our first kiss and it lasted until dawn. For so many timeless hours our lips remained pressed together, nourishing each other's lips, each of our tongues drank the breath of the other's tongue. I peeled the blankets from our hot bodies and slid the nightshirt off Pénélope's chest and over her shoulders. She happily let me undress her as she undressed me herself and we delighted in every curve and soft and firm place on the other's body. She passed her eager hands across my muscles and taut skin, exhaling with sensual joy. As I inhaled the fragrance of her hair and mouth, I sent my happy hands over each curve of her humid body, across her small breasts and the firm curve of her hips. We breathed together with desire breathing more desire into one another as our lips hung together. And when I came to the scalding wetness between her legs, she whispered that I needed to stop, for she had never made love to anyone one before.

"You haven't?"

"No, I haven't."

"Okay," I whispered, "Go to sleep, little girl." I turned her over and kissed her a final time.

The next day Pénélope and I didn't see each other. We swam on different beaches. I dined in town, and I assume she too ate in town by herself somewhere. At night, while I sat working at the desk lit by a kerosene lamp, I heard her coming up the path to our villa in the silent night. It was that same silent night that I would rob the virginity of our dear Pénélope. She was yet unbroken. I laid her down beneath the moon and the window and unclothed her. Her firm hymen blocked the passage of my fingers which I passed between her legs, and it felt as though nothing could enter inside her. I took my fingers out and watched her eyes as they looked steadily and affectionately at me. Taking her humid hands in the palms of my own, I pressed them against the sheets and tried to enter inside her. It felt as though it couldn't be done. I almost became frustrated. Then, with the suddenness of a dam breaking, her hymen tore and broke open. I felt a snap of skin and a release of fluid—almost cold was that fluid that passed over my groin and onto the sheets—and I knew with certainty that she had in fact been a virgin before that night.

Pénélope enjoyed making love, although she admitted it was strange; and I was soft with her, taking care to be affectionate to an extent that I'd been with no other woman. We passed two more blissful nights alone together before Themia returned. They were idyllic nights—hot with the Mediterranean Sea air, fragrant with the summer leaves. We wore nothing and explored the world together like brother and sister, and made love like man and woman. When Themia came back to the villa, we tried to act as though nothing had happened and resume our roles of before, but it was impossible. Like foolish kids, we tried to hide our new passion. One afternoon, Themia caught us kissing wildly in a coat closet and she began to cry and neither of us knew why she was crying. Pénélope went silently upstairs with a bowed, moping head, and I left to walk down by the beach.

Finally the time came for us all to leave the villa and for me and the sisters to go our separate ways. I returned to Paris alone. I think Pénélope went to Norway to see her father. I'm not sure what happened or where the time went. Season overlapped season. We were distanced by time and other things. But no use filling in the gaps, Pavel. You know the stories that come to separate lovers. No point in tiring you with a well-known tale. We did meet once more, Pénélope and I, to live together on a far-flung island—a place in the middle of the Pacific, about as far from mankind as one can be. But that's a story for another time. I will not tell it now... just that I recall biding my days on the beach on that island looking out over the lapping waves, feeling sad; that anguishing feeling that I was missing life. I was a prisoner separated from society by an uncrossable expanse of crystal blue sea. Desperate was my desire to be amongst the people again—*in the polis*, if you will. So, giving up what I had, saying farewell to Pénélope, I returned again to Paris, by myself, to continue my wanderer's life.

Now you see me here. Though much has changed, I am still now who I was then. When I saw Pénélope later in France, the next year, she was still devoted to me and swore to me that no other man had touched her. I gave her the necklace that you are keeping in that case for her. I still remember perfectly the last time I saw her: she was leaning on the windowsill in a room on rue Montfaucon. The sun washed her face with creamy light. She was naked except for a pair of white panties and the amber necklace clasped around her neck. We had just made love and she asked me to remain always faithful to her, to quit my wandering life and settle with her. I told her again I could not do so, and we cried together. She turned away after, hiding her tear-stained face in the crook of her arm, and left without looking back. Afterwards I broke down. Never again, I knew, would I find what I'd had with her. Every time the realization returned that Pénélope was gone from my life for good, I felt eaten by that sadness and hollow feeling. Just as a woman living alone weeps bitter tears in the night when she wakes from a dream in which she was a youthful girl living in her home country, a dream in which she was walking in the afternoon hand-in-hand with the young smooth-faced boy she'd once hoped to marry, so many years later she now wakes in the middle of the night in a far away country, now old and decrepit, with brittle bones and shriveled white hair, she weeps and weeps with the realization that she is no longer a beauty and no longer a youth and no longer near the home where she was raised—so would I weep bitter tears of lamentation each time I realized that I'd truly and forever lost youthful Pénélope and the innocent love we had shared. Gone was my Eden, and gone is my Eden now. Wandering the streets, after that time, I looked for her often, though I never again saw her or found anyone who knew her.

An old copper mantle clock rattled on a nearby shelf to chime out the sixteenth hour as I finished telling my story to Pavel. While the sentences ran dry, the rosy light of my story dimmed to the dank and dusty pallor of the dirty Bone Shop where us men sat on the old cowhide seats next to the film covered window. As I finished my tale, I turned over the empty clay cup that had somehow appeared in my hand during the telling of my story—once hot and brimming with bitter tea—and I tapped it against the plate on the table the way one ashes a pipe and watched the dregs of the black tea tumble over the plate. I looked at Pavel Ivanovich who said nothing but sat trembling across from me. He trembled and looked into my tired face with bulging eyes while the veins caked on his forehead. We men stared at each other in perfect silence until Pavel let fall the house key I'd handed to him. The key fell and chimed on the plate and then clanked on the table. This event made me smile wryly. I picked up the key and said to Pavel...

"Well, you've heard the story. I didn't try to soften it on anyone's account or tell any false tales. I see my gift of the apartment at the Place de la Madeleine doesn't interest you. *Bah, tant pis !...* I'm afraid I can't stay to talk anymore. I slept an hour at best last night. I'm starting to hallucinate a little bit. I think I'll go back to my bed at Madeleine and sleep one off. I'd like to forget so many things. It's been so long since I've had a good night's sleep, etc."

This casual banter of mine just made Pavel tremble all the more furiously. With a crescendo of anger, he finally leapt forward so that his eyes were a mere hand's breadth from my face, and he cried, "You damned thing! Why would you tell me such a story of you and Pénélope together? Do you enjoy this cruelty? Do you relish in tearing the organs in my gut? You are a God-forsaken bastard to tell me this. Sure you loved her. But I love her now. And you speak about taking her virginity with such vivid words—breaking her hymen and feeling her lips on yours with eternal devotion. This is the girl that I am going to marry! And you tell me of your adventures in a way that makes me think she will always be devoted to you. You want to see her again to convince her to run away with you. You want to win her back! Oh, but you would have to steal her like a thief, for you do not deserve her. You cannot give yourself only to her—yet *I* can! So give her up and do not talk of this crap about her white panties and the way the stars gleamed in the sky. Your poetry makes me sick!"

"Ah..." I sighed, smiling, as I recoiled in my seat. "It's just a little verbal jousting, my dear Pavel. Don't worry. We're just butting horns, you and I. A very manly thing to do, no? Listen here... Pénélope has only slept with you and me. I was the first, you were the second. A while ago you gave your confession to explain the necklace in your shop and I had to sit here and feel *my own* organs being wrenched as you told about how you spoiled the one thing in this life that I love beyond all else. Pénélope was the one person who was pure and who belonged only to me. You took that away from me and I had to listen to your story of your body mucking-up her purity here in a sweaty heap of sexual fury while your friend August lay upstairs snoring away. Do you think that story was easy for me to take? No, it wasn't! So in return, you had to listen to my story of how I deflowered your fiancée. Such is life! Now do you want the key to the apartment or not? Tell me quick because either way I'm leaving this ragged shop to go sleep in about five seconds."

At this, Pavel's eyes darted around and then fixed on my face. "If I take that key," he spoke, "and when Pénélope returns to Paris, I take her to live in that flat, then I have to agree to let you see her for a final dinner—a 'Last Supper' as you call it—where we three will eat and drink together. That was your condition. Can't you see that I cannot do that? I worry that you two will be stirred by old feelings if you see each other again."

"Aren't you convinced she loves you?"

"I am. Yet she and I have known each other only a short time. You have known her longer. You will use nostalgic tricks to steal her. Can't you see I am afraid of this meeting? I cannot do it!"

"Nostalgic tricks?! Aye, you are a fool, Pavel! Can't you see? Can't you see what has come to pass and what can be no longer? Pénélope is no longer pure for me, her body is twice-used and ragged. *Je n'ai plus envie d'elle !* I only want to see her again so I can finally leave Paris. So I can leave this Parisian life, this life of intoxicated pleasure I am living. One Last Supper, a *'feast of friends,'* then I can go away forever. I dream of going away to live in a fishing village in Cuba. I will rise early and make my body hard and brown from sport in the sun. I will wear a pair of white linen trousers, a black t-shirt and a straw hat, and eat yellow rice and beans with fried plantain bananas; and on hot afternoons I will drink cold frothy beer with the local men in the barroom where a ceiling fan will flap and a jukebox will play. We will have arm-wrestling contests. I will beat the Great Negro in a show of strength. There is a girl there I'm going to marry. She has a freckled nose and rosy cheeks. Her name is Gonçuela, etc...." All the while I was telling Pavel of this Cuban revelry, my brain was frothing with exhaustion and delirium. I began to sputter meaningless words while the calls of seagulls sounded in my head. My story was going into unchartered territory…

"You are a wanderer like me, Pavel. You can relate to this dream. I need to get out of Paris. It is a never-ending cycle here. An endless series of decadent nights with hung-over mornings. I work and I feast and I make love—I never sleep—and all the while I am losing my youth, draining my health, and life is passing me by. Can't you see I need to sleep? Can't you see I need to get out of Paris and run away from here? If you love Pénélope, if you want her to have a comfortable life—not a life of misery in an American radiator shack, holed-up in a Staten Island ramshackle icebox or a Brooklyn basement—if you want to help Pénélope, and also want to help a world-weary wanderer tired of orgies and the fierce nets of loose Frenchwomen, for God's sake take this damned house key from me, take that suitcase of yours that is packed to go to America, sitting by the ladder over there, (I see you're all packed!), and get the hell out of this rotten Bone Shop!—this miserable place filled with broken kettles and old dirty rags—go to your new life at Madeleine. Go, for God's sake!"

With that, I broke down. My body crumpled into a heap on the floor, where I felt my lips swell with fatigue and my eyelids grow into heavy lead fry-pans that flopped over my wretched eyeballs. After the exertion from my fevered speech had settled and I my heart-rate calmed, I felt a clarity begin to seep into my brain. Still I lay in a heap on the floor with the keen awareness that Pavel was hovering over me. I lay there, thinking: 'It was a good story I just told. Only the little the worse for all my exhaustion. Still I think it will have the result I want it to….' And it did. Charged with sudden emotion, Pavel leapt down on me and embraced me. Crying with joy, he spoke words of brotherhood as he helped me to my feet. Dusting off my shirt and clasping my hands, Pavel gushed sweet words of friendship and shook his silly, ridiculous face…

"You really are good at bottom, my friend Dmitry! You really are good!" he blubbered, then… "I'll go right now to Madeleine. I'll take my valise this instant and this key and go to Madeleine and start getting the place ready for Pénélope. Oh, if there aren't yellow curtains in the windows I'll have to get yellow curtains. Pénélope will certainly want yellow curtains. And some blossoming plants, too. Oh, I'll go right now!"

"Right now?!" I cried. Suddenly, a clear realization surged into my head, parting the last waves of fog that had been suffocating my brain. I realized that I couldn't let Pavel go right then. It was not yet five o'clock. "No, Pavel, not right now! That is... I mean... there is still one thing I have to move out of my place before you go there. What?, you ask? An old piano. Yes, an old piano. You see, I'm moving my writing-room from Madeleine to Saint Germain and I have the whole apartment empty at Madeleine except there is still this piano I have to move. It is a very precious piano. I wrote my third and forth symphonies on it. I need to go there right now, I have an appointment to meet the piano movers. They must be waiting for me. I'll go now and you come later. Here, let me write down the address. As for the door-code, buzz: '1917.' Ha, fancy that! That's the year of your revolution. Quite a coincidence! You were meant to live there, I guess. Just make sure Pénélope keeps coffee in the cupboard and paracetamol in the medicine cabinet. How do you find which door it is? Okay, when you enter, take the stairs to the fourth floor, and it's 'en face.' Please wait until tonight before you come though, don't come now. In any case, don't you have to wait here for August to return? Shouldn't he be back from burying his uncle by now? Yes, please wait here and do not come to Madeleine before seven in the evening, tonight. I should have the piano out by then. It's a very precious piano, you see!"

17th Soliloquy

"No nonsense today!" I decided, "I have to do this job right. Then tonight I can sleep early. Twelve hours of oblivion, that I shall have soon, soon beneath the cradling moon—but first!..." As my feet scuttled up the rue de Rivoli, I clutched my thoughts the way a traveling salesman clutches his sample case as he runs to catch a departing train.

"Slow down, Monsieur!"

...This came suddenly from a figure blocking my path. It was a scrawny little street-urchin, about five years old. He was flopped on a patch of sidewalk. "Buy some of my stamps, will you?"

Stamps? So sits a street urchin on a dirty patchwork quilt selling counterfeit stamps... Amusing! . . . "They're not real stamps, little kid. Do you have a map of Greece for sale? I'd buy that. How about a wig? Some sunglasses at least?...'

"No, monsieur. I have none of those things!"

"It's a hot day, kid..." I stretched my arms and elongated my spine. I wiped the salty perspiration off my brow and observed the quality of the summer air and the scorching sun overhead. All the while, the little rascal stared blankly at me from his quilt. "Do you have enough stamps to mail that sun somewhere? Aye, it's a hot one! I want to send that sun to a friend."

"No Monsieur, I don't have enough stamps for the sun." This last phrase trailed behind me like the tail of a kite as I walked away from the urchin to get on with my business. I'd been worried before that it was too late. I'd asked the urchin for the time and he informed me that he didn't have a watch but he brought to my attention the window vitrine of a nearby *horlogerie* where a hundred clocks were huddled together like a hoard of gabbing sisters, ticking the time away. Four-thirty in the afternoon? I can make it, but I'd better hurry!

The golden sun roasted the rooftops of the apartment buildings I passed on my way to La Madeleine. As I walked my brisk pace, my head rolled around on my shoulders so as to enjoy the sight of these rooftops all stacked together—their sheets of zinc were crowned with chimney-pipes and all their surfaces glimmered with the rich gold of the sun's rays. "Holy city!" I exclaimed aloud as my body surged with tremendous joy. "...So enthralling it is to be alive, is it not? Glory it is to be tossed down onto the surface of this bountiful and impossible earth where one can wander as one pleases and spy the rooftops of the city. All it takes is a glance at the rooftops of Paris to fill one with heroic ideas that can be fashioned into works of genius!"

Now I knew how I wanted my hero's tale to go. Stopping on the street I searched in my pocket for a pencil as I recapped where my hero had been. Where had my hero been? Oh yes!...

'When our hero awoke on his lonely ship in the blushing light of early dawn, he could see his native land not far off. On the shore, he watched cooking fires burning and saw stately cypress trees growing. These things he'd often dreamt of when on his seafaring journey. Around the fires, people were gathered, playing pipes and charring food. Sweet music billowed into our hero's ears from over the calm sea. The smells of the savory foods being roasted on the far-away fires billowed into his nostrils; and with a glad and nostalgic heart, he watched the flames toss lofty smoke puffs into the peaceful sky. The pipes played on—Ô, how they played! And our long-traveled hero knew he was finally home!'

"Yes, good..." I mumbled, "But now our hero enters the city and something needs to happen involving the old rooftops..."

'The city on his native island is surrounded by walls. The houses are tall and ancient, stacked together, with tiled roofs. It is late-afternoon and the hot sun bakes the roofs as our hero shuffles in the guise of a shepherd towards the palace. He had stolen this disguise after anchoring his ship. Sneaking quietly around the bay, he found a sleeping shepherd and stole his clothes and went up a hill and found one of the shepherd's lambs gone astray, and he killed the lamb and draped its carcass over his shoulder. Now he is walking in the bustling town, disguised as an old shepherd—a usual sight as many rural shepherds come to town with their freshly killed beasts to sell the meat in the marketplace.

'A lot has happened since our hero left his native land. There was a new ruler in the palace now. Should our hero return and claim his rightful place at the throne, the new ruler would imprison him and have him put to death. I have to say somehow that the beloved young wife of our hero was forced to flee from the palace when the island and city was besieged. She fled from the palace in the middle of the night in her own disguise, dressed as an old beggar-woman. She now lives as a poor laundress in the attic in the town. That's where the rooftops come in. The lofty wife of our hero now washes clothes for the poor city-folk all day long, and in the evening, while the hot sun makes its bulbous descent over the city and the nearby sea, painting rosy light over the ancient rooftops, our exiled queen sets down her work and climbs out onto the rooftop and looks far out over the sea in hopes of seeing her husband who will finally be coming home any day now, she prays, by way of swift ship. Years he's been gone, yes, and others believe he is dead. But as our impoverished queen stands on her rooftop and weeps, she knows he is still living and is striving to come home to her. As the tears fall from her tender eyes, she hopes that today of all days will be the day her husband sails into the harbor.'

"Yes, this is all good work!"

'...Now, the curtain falls and rises again. Years have passed. The chorus is singing as our hero walks in disguise of a shepherd with a slaughtered lamb over his shoulders. The city is bustling, yet the chorus must explain that it is in disorder. The new ruler is doing a bad job. The people need their rightful king. Now the king, disguised as a shepherd, enters a random house in the city and seeks refuge in the attic of a poor blind woman who offers him *xenia*. While they are eating, she, believing him a stranger, explains to him the situation in the palace. She mentions, by-the-bye, that everyone in the town knows that the beautiful queen was dispatched into unfortunate exile within the confines of her own city, yet no one knows where she is; thus no one can help her—though they would if they could. But she will reveal herself to no one. All that is known is that she is now living somewhere in an attic, working as a laundress, But which attic? One can only guess! So many laundresses are scattered around. So many attics there are in the city. So many rooftops. So many houses crowned with gilded tiles, golden chimney pipes, rooftop windows with open panes, perched like mouths drinking the wind of the skies. How can one fail to create beautifully when one looks at the rooftops of Paris?!'

I had managed to drift into strange side-streets as I dreamt up these ideas for my hero's tale. No time is better spent than when lost in the land of creative invention. I had a clear picture of the shepherd leaving the blind woman's attic to find his beloved wife. A few details to work out here and there, but overall I had my hero's life going beautifully. The work was nearing completion. Just had to get it into dactylic hexameter... That would be easy enough. Certainly by autumn it would be done and I could begin a new work. What would my next work be? Next I'd begin my masterpiece!... 'The Vermian Opera.' ...The what?!

"The Vermian Opera!" I cried out suddenly, realizing I'd slipped off track, "Christ! I've forgotten Pavel!"

I caught myself standing in front of the Opéra with my hands hanging like the drenched arms of an octopus over my turned-out trouser pockets where I'd been fishing for a snub of a pencil and a scrap of paper in order to jot down these narrative ideas I'd been concocting for my hero's tale. I'd gotten lost in creative bliss and had forgotten Pavel and the chore I was undertaking. The muses had apparently led me to the opera house when I should have been going straight to La Madeleine. No matter, one could quickly get to the Madeleine from the Opéra Garnier. But was there a passport in my pocket at least? The work I was about to undertake would require a passport—and a good one at that! I would need an identity such as that of Dmitry, resident of Belgrade. I certainly could not use any old identity that may link me up later. Not with this plan I was going to carry out. Now I remembered… Dmitry's papers I'd hidden in a box in a room in Saint Germain. What time is it now? A clock near the Opéra ticked five minutes short of five o'clock. No time to go to Saint Germain…

Rummaging through my leather satchel, I found the packet of Grecian foxglove, that potent and toxic herb I'd taken from the Bone Shop, along with a hefty roll of cash and a clever passport sealed in an envelope. It was an honest passport, fabricated at the embassy in Bratislava; one I never used except when stuck in governmental predicaments. Why I had it on me this day, I don't recall. I lifted the navy cover and saw my face and read *Mr. Such-and-such* printed in neat letters. Ach! That name was one registered with the French Police Commissariat, along with the inky prints on my fingers, from that time long ago when I got tangled in the schizophrenic affairs of a muscovite fashion model and was imprisoned on a sunny day in the fifteenth arrondissement of Paris. They held me for questioning and made copies of the passport and made me sign documents when they finally released me. Yes, that identity was thoroughly fried, but I had no time to get to Saint Germain to get another. Tucking the roll of cash, the packet of herbs, and the passport back in my satchel, I took to heel down the Boulevard des Capucines…

I passed a pension on the boulevard where a sign read:

INN FOR TRAVELERS AND STUDENTS.

Just adjacent to this inn, there was a novelty shop. I hurried inside to find a disguise…

"I'm on an adventure and I need a proper wig—and some glasses." The clerk brought me a monocle and a mound of tinsel with some patch glue. "Aye, what do you think I'm off to do, buy a box of bandages? Friend, bring me a good disguise!"

The clerk returned again with large sunglasses with lenses like blue cellophane platters, and a white modish wig. "That's more like it!"

He sold me too a slender hobbyist's telescope. This I tucked it into my belt, and off I fluttered, down the road, admiring the sky that flowed around my head like swirling blueberry-milk.

I punched the year of the Russian Revolution into the door buzzer at Madeleine and was transported instantly to the back of the courtyard. I took my telescope out held it up to the blue lens on my right eye to get a closer look at everything. My satchel flapped against my waist as I hurried up the stairs to the fourth floor.

'It must be not too late,' I thought as I came to Sybille's door and saw that it was open, allowing entrance into the bare and well-lighted salon. 'The *propriétaire* is still here....'

"Madame?" I called aloud, fixing my wig and entering the room. My wood-soled shoes clapped on the bare parquet as I crossed to where a squatty old woman with a face like wrinkled fruit stood examining putty on the walls. "You must be the *propriétaire*?" I asked.

"Yes, I am. You're looking for what?"

"Let me introduce myself. I am Julio So-and-so. A famous cinematographer from Buenos Aires. You've heard of me? I've come to Paris to film my new movie. I'm here scouting locations. I see this apartment is available for rent..."

"Who told you it was for rent?"

The old *propriétaire* inched up to me to examine me closely, but I slid off by the window and extracted my telescope to examine the view from the room. "Buenos Aires you say? You must know the girl who was living here: Mademoiselle Sibylle. She was supposed to meet me here with the key. Where is she? I need to recover the key!"

"Exactly! It was Miss Sibylle who told me this apartment was for rent. She is one of my actresses. She left today for Argentina to star in a picture..."

"What?! She left...? She was supposed to be here at five with the key! What did she do with the key? Did she give it to you?!"

"No, Madame." I slithered over to the old woman; and taking a crisp fifty euro note from my pocket, I slipped it into her hand, "Here's for the trouble with the key. Sibylle's a forgetful child. She probably packed it away." Then... "I'm going to need the apartment for four months. It is available, correct? Oh? Hmm?... You do say! It can be *made* available, then?? That is a fine thing! But it will need to be made available immediately. Is there a bathtub? Yes? Big enough for a king? I'm filming '*The Return of Agamemnon,*' you see. The bathtub in the murder-scene needs to be big enough. Yes, a murder-scene, that's right. I'll just have a look at the bathtub, if you will be so kind to go and get the 'Rental Agreement' for us to sign."

"Young man, I don't want any murder-scenes in my building!"

"Don't worry, Madame, it's all movie magic. The neighbors won't hear a thing, and we have 'people' for the mess...."

The old *propriétaire* batted her eyes around in confusion for a few moments and then propped her shoulders and smoothed her wrinkles on her cheeks to say: "It will cost you one-thousand euros per month."

"That is fine. I'll pay four months up-front." And that was all. The old woman scampered off to find the Rental Agreement. While she was gone, I went into the bathroom to have a look. There, I saw the sink where I'd taken pleasure on a couple of occasions to wash my face and hands with the fragrant products of the young Sibylle after making love to her fragrant body. The tub was really too small for any King Agamemnon to bathe and die in. Lifting my modish wig, I rubbed the sweat from the top of my natural hair and repositioned the wig on my scalp in the mirror. I then unbuckled my satchel and took the packet of toxic Grecian foxglove from inside and, opening the mirror, placed that fated packet in the empty medicine cabinet, right in the middle shelf. And there the packet sat, looking at me; and in my sleepless delirium, I could see that the packet was smiling.

"Mmm... chic and debonair," I said, smiling at myself in the medicine cabinet mirror, with my rosy mouth and my blue cellophane eyes.

"Eh, Monsieur? . . . Monsieur So-and-so?" called the shrill old voice of the *propriétaire* as she stamped across the parquet of the salon. I went out of the bathroom to meet her. She was holding a stack of papers.

"It's a fine bathroom, it will make a fine movie."

"I didn't know Mademoiselle Sibylle was an actress. Makes sense though, she's such a handsome girl!"

"Yes, Madame, she is starting to be very well-known in Argentina."

"Bah, dis-donc !" the old woman chimed, obviously thrilled to receive the stack of fresh European currency I was thrusting in her hand. "…but she said she was going to South America to study art-history, I thought, not to star in pictures."

"She is modest, Madame. Is everything settled? Please sign the agreement then."

"Just one thing, Monsieur. Do you have a passport? I'll need to see your passport to put the information down on the agreement. We do everything by the books in my building…"

"Yes, Madame. Of course, Madame." And with that, I took a passport sealed in an envelope from my Moroccan leather satchel and showed it to the old woman.

"Oh!" said the woman, scrutinizing the passport, "Monsieur Such-and-such… hmm, your hair looks different in this picture!"

"That's the movie business," I replied, lifting up my sunglasses to let the old woman see my eyes, "One can't walk around town in one's natural form, you see. Fame and notoriety, Madame. Godly sights incinerate mortal men. I see you understand…."

"Yes, yes… I thought you were from Argentina…"

"I grew up there, yes. But I wasn't born there. I had a turbulent childhood, you see Madame."

"Hmm, okay. So Sibylle didn't give you the key then?"

"No, Madame."

"Oh, that girl! Well I have another one here. Four months you say? And no loud murder scenes? And your 'people' will clean up the mess? . . . I'm going to have to tell my sister I know a famous person; and that a movie is going to be made in my building. Can you put me in the film? I'll play the landlady!"

"You'll play King Agamemnon's landlady! Ha!" This idea made me roar with laughter. Ridiculous air streamed through my nostrils with the very thought of it; and turning around, I said goodbye to the old woman who was already leaving herself. "But wait!" I called after her, "This bed in the corner... I'm afraid it doesn't fit. Can it be moved?" Lifting the sunglasses from my face, I surveyed the wooden frame with the mattress where on two occasions, I'd had sex with sweet Sibylle.

"No, I'm afraid it cannot be moved, Monsieur. This bed is rooted to the spot. Such a sturdy old bed it is. No, certainly it cannot be moved!"

So hearing, I walked over and pushed at the bed, and sure enough its wooden frame was rooted to the ground. So sturdy was that bed in place, one would say it were carved from a single olive tree, and after it had been laid, the rest of the apartment was built around it, and the building around that. "Fancy that! Well, we will leave the bed then! Goodbye, Madame!"

"Goodbye, Monsieur!"

Alone in the apartment that now belonged to me and my fated guests: Pavel and Pénélope, I took a last look around to make sure no remnants of Sibylle remained. Except for a box of washing-soap in the kitchen, a stapled packet of Grecian foxglove in the medicine cabinet, and a plunger behind the toilet, and the bed, the place was empty. Smiling at my clever devices, I walked out of the apartment (locking the door behind me) and scampered out into the Place de la Madeleine with great style and grace, as would stroll any famous cinematographer who had just discovered the location where he would film the climactic scene of his greatest masterpiece. Overhead, the sky was cooling off. The summer sun went and hid itself behind a stone building the way a child hides behind a bush. 'Is there nothing in my life that isn't brimming with perfection?' I asked myself, tossing my wig in my satchel with the blue-tinted glasses. I skipped down the rue Royale in the direction of the Jardin de Tuileries with a joyful heart, while my pleasant thoughts mused on eternal questions…

What would I need with rice and bananas and cool frothy beer? Answer me that! And why would I want to get out of Paris? Some idea that was! . . . I sure was a clever one today! I wonder if that old landlady will be spying on that apartment, hoping to catch a glimpse of King Agamemnon. She'll wonder who Pavel is. I'll have to cast him as Menelaus. Menelaus the cuckold!—Ha! "What did you say, Madame?" Pavel will ask, "A famous cinematographer has rented this place? I thought I was a guest of Dmitry. He's a composer, not a cinematographer. He had to go away for awhile, to 'take the waters,' I think. Said he needed to escape this 'Parisian life of decadent nights and hungover mornings.'" Sure, Pavel! Fancy such a thing as leaving Paris! Why would I leave Paris? I would be nobody lost in some Cuban fishing village. The heroic life is lived among the people until the end. Let old bearded Epicurus run away from city-life. Let's see what kind of foolish epics he can write with ladybugs for muses. I'm staying here in Paris— 'in the polis'—where I'll squander my health and my sanity. Morning after morning, waking up in a bachelor's mansard, washing my face in a basin while the fat boulangères open their bread shops down on the street below, the plump pigeons coo and mate in the planters, weaving nests with poppy stems and panty straps and other relics of last night's feasts. I'll squander the final rays of youth rolling in the flesh of passion, and the sun will eventually set, casting shade over my soul. But rich will be my life if I can keep my memories full and brimming, and record them on clear-eyed mornings while I set joyously to work setting pen to holy craft. Look around you! It's summer! The one time of year when you are truly alive! . . . Yet I've said that very same thing in other seasons. But flourishing summer . . . life is perfect and nothing is lacking. Look at the babes drinking joy from their mother's legs. Look at the sky milking itself like the breast of a baby-blue goddess. Look at the leaves in the high-up trees, brushed with yellow smudges of sun! I stroll past the stone figures in the park, over the hot dusty floor. The heat is sweltering and in my lack of sleep I imagine the sweat on my crown is blood which the sun is wringing from my skin. I am sure that any moment the sand beneath my feet will begin to boil and overwhelm me—yes!, the sand will overwhelm me!

That day, I walked among the statues in the park and saw Theseus wrestling the Minotaur—a brave occupation! There I saw Cain who had come to kill his brother Abel. His hand was pressed to his violent eyes to shield the murderous sun. As the heat pounded visions into my brain, and the hordes of tourists in the gardens scattered across the corners of my eyes, I saw the statue of Cain take his hand from his face to cover his fiery genitals. "That's not Cain, but Adam!" I cried, surprised to see such a sight. Here I was, walking through the Tuileries Gardens and there was Adam treading across the gravel path as he was being expelled from the garden. Fancy happening to walk through the Tuileries on the same very day when Adam was expelled from the garden! I marveled at my luck!

'Hmm . . . but I didn't know Adam was expelled from the Tuileries Gardens! Is it true? I would've guessed he was exiled from Luxembourg. Poor Adam! And I thought I had it bad—ill as I am from lack of sleep. I guess he'll just have to go make a life for himself elsewhere. Sure he thinks it's rough now, but years from now, after a wandering awhile in search of a home, he'll wake up on a sunny shore next to a clear blue sea, and remember all the loose girls named Eve he'd met bathing nude in the coves along the sea, and all the sisters of these Eves whom he'd kissed and fondled; and happy, he will rejoice and give thanks. He will remember Paris, but will be glad he left the Tuileries Gardens. Perhaps he won't even remember Paris. He'll remember Istanbul though, and his mistresses there; and his sweetheart in Alexandria. Yet that late-afternoon he passed me in the Tuileries Gardens holding his genitals in disgrace, he won't remember that at all.

'...And should I be disgraced to leave this life without a victory? But who said I was leaving this life? This life is mine till the end! It is a perfect life, and it is a perfect day, and now the day is over.'

The day was, in fact, over; and it had been a perfect day. It had been a perfect day, and the evening too was perfect. Though before I could feel myself a true god among men, I knew I would need to sleep.

18th Soliloquy

Longing to rest and sleep my weariness away, I trudged on my solitary evening walk from the Jardin de Tuileries, up the rue Bonaparte, until I came to the stately apartment-house facing the St-Germain Cathedral where I worked much of the time. A sturdy elevator took me up to the top floor. When I came down the hall, I heard the stirring of some critter near the door where I was headed, and I saw plopped down on the floor, a tiny blonde girl in a bright-yellow dress. I looked at my watch, it was nearing seven o'clock.

"Aleksandre, you've finally come!" The tiny girl picked herself up off the doormat and wrapped her arms around me. She smiled a great big grin. Her mouth was plush red like a painted doll and her cheeks too were made-up. Her cropped yellow hair sprang on her ears as she leaped on her toes to kiss me.

"Hello, little gypsy! What are you doing here?"

"Waiting for you!"

Her name was Palomita. She'd come from Andalusia to study fashion in Paris. I'd made love to her a few times here in this apartment, having only recently met her; and now she felt herself welcome to slip in through the security-door and sit on the doormat and wait for me at any given hour. She had been waiting with her box of colored pencils, and there were sheets of paper and pencils thrown about the hallway. The papers were filled with sketches of fashion models dangling purses and wearing evening dresses. Like a child with a mouth full of sugar and hands full of crayons who sits on the stoop as she waits for her parents to come home from work, eagerly thinking they'll arrive at any minute with parcels and groceries in their arms, so was my little Spanish dovelette sitting in wait for me this early evening with her sketches and her childish dress. Seeing this ridiculous sight made me wonder whether or not I should continue to sleep with girls so young.

"I've been waiting here for over an hour!" laughed Palomita, pushing her tongue into my mouth. Our lips pressed each other's and our tongues entangled. After the kiss, I set her down and turned the key in the lock started inside and she followed after me.

"But *why* have you been waiting here? And did the neighbors see you spread out on the mat with your coloring pencils like a little latchkey-kid who'd forgotten her necklace before school?"

"My girl-friend, Marina, who's letting me stay at her place, she doesn't want company right now, so I have nowhere to go. I wandered around St-Germain for a while and then came here to see you. Why do you look like you haven't slept in forever?"

"Because I *haven't* slept in forever. Sleep is a stranger to me, Palomita. I have a lot of work to do, so you can't stay long. But we'll drink a coffee."

"Are you happy to see me at least?"

"Of course I am!" I picked up Palomita's skinny little body and glided her across the room, and set her finally down on the bed beneath the window—a window that let in bursts of wind, now warm from the summer day that'd passed, now mild from the evening to come.

After we caressed each other's skin and felt the moistness growing from tender places in the softly dimming night, I went and brewed coffee. Then retrieving a well-strung guitar from the corner, I began plucking a wanderer's song. It was a gypsy ballad I wrote back when I myself was a wayfarer of a youngish age—a traveler who was no more than a boy, who knew nothing of the future, and cared only for the songs in his head, the colors of the trees on the landscape, and the feeling of a highway beneath his youthful soles. Palomita perched on my bed and listened to my gypsy song as she sipped the coffee I had made for her.

"I like that song. Why did you stop? . . . You know, if I don't get into fashion school, I have to go back to Sevilla to my parents' house."

"Nonsense! You could stay in Paris and join with some other little gypsies like yourself. You all can run around Paris in colorful dresses picking pockets and telling fortunes. Tell me the future, my beautiful Spaniardess, and I'll furnish you a fine Parisian mansard with a high roof, and enough precious gold to allow you to live with high morals."

"I don't want morals. Why do you need to know the future?"

"I'm nearing the end of my hero's tale, dear girl, and I need to know if my hero, having returned home from his journey, rejoins his culture and society and finds bliss in domestic life—loving his wife, tending his flocks and working alongside his fellow men—or does he set off again with his wandering ways: flitting over the sea and traversing hefty continents, a warrior of men, a lover of women, a stranger of many alien tongues and myriad tricks, a man given welcome in all lands, a man-of-the-world? You know, little blushing Palomita... one thing is for certain is that my hero's words will live long after he is dead. Likewise, these words we are speaking now shall live after the sun has set on the landscape of our souls, casting shade over our eyes. In the ruins of our great cities, these words..." ...rambled on and on without care for where they went, and seemed as though they'd never stop dropping out of my mouth, skipping this- and that-away, and soon my poor little dovelike Palomita, having had suffered enough, blew a familiar name loudly in my sleeping ear...

"Aleksandre!"

"*Eh ?! Quoi ?!*"

"Wake up, Aleksandre! You're not listening to me! You're mumbling about strange things. You were thinking about something else this whole time!"

"I was?"

"Yes, I was talking about my fashion school, and you were mumbling something about the Dardanelles and some buried cities that no one's ever heard of."

"I was?"

"Yes, now please listen to me or play a song or something, but don't bury your head back in the blankets."

"My dear Palomita, I think I need to sleep. Run along for a while, I need to sleep. It's been a long life so far. I feel like a hundred decades are dangling from my eyelids on chains. If you're still in Paris in a few days and haven't joined the gypsy-wagon, come and see me and we'll travel to the Dardanelles together. I'll introduce you to a girl I know whom you will like. She too is the color of pollen. We can stay at her house in the desert. You'll like her. You two will laugh."

And so the sweet night fell. As I listened to the soft little sounds of Palomita's feet as they stamped across the empty square of Saint Germain below the windows of the room to which I held key, and where I lay; the sky and the summer stars inhaled and exhaled, blowing upon the night. It was the type of night that makes lovers of wanderers and puts heroes to sleep. And so I slept. For three days, I slept. And when I awoke on a late July morning, I felt as a newly-grown youth ready to lace his sandals, drink from a basin the water of life, and leap high into the sacred day.

19th Soliloquy

Daylight poured into the room where I sat up and clasped my hands...

"Glory to be alive!"

I had just slept for three days in a room in St-Germain-des-Prés—my dreams were wild and free! It was a rest of the sort that only falls upon those who come to sleep after a period of especially triumphant living. So pleasant were my dreams. Here I was chasing rabbits through laughing fields; there I was being chased myself, away from a fortress prison from which I'd escaped . . . I soared down the hill while guards pursued me tossing javelins. When my swift feet reached the riverside, I duped my pursuers and jumped a steamship that carried me through the delta, then out into the open sea. I sailed unhindered and safe through the wide ocean until I reached Arabia where I became king. I awoke clear-minded, fresh as young Apollo, and strong too!

So I slept for three days; and after I began a period of work that lasted three heroic weeks. Only briefly did I pause, three times per day: once in the morning, once per evening, and then again in the little-hours of night, so as to take part in those activities that are of meaning to us, we sons and daughters of men who dwell on this mortal earth.

After joyfully working each morning, I would leave off around midday to challenge myself to a footrace. Speeding along the sunny paths of the Jardin du Luxembourg, ideas would breed like aphids in my head—for creative invention is easy and sublime when air cycles quickly through the lungs and the body is busy at noble tasks.

In the rosy light of evening, I would stroll to the markets at Buci to buy sweet tomatoes, tawny citrus and green herbs. These bounties I would stir together to eat at the hour the sun fell—for the fruits of the vines and the trees and the little bush, at once cool and well-perfumed, provide the eater with an experience that resembles an act of worship when they are eaten slowly in the hot summer months.

Back at work, I would sit at the desk and compose my verses, wide-eyed from the coffee and the hysterical tinctures that fueled my blood. Day and night, I would work, weaving heroic couplets with forlorn melody.

"Muse! Where is the line I'm trying to find?!" Leaping from the chair to the window one afternoon, I flung the shutters open, eager to see if the next verse would tumble in from over the rooftops. "I have to get our hero out of that attic! The lamb is going to rot on his back if he stays there too long gibbering with that old woman. Make him jump!" Now my hero's tale was quickly coming full-circle. Everything had become crucial and I needed to bring it all together just right. I called to the ideas that were floating like puffs of cotton over the rooftops, but before they would arrive and fall in my cupped hands, I would be gone!—off to the kitchen to wrestle a cup of coffee from the counter. Then I would strangle the house plant. Perhaps pose a few questions to the hinges on the bathroom door. Then I'd begin to pace the floor, pace after pace, talking feverishly to myself as would any proper genius or fool...

"Do you see what I've done? My hero is now safe in his native land, you see, reunited with his beautiful wife. His son has come of age and is ready to rule alongside his father. It is time now to weave the double-narrative. A composition of this caliber needs a double-narrative. But how should I transition? The primary narrative is *epic*. The secondary should then be *tragic*. I've already decided that! But why? Because the whole thing is *lyric* in mood. So weave together the *epic* and the *tragic* (over the *lyric*) and you have all three! Now, maître, focus your thoughts... We must perfectly blend together these poetic elements. But what on earth is that beast?!" With the interruption, my eyes stole to the window where I thought I saw a giant falcon pecking his way through the glass. Nonsense!, the glass was open, and there was no falcon—just some fluffy pigeon sitting on the eave munching a piece of cord.

"...So our hero has come home after years of wandering. He reunites with his wife, reestablishes order in his kingdom, and installs his son on the throne. Now he must go back out into the world. But why? If he has spent all these years striving to come home, why would he leave again? Why? . . . Because he has the soul of a wanderer, that's why! And now, back at home, he is a stranger once again in this life. He must go back into the strangeness of life. Yes, this is it!..."

Happy with the way things were going, I went to rummage through a box where I found a potent pill that I quickly mashed between my teeth to soothe the muscles in my back that were twisted from pacing the floor half the day and sitting in a chair the other half. I took my pen in my hand anew and began to put the pieces together...

'The chorus sings of the fall of night, as our hero wanders through the peaceful city, his heart full of melancholy. In search of understanding his place in this confusing life, he ventures alone to the outlying fields where he hunted as a boy, and feels himself a stranger there. He walks to the harbor where he used to fish and build boats and map the constellations at night, and he feels himself a stranger there too. Estranged to the earth that feeds him, to the sky overhead that confuses him, and the moon and the stars that drive him mad, he decides he needs to leave again. He is estranged to all but the wandering path, and realizes his heroic journey is not over. And so our hero leaves again his native land and wanders far and alone...'

"Aye!, I have the end of my hero's tale!" I rejoiced as I leapt from my chair. Although it wasn't there in words, I had it in concept. It existed as a feeling in my head and I knew I just had to draft a few lines of poetry to put the concept into verse form. So happy I was to have found the end. No, it didn't yet exist on paper, it was only a feeling in my head, but that feeling had finished steeping and was ready to be blown onto the page. I had it, and nothing, (not even the savage city outside), was strong enough to take it from me.

Fueled by my inspiration, I ran across the room to liberate the cup of coffee the bookshelf had taken prisoner. Lapping the black watery brew like a hyena, I tossed the empty cup aside. I then returned to the chair to continue my divine act of creation. Hot blood swished in my head as my mighty pen stole across the page...

Now it is time for the double narrative to begin. Here it goes:

'The curtain falls on our hero after he is once again far from his native land. But where is he? Why, he's in a foreign city, that's where!—lying on a cot in a rented room, over a marketplace where merchants trade salts, oils and saffron, where vagabonds flit with stolen purses in the shadows behind carpet stalls. Goats are bleating, dancers are blowing fire, musicians are strumming lyres. It is nighttime and the air is spicy!

"'Twing... twang...'" The oriental song continues as our hero sings himself to sleep on his heroic cot. All of a sudden...'

"Wait! How is this different from the beginning of the hero's tale?" ... "I'll tell you! The difference is that now our hero is old—no longer a boy. You know, It's good that one grows old in this life. If there's one thing to take pride in, it's that. It's a fine thing, this life. Good God, and it's summertime too!"

Running to the window, I opened my mouth as wide as a saucer to take glory in the season that was before me. I perched myself on the ledge and rejoiced for I suddenly recalled where I was and at what glorious stage in life I was at; and as it was all too much, my cheeks became inflamed with pleasure. I sprinted to the cupboard to retrieve some bread kept in a Moroccan breadbasket. I took the seeded loaf and went to back to the window and began to snap the bread and eat.

"Oh, holy city!" I sang as I sat, snapping my bread. Wherever the seeds fell, up sprang a forest. Darting off to the kitchen, I found some grapes and began munching the skins back at my place on the window-ledge. I flung the seeds to the street below and up sprang vineyards. I was now wandering through sunny orchards, nourishing myself from the fruits that piled in the lap of sleeping Eve. Her soft pubic mound bathed in the sweet juices that dripped from the figs in my mouth...

Snapping my bread, delighting in the soft wheat melting in my mouth and the shower of poppy seeds tumbling down to the street, I watched the seeds land on the sidewalk. Then up springs a land of opium flowers! . . . Ancient lotus and forgetful herbs began to flourish from the Parisian concrete. I was creating a world of myth and found myself lost in sweet oblivion. Enough of this! Time to work!

Back at my desk, I took again the pen to my happy hand...

'Goodnight to our tired hero. Again he is far from his native land, just as he was ten years ago, back when he was young man. Now, mature in years and experience, he lies on a rented bed over a bustling marketplace in a foreign seaport. The curtain falls and rises in Athens....'

"Athens?!"

Yes, let me explain...

'Like the night, the curtain fell on our hero and rose like the dawn on a pair of young lovers fleeing their home on the island of Salamis to live together in Athens. One of the lovers, the girl, had been married young to a wealthy Salamis merchant who was already old and disagreeable; but she was in love with a poor, yet handsome, youth—who was very romantic (as poor youths usually are)—and she wanted to be with him. Should they stay on their island and meet in secret in the town or in the gardens? Why, they would be certainly caught by the girl's husband, and the two lovers would be tried for their crime and put to death.

'"Come with me to Athens," the girl sings to her lover, "and there we will forget my husband and we will consummate our love and I will bear thy children." So her wishes were sung and her lover gave heart. The two made haste to sail away.

'But while they were at the port, they were spied by an acquaintance of the wealthy merchant: a scheming, shrew-like man who hoped to grow rich from this discovery of seeing the merchant's wife with a lover. He quickly ran to the merchant at the latter's home and spoke thus... "Sir, I saw your beautiful wife in the arms of a young man, this very day. It's true! They were at the port buying a ticket to sail to Athens on tonight's ship. When I left to bring you this news, they were embracing affectionately by port with luggage to travel. I watched them sitting on the slick pier. It has been raining today. Should I go and bring your wife to you? I know, as you are rich, my friendly merchant, that you will reward me for this task. I will not only bring your young wife to you by the scruff of her fair neck, but I will also have some ruffians drown the young man who accompanies her. Shall I do this?"

'"No, no," replied the merchant, wiping the single tear from his eyelid which had formed when he learned of this news. "No, do no such thing. Neither bring me my wife, nor drown the young man. Rather, take this money... here... some silver pieces. Go, and board the ship and follow the two to Athens. When you arrive at Piraeus, you will find a monk named Ascidas in the monastery there. He is a childhood friend of mine and is to me like a brother. *He*, rather than *yourself*, shall bring to justice my wife and her young friend. He is a holy man and will know what action to take. You stay on as an observer. After the work is done, return and tell me of all that has passed and I will give you ten times as much money as what I am giving you today. Here, take this currency and go to the port!"

'"I will do as you say, my dear sir. I will find Ascidas and observe his endeavors, and the account I give you upon my return shall be worth all the money you reward me with." And so the man took leave of the merchant and returned to port.

'Along the docks, night was overtaking evening and the boat was loading with passengers. It was then the two lovers began to cross the sea. The journey was tough, the night was rough, and the storms shook the vessel and threatened to pull it under water and devastate it. The lovers embraced each other desperately for they were sure they were going to die and believed they were embracing for the last time. When, however, they reached land in safety, they gave thanks and kissed the soil and ventured off together in merry love towards Athens.

'The first person they met was a monk who was traveling up from Piraeus. The monk said that they looked like they were in trouble, fleeing something perhaps, and asked if he could be of service. He swore that as a monk, he was bound to keep their sorrows between him and God and would reveal nothing to the Law, should they be in violation of some moral code. The lovers, believing they had found someone whom they could trust to help them, told the monk the whole story. The girl explained that she'd been married young to a rich merchant whom she did not love, and was running away from him to be with her young lover who was so handsome and romantic; and that because it was love that caused them to run away from Salamis, their plight was from the heart and was divine and sent by God and the monk should do everything in his power to help them. The monk nodded in agreement, and said that it was indeed his duty to God to help lovers who were committing adultery for sacred reasons, and he told them he would give them sanctuary at the Acropolis.

'"Meet me on this path at midnight tonight," the monk told the lovers, once the three travelers had arrived at the Athenian market-stalls at the base of the Acropolis, "and I will guide you to a little house where you can be alone and in love together, away from the world. For that is all lovers really want, no? A place to be alone together and away from the world? I will prepare for you a holy bed and bless it and there you may consummate your love for the first time." Then the monk paused, "you haven't *yet* consummated your love, have you? For if you have, I mightn't be able to help you." ... "No, we haven't!" the two swore to the monk, while clenching the hem of his robe, pleading, "We wanted to make love together on the ship, but the storms were so violent, we couldn't! No, we have yet to sleep naked together." . . . "Very well then," said the monk, "Both of you, meet me at midnight atop this hill, and I will lead you to a place where you shall soon sleep naked together—as two lovers ought to do when driven by the heart's holy passions."

'So spoke the monk, and took leave of the lovers until midnight. In his absence, the lovers fondled each other, but no more, as they waited their holy bed. When the monk returned with a lantern at midnight on the path, he began to lead the eager lovers up to the Acropolis. They followed him; and as they did, they kissed each other and praised the monk for helping them. They praised the monk and they praised their fate and they praised one another and renewed their vows again and again.'

"This is good!" I cried, leaping from my desk. I was tempted to pile some towers of wax around the edges of the desk and enflame their wicks, to brew bowls of steaming things, and coax my hands with creams and other pleasures, so that I could stay awake to work all night and finish the hero's tale once and for all... "No!" I decided, "I will sleep and work again in the morning. Working at night is for amateurs. Amateurs and madmen. Holy are the creations of the fine morning. I will sleep and retake the pen tomorrow!" And thus I did.

'

20th Soliloquy

So I slept the night, and when I awoke in the cool of morning, I mixed packaged crystals of coffee with scalding water and drank the steamy solution at the window.   The shutters and the glass were open, and below, one could see the specks of citizens scuttling across the Saint Germain Square.

At my composing desk, I set to work with the confidence that I'd finish my hero's tale that very day—or if not that day, the day after. *Très bientôt, en tout cas !* It would be the best thing I'd ever created and the public would receive it with open arms. I closed my eyes and listened to the rooftop above me trembling like a nervous child. Outside the breezy window, I could hear the city of Paris rubbing its moist avenues together and stamping its intersections in anticipation for the gift I was about to give it.

"Aye! . . . more coffee!" Howling thus, I kidnapped a cup and filled it with that potent black beverage.

"*Bon sang !* I have way too many clothes on! Let me be less dressed. I need to feel more sensual as I finish my hero's tale!" Saying this, I disrobed except for tiny black underwear and a handsome-fitting, and very thin, cotton shirt that let my firm skin stretch and wind like packed desert hills, browned by the sun. Following this exercise, I rubbed a masculine potion on my face... a special sort of cream. I then went to the piano to pound out the refrain of my hero's tale... open fifths... open fifths...

"So where was I? Well, our long-traveled hero went back to his wandering ways. And now the double narrative comes in concerning the two star-crossed lovers. My job here is to simply introduce the lovers' plight, lead them to climax, and then kill them off...

"But where were they? Oh, yes! They were waiting on a path for that old monk, Ascidas, to come lead them to sanctuary on the Acropolis. It is there they will meet their untimely death. This is how...."

'Midnight greeted the land of Greece as the two lovers were fondling each other on the Athenian path. They were oblivious to all until Ascidas the monk appeared from the mess of trees lining the path and urged them to follow. The climb up to the Acropolis was steep. At the vista, the three stopped to drink a cup of wine, admire the full moon, and pray. The two lovers now found themselves standing in front of a crude stone house that faced the Parthenon. "Here is where you two shall have sanctuary," spoke Ascidas. And the lovers stood before the stone dwelling and looked at one another with great joy in their eyes. The stone looked solid, and would surely keep their love within and the rest of the world out...'

"But wait!" I cried with a sudden panic that made my arms flutter enough to scatter the papers on my desk. "How am I going to have Ascidas the monk do away with the two lovers?" I was baffled. I paced the floor and chewed my brave knuckles. Then I retook the chair and pen and tried an idea...

"'Not so fast, my young friends," Ascidas whispered in the darkness of the path, "I must prepare the sanctuary and bless the ground, as well as the bed where the act of consummation shall take place." . . . Here, the lovers were bouncing on the balls of their feet, they could hardly stand it! . . . "You two go into this little barn over here... you see this little hovel with the straw on the ground, yes there..." Ascidas led the lovers into a nearby hovel where they were to hide from the night and strangers alike for a few minutes while the monk blessed the sanctuary and made it holy. The monk then stamped off and entered the stone house alone.

'Upstairs, Ascidas turned the key that was on a cord around his neck and entered a large room with stone walls and a stone floor. It was bare except for a bed and a window carved in the stone. The window looked out over the Acropolis....' (Writing this, I thought of Sibylle's apartment looking out at the Madeleine.) '...The window looked out over the Acropolis with a stately view of the Parthenon, which was lit by a broad and gleaming moon that soared in the clear sky. The small bed in the corner across from the window was carved of twisted wood sprouting from the ground. It had a plump mattress of a muslin cover stuffed with straw, and a stuffed muslin pillow. Elsewhere, the humble room was bare. There was no need of a lamp, for the full moon beaming through the window washed the stones with silver light.'

Now I thought of the medicine cabinet in Sibylle's bathroom at the Madeleine, in which I'd left the digitalis herb. I wanted the same feature in this room on the Acropolis. But how could I? Such a long-ago and faraway place could have a wooden bed with a stuffed mattress, yes, and stone walls, but it couldn't have a medicine cabinet with a mirror over a sink with running water. No, that would be absurd! Let's see...

'...And so while the two lovers were embracing in a crude hovel where animals nested, awaiting the return of Ascidas so as to be led to their own nesting place, Ascidas himself stood in the high-up room and thought to himself carefully. He peered out the window past the Parthenon and thought he saw someone far below scuffling in the bushes. "It's that silly acquaintance of my friend the merchant," he said to himself and ceased to pay it any mind. And reaching into his burlap robe, he took out a heavy packet containing dried herbs. It was a mixture of Grecian foxglove and poppy leaves.'

"Now what can I have Ascidas do with the herbs?!" I wondered aloud, abandoning the desk anew to pace the floor. "I can't very well have him spread the herbs on the window as though it were bird seed! Those two lovers simply aren't going to go pecking at seeds on any windowsill! Can't I put a mirror on the wall and have him place the herbs behind? They aren't going to go looking behind any mirrors!"

…Here I was almost done with my hero's tale and I was baffled with the conclusion. I had two fugitives hiding in a flea-infested barn, and a monk with a packet of deadly poisonous plants pacing the floor, (just as I was doing!), thinking of how to lead the former to the latter. (Just then there was a knock at my apartment door in Paris!)

'Who is that?!' I stopped cold in my tracks in the room in Saint Germain and stared at the closed front door. All the while, my heart leapt with terror in my chest…

'Detectives?! *How* detectives? Already?!'

How, I wondered, could detectives have found me so soon? It'd only been a mere few days since I'd weaved that grand scheme involving Pavel and Pénélope in that apartment at Madeleine. The lovers were quick to have a dispute, I take it. Someone did someone else in with the packet of digitalis I hid behind the mirror in the bathroom. Detectives are quick to trace events in this city! *Oui, oui ! …On ne plaisante pas avec la police parisienne !* …Holy Christ, Detectives! I'm finished!!' …Again the knock pounded on the door, and each time it did, I felt that the pounding was a dull hatchet-blade thrashing at my lungs. Here I stood almost finished with my oeuvre that had taken me years to create, and the authorities were here take me away in shackles. 'Should I gather the papers and climb out the window?' …Again the knock at the door. I stood not far away, petrified. "No! I will not climb out the window," I decided, "when they come for you, you go. It's as simple as that. That was the rule in Galicia, and that is the rule here. When they come for you, you go!" So mumbling, I gave up all plans to escape. I walked over to the door and opened it to turn myself over to the detectives…

Ô, sweet are the angels and devils alike, who feud in the rafters of Heaven!

To tell of the joy I had that moment… when I saw before me not a pair of detectives ready to trap me in handcuffs and drag me away to some squalid prison, but rather it was just the building's concierge! A plump Portuguese woman with red splotchy cheeks. She was holding some letters and a little package, and wanted to give them to me.

"Sir, the mail. I didn't want to leave them by the door as usual because there is this package. *C'est peut-être cher !* It's better to take it inside. *Au revoir !*"

And with that she was off, leaving me in the doorway with a stack of mail and a heart shivering with relief. "I'm saved! I can finish my hero's tale, after all! The air smells nice here...." so I chattered with myself and closed the door and bolted it and went to the window to open the mail. Pleasure it is to read one's mail by an open window—when summer lays beyond and sunlight is abound!

The envelopes were uninteresting. Some commercial offers. A discount on Marie's Provincial Tartines at the local grocery. One crisp envelope informed me that the city was experiencing an abundance of stylish neckties at all-time low prices. I tossed these aside and started opening the package. Pretty was the paper—and scented too! It was from my fair-skinned Daphné, favorite daughter of a far-away father. She was by his side now, and by her mother's two, at the family's home in the south near Marseille. She missed me and had sent a little gift—two puffy soft pillows, each the size of a plum. I took out the card and read...

Bonjour mon petit Aleksandre...

How is Paris ? I sewed a couple of little cloth "pochettes" for you. Smell them! They are filled with the lavender that I picked on the hill near our house. My mother and I went out with big white hats and flower baskets and gathered lavender on the hillside all afternoon. Then we came back and my mother went to drive into Marseille and my father came and chased me around the garden as if I were a little child. He was running fast and I went straight for a large palm tree in our yard and tried to climb it to get away—but alas!, I can't climb palm trees! . . . and so I fell on the grass by the trunk of the tree and my father came and rolled around and laughed with me. After he left, I stayed to take a little nap. But then came a rustling from the top of the palm tree and I looked up and saw rats up in the tree! It's disgusting how the palm trees in the South of France have rats in them. Now I'm in the sunroom drinking

Campari and writing this letter. Anyway, enjoy these lavender "pochettes." They are for your sock drawer, so your socks always smell nice. I send you lots of sun from the south. In September I'll be back in Paris. Je t'embrasse fort!

- Ta Petite Daphné

Setting the letter aside, I picked up Daphné's lavender pouches to examine them. Fine was their needlework, tightly stitched cotton tied with silk ribbons. I pressed them to my nose and the sweet fragrance of the lavender poured through the fabric. 'Gentle Daphné, thank you! I will go put them in the drawer with my socks just now … but why should my socks have both of them? Giving both of these pouches to my feet would be like putting all the bread at one end of the table. No, I will put *one* in my sock drawer, (which I did), and *the other* I'll put in my pillowcase so that I can smell it while I'm going to sleep and when I'm waking up…' With that I took the second pouch and slipped it into the pillowcase belonging to the pillow which I used those nights when I slept in this room in Saint Germain. I then went back to resume work.

I worked for the rest of the afternoon but it was no use. I didn't know how my little monk would exterminate these happy lovers. There could be no medicine cabinet on the Acropolis. Even a simple mirror on the wall would seem out of place. In the end, I thought to have the monk go find the lovers in the barn, and while leading them through the dark hallway to their room, he would stick a knife into each one of them—spilling their guts.

"Nonsense!" I was going nowhere with this double-narrative.

Frustrated, I went to the kitchen to eat some sweet brebis cheese and take a glass of water with gas. I paced up and down the room until I was exasperated. "Goodness gracious," I finally sighed, "It's senseless to think I govern my afternoon." Then I went to lie down quietly for a moment to rest my thoughts.

"I won't sleep though. I have work to do. I'll only close my eyes for a few minutes." This I promised myself, but when the lavender fumes began seeping into my nose through the pillowcase, I grew lightheaded and sleepy and a pleasant sleep overtook me.

An hour later, I awoke with a great start... "What is this? I was put to sleep! Those lavender fumes dissolved the city of Paris and sent me roving the flowering hills of dreamland Provence!" And with this realization, I leapt from the bed with the solution to my hero's tale! Daphné's pouch in the pillowcase had just solved all my problems! At the desk, I picked up my mighty pen and began to write...

'And so while the two lovers were embracing in a crude hovel where animals nested, awaiting the return of the monk Ascidas, so as to be led to their own nesting place, Ascidas himself stood in the high-up room and thought to himself carefully. He looked at the bed far against the wall, opposite the stone hole that served as a window, and a smile crept over his face. He walked over to the bed and took out his knife and made some careful slices in the muslin tissue of the mattress. Then he took the packet of Grecian foxglove mixed with dried poppies and began pouring the herbs inside the mattress to mix it in with the straw and wool and other stuffing that gave the bed its bulk. With his old hands, wrinkled from prayer and calloused from tending the plants in the monastery garden, he worked the deadly herbs into the straw until the mattress was completely riddled throughout. He then closed up the muslin and stitched the mattress back together with a needle he kept in his slipper. Happy with the sight of this poisonous marriage bed, Ascidas scuttled out of the room and down the stairs to the yard to find the lovers and lead them to their sanctuary.'

"A poisonous marriage bed? That's genius! Let's continue..."

'They were fondling each other next to a hog in the barn. "Come, come!" The monk pried them from their embrace and led them to the entrance of the stone house that would be their refuge. Inside, save for a mattress on a bed-frame carved from a single olive tree, the room was empty. A single hole was carved in the far stone wall to serve as a window. It looked up at the formations of the Acropolis and the night sky.

'"Here is your bed and here is the key to lock the door once I leave." So saying, Ascidas handed the slender key to the youths.

'"But why isn't our bed beneath the window?" the lovers asked in unison, "The first time we make love, it should be in a bed beneath the window. That way, between our breaths, we can look up and see the moon in the sky."

'"There is no need to put the bed beneath the window," said the monk, "The moon is full tonight, and so its light fills the whole room. Besides, the bed cannot be moved. Its frame is carved from one single olive tree planted beneath the house. To move the bed, one would need to move both the tree and the house and this cannot be done. Go, you two . . . lie on your holy bed. The moon is vast and steady tonight. It will bathe you in its light. Everything here is beautiful. Take the key, I am going now. Be still."

'Once Ascidas had left the room, the young man locked the door and led his twice-wedded bride to the bed and lay her down on the mattress and cupped her knees in his hands and kissed her. Their bodies were washed in moonlight as they made love together for the first time. It was beautiful and it was holy and they prayed upon each other's firm and sweaty bodies and though the bodies were beautiful alters of flesh. And after they'd finished and were lying beaten and worn like animals, they entwined their bodies to sleep the morning through. Both were enraptured, happy that they could sleep all the next day together without the fear that the girl's husband, or anybody else, would discover them; for Ascidas the monk was the only mortal alive who knew where the couple could be found; and he, after all, was on their side.

'So they lay after lovemaking, breathing, panting heavily together. But soon the poppy leaves in the mattress began to overcome them with their lulling fumes. The foxglove too leaked fragrant smells and made them sleepy. The lovers soon were overtaken, overwhelmed. While they slept, they drank the fumes of the potent herbs that came from the pores in the mattress; and so entwined, the two lovers died. It was the happiest death that two people could ever have.'

"Oh... it's a great story," I sighed, putting down my laboring pen. Satisfied with my work, I crossed the silent room and sat at the piano to tick out a tune: a lullaby in A minor to lull my senses. Soon I was ready to crawl off to sleep on my own fragrant (but not poisonous) bed. There I lay, while the sky outside puffed night into the airy room, and puffed dreams into my happy soul.

21st Soliloquy

So all things come to an end. After years of delirious and exacting work, I finished composing my great hero's tale. It was only a week later that I found myself sweeping up a pile of ashes in the rooms where I worked in Saint-Germain-des-Prés.

A document had caught fire—or rather it was me who set the fire. I had burned a passport I no longer wanted or needed, and was brushing the soot off the floor into a dustpan. You see the reason for that was simple...

The night before, some friends came to find me with armloads of champagne to celebrate my finished work and to take pleasure in my company. We drank heroic amounts of that gorgeous bubbling wine. Arm in arm, we ventured out beneath the blushing streetlamps to feast in the city.

"You really finished it?" they asked me.

"Yes. It just needs a few lines worked out here and there. I'm taking it with me to the countryside in a week. When I'm back in Paris in September, I'll seal it in an airmail envelope and send it off to the great Patron Saint of Composers..."

"Where is the Patron Saint?"

"Bah, Saint Petersburg, of course!"

"Of course! More champagne?"

"Of course!"

It was true, I only had to polish up the dactylic hexameter, add a few colorations to the musical score. A week's work at the most. Now was August and the whole city was emptying itself to go to the country. I'd take my hero's tale to the soft shores of the Mediterranean, or Lake Como, or to Certaldo Alto and the green hills of Tuscany—there I would finalize the work!

"Am I in your hero's tale?" each of my friends asked me.

"Yes, your words will live forever."

"Splendid! We'll all go see it together when it's performed in Vienna, etc."

Meanwhile I was thinking of how I should go to Verona to polish the work chez Tommaso. '…As a philosopher, he'll understand the meaninglessness of my finalizations and other occupations; and the two of us will laugh and enjoy the season. I will work in the mornings while his household is asleep. The air is clean in the Verona hills. And besides, Tommaso's maid is a good cook. First of September, I'll mail the piece to Russia and that will be that! Then I'll begin a new project—one even more ambitious than this last one. I'll write *The Vermian Opera*, which I promised Pavel I'd write. Or maybe an allegorical play: *Adonis' Seduction of Persephone*. My work will flourish as the days grow cold. Let Autumn wipe her moist glove on my cheek, for I will subdue her with the heroic work that will soon gush from my mighty and inexhaustible pen!

'…But what if I shall not be allowed to make the final corrections on my work? What if my train leaps off the rails on the way south and my body rains down in shreds over the Italian countryside? The world would be deprived of my hero's tale! Even if I were to entrust a friend in Paris with a copy, it would be missing the final corrections and that would make it an imperfect oeuvre. After all, is it really perfect as it is now? Is it right, for example, that the Salamis merchant should provide his adulterous wife with such a happy death? Why did he have a monk bring his wife and her lover to a poisonous bed? He could have simply paid the ruffian down by the docks to lop off their heads and toss their bodies into the sea. Why that and not this? No, it's perfect like it is. Still, what am I doing out *playing* while the manuscript is left alone and vulnerable? Good Lord! I'm out cajoling with loose women in skirts and high heels, guzzling champagne, when I should be locked in my room until my hero's tale is posted first-class mail!'

Yet, as life treats me gently, I didn't think I needed to worry about a thing. And so I continued cajoling, caressing thighs and drinking wine. In the morning, I woke up tipsy and happy to be alive. The Bialetti kettle chugged coffee on the stove. On the table sat a first-class ticket to Florence. I'd decided on Tuscany after all. I opened the window and inhaled the summer air that poured in. My clothes from the night before were tossed around the room. A traveling case sat open for the packing on a desk where I had spent so many hours setting pen to holy craft.

After I drank a bowl of potent coffee, I went down to buy some books which I planned to read beneath the leafy trees at a café terrace on the Faubourg Saint Germain. While I was on my stroll, I stopped at the kiosk for a newspaper. I wanted to see if anything had happened during these long seasons I had been submerged in my own current events, hearing only the news of my own invention.

The birds were feisty in the leafy branches of the swaying summery trees. A little finch landed on my table at the café and chomped on the sugar that went unused on my coffee saucer. When I tried to claim the sugar, the finch chomped my fingernail. I turned to the *Curiosity Section* of the newspaper and began to read. There was an article in it I found startling. It began like this...

GIRL FOUND DEAD NEAR THE MADELEINE—BODY STUFFED WITH POISONOUS PLANTS.

My eyes flashed at the headline. I read on. It seemed that a young girl had been staying in an apartment with her boyfriend at Madeleine. After some emotional turmoil, the girl had "voluntarily" ingested toxic amounts of a dangerous herb called 'digitalis.' She was found lying on the bed by a janitor who was passing on the stairwell and saw the half-naked corpse through the open door. Police were called in.

It seems there had been some dispute between the lovers. By the time the police arrived, the building's proprietor had entered the scene and the old woman denied that the girl was dead and said she was just acting in a movie, that her lack of respiration was, quote, "movie magic," unquote; and that the police were interrupting the scene... *and could they not please leave?!* When police asked the landlady where the movie crew was, the old lady became flustered and ran out of the apartment. She was found at her sister's place a few hours later asleep on the floor.

The police apprehended the dead girl's boyfriend the next afternoon in an occult shop along the Seine, where among other items, medicinal plants and some poisonous herbs were sold. Police held the young man as a suspect for two days of questioning and then, convinced of his innocence, released him. Back at the apartment at Madeleine, next to where the body had been found on the bed, were a couple of suitcases that the couple had been packing to travel. In the luggage, police found two third-class tickets to America. They also found some passionate letters that were mailed from the occult shop.

When police investigated the shop, they found the victim's boyfriend who was completely unaware that anything had befallen the girl. The news of her death threw him into a fit of hysterics during which he tried to stab himself in the eyes with a copper letter-opener. Police retrained him and put him in a cell at the local prefecture's, where he remained locked-up until he could give a coherent statement.

Two days later, the young man signed a formal declaration saying that his girlfriend had ingested the poisonous herbs after a dispute arose when she refused to accompany him to America. He had asked her what plants she was munching, and she said they were "spearmint leaves" which she had found in the bathroom when the couple had moved into the apartment. She then began to cry and collapsed on the floor and the young man helped her to bed. Once she was on the bed, he stated, she began to kiss him passionately with swollen lips, telling him how she loved him. He said her mouth had tasted disagreeably bitter, "not like spearmint." Between kisses, she said she would follow him to America—

or to anywhere else, on earth, or in heaven or hell—under one condition. The young man was to leave the apartment right then and go back to the curiosity shop where he worked. He was to turn his back to her just as Orpheus was asked to turn his back to Eurydice. Could he do that? Why not? He trusted her, didn't he? If he *didn't* turn his back, she would leave him forever and never go with him anywhere. Otherwise, once he reached the occult shop, he was to wait for her to come. And assuming he didn't give up faith and turn to look at her while leaving, or return to find her, she promised she would come right away and the two would reunite at the curiosity shop and then travel on to America.

Well, he had no choice but to leave the sorrowful girl on the bed. He kissed her one last time, tasting the bitterness on her lips, very unlike spearmint, and then turned to leave. Once he was in the stairwell, he realized that in his haste he'd not closed the door to the apartment. But he could not turn around! If he were to turn back and go close the door, he'd lose her forever; and so he let it remain open.

Leaves blew around the young man's path as he crossed the Place de la Madeleine, heading towards the rue de Rivoli; and he walked hot with emotion to the curiosity shop. It was at this same time the girl lay dying on the bed in the same position he'd left her—poisoned by the potent leaves of digitalis she'd consumed. The door to this fateful apartment, however, was standing open and a janitor was soon to pass by and notice *"une chose très bizarre !"* lying on the bed, but it would be too late.

The case has not yet been dismissed as an accidental occurrence, or suicide, however, the newspaper stated. The victim's family currently are aiding police in an investigation to find out the situation of the apartment where the girl died. Apparently, the apartment belonged to a well-known composer, whose name cannot be disclosed, who is believed to be a former lover of the victim. The apartment was allegedly lent to the young couple, as they were without means and needed a place to live. Although the poisonous herbs are believed to have come from the curiosity shop, the young man employed there attests that he didn't put the digitalis in the girl's possession; rather, her former lover, the composer, took the poisonous plants from the shop on a visit he paid, and "intentionally" planted them in the apartment before the couple moved in, to create, quote, "scandal and intrigue," unquote. The landlady of the apartment supported this theory when she told the police that the composer, quote, "paid cash for four month's rent in advance, saying there were going to be some murder scenes taking place," unquote. The crime investigation continues...

"For heaven's sake!" I gasped, "What drama they print!" I quickly shut the *Curiosity Section* of the newspaper and threw it aside. "It's a shaky plot! So they call that young man an Orpheus, eh? Well if he's Orpheus, I must be Apollo! Can't they see their Orpheus working in the occult shop was the one who laced his girlfriend's spearmint with poison? Ha-ha! Can't anyone see that? Ha-ha-ha! Well, the boyfriend told on me!—the tattler! It's all over between us! Ha-ha-ha!" I rocked in my chair and became hysterical with laughter. All the while, I asked myself why so much of that story seemed familiar... "It reminds me of something I may have composed once upon a time... *Eurydice of Madeleine* ...didn't I write that once? Is this the-world-imitating-my-art again? Why does it seem as though there are these days when all the news of the world is nothing more than echoes of the thoughts in my head? Well, tell me! . . . I'll tell you, I won't be going to call on Sweet Sibylle anymore. I hope she's fairing well in Argentina. Pity about what has happened at her apartment while she was gone. All those murder scenes! Movie magic! As for me, I'd better go back right away and get rid of that passport that I used to rent that apartment. I should go burn that up right away..."

And that is exactly what I did. Leaving the terrace, I scuttled across the street and flew up the stately elevator to the room to which I held key in Saint Germain. I unlocked the sheet metal safe in the armoire and took out my honest passport I'd used to rent Sibylle's apartment at La Madeleine. A horrendous match set fire to that passport—a ball of flames blazed before my eyes. After, I stamped the mess out.

In the smoky room, I crouched down to sweep up the ashes in the dustpan. Ashes coated my hands. "Ashes!" I cried, scooping a handful of the sooty mess. I sprinkled the ashes on my head in imitation of Job, that unfortunate man on the dung-heap, and felt a rush of euphoria realizing my fate. Twisting my head up towards the heavens, my spine bent like a serpent, I cackled at the ceiling as if it were a god, and I were the man on the dung-heap. "You think you can defeat me this easily?" I shouted, "I too can fill Leviathan's mouth with harpoons!" I blew a mighty breath at the ceiling as if it were the sky and I were blowing away the clouds. My breath was an atom-bomb and I knew that my hero's tale was finished—rough-edged, yes, but finished—and I felt invincible to all the world and heaven too. I cackled louder than ever as I rubbed the ashes into my forehead and scratched my scalp... "I too can fill Leviathan's mouth with harpoons!"

All that out of the way...

Calmly, I walked over to put a record on the phonograph. I found some white candles in a cupboard. 'Should I go out to buy some red wine?' I wondered. "Tonight is my last Parisian feast for the summer. And who knows if I my fate has written it so that I'll return here to this sacred city and this life. Tomorrow, come early morning, in the crisp air of predawn—yes, tomorrow!—before the bulbous yoke of Helios rises and swells to crack and bleed over the earth, tingeing the sky with rosy light the way a young menstruating girl tinges the water rosy when she dips her sweet legs into the bath. At this crisp hour of morning, I'll wake and drag my mighty body to Orly and say goodbye to Paris. Off by swift airplane for the enchanted land of Italy. I will gallop like a youth in love. I will glide gorgeously, soaring like an albatross, until I land on a sunny, pleasant hill inside the Florentine walls!

22nd Soliloquy

With my head rinsed of ashes, my legs veiled in fine trousers, handsome in a shirt of silk and perfumed hair, I stepped out through the courtyard and hailed a taxi to take me to the rue Saint Honoré. There, a banquet table would await my friends and me, laid-out on a lighted patio, laced with crystal vases and golden plates. There, we would share a final feast. Come morning, we would go our separate ways. For better or for worse I would slip across the French border—either for a brief respite, or for the rest of my fleeting days, which collect to form my cherished life.

Long-tried comrades assembled at the table...

Sami, the mighty Syrian boxer with fists of iron was with us; and Marco V—, the illustrious Italian pianist, as well as Prince Samuel N— who'd returned from Ghana where he'd spent years in exile. Also with us was Etienne of Saint Sulpice, Daniel R— the lord of Castel; D. Totté of Antwerp, Safouen of Tunis, S. Lassissi, P. Lijour, the Breton poet, *Ouan-le-Menteur,* and the Baron Jean-Marc T— (man who'd left a broken heart in every European town north of Madrid, south of Amsterdam). *Gros Minet* too was with us, and Martin de L—, whose shade now haunts the Château de Vincennes. Some of us were rascals, others noble. All in all, glory was seated at our table and happiness was abound!

Aged wines and expensive liqueurs were poured and drunk. We laughed and talked of our summer travels to come. To supply us men with those pleasures that come from flirtatious and sexual dalliances with the gentle sex, we invited several young nymphs to join us—girls with supple skin, flourishing heads of hair, and eyes as large as planets. Our dinner was served early and was cooked to perfection. Waiters attended to all our needs. Spanish guitar players strummed the songs of Granada. We filled our stomachs again and again with sweet melons, the flesh of figs, blushing strawberries and ruddy grapes. We ate the good grains of the earth, nourishing our bodies on bubbling roasted cheeses stuffed with saffron and garlic—dishes laced with warm sauces of cream and summer gourds filled our bellies. We dipped again and again the hearty breads to fill our mouths; poured heaps of bountiful wine also into our mouths from high-held sturdy vessels made for such feasts and symposiums as only gods attend. We sang the joys of witnessing the abundant life. Overhead the sky was littered with haze. It carried the remnants of stars and the echoes of city lights. There we laughed and told stories—though only briefly. Two hours before midnight I parted from my friends. I kissed the girls' lips and said goodbye and good luck, I then made my way to the Faubourg Saint Germain to pack for my voyage and to let sweet sleep descend upon me.

Eleven o'clock at night, I entered the door to the room I kept in Saint-Germain-des-Prés and began preparing my suitcase and my clothes for Italy. "In a few hours I'll be gone I must clean the rooms until they are bare and fresh!" Beneath a floorboard, I took out a clever passport which I'd forged one spring while in Marrakech. I put it in my suitcase. "That will get me across the border." The suitcase I put by the door.

Around midnight, Nadja came to see me . . . "to say goodbye," she told me, "and to thank me for showing her around Paris, helping her make friends, etc." She arrived bearing gentle gifts: Ceylon black tea, as well as a potent rose liqueur from her native country. The tea I let steep and then poured into two heated bowls until they were made brimming. Pleasant steam poured into our nostrils. Two slender glasses of crystal, I filled with cool sparkling wine and Nadja's rose liqueur. The chilled alkaline fluid brushed our tongues and made us light of heart. She laid her long and slender back on the bed and reclined while I opened the windows wide to let the spicy summer air come to season the room.

"I've left the Beaux Arts School," she informed me, "I'm going back to live at my parents' in Croatia in a couple of days."

"You're abandoning Paris?"

"For now. I might move to Moscow after that, I'm not sure. My father doesn't want me studying painting forever. He thinks it's time for me to start doing something serious."

"I see. So this is farewell, my dear girl."

"I don't know. Will you come visit me?"

"Of course I will," I promised, "Someday." And with the wine we drank and the laughter we took, and the freedom night allows—also with our caresses, and with Nadja's soft and golden skin, and the wetness of her gorgeous mouth—I really believed I would go visit her someday, in her far-away home on the Adriatic Sea, or in Moscow, or wherever the future happened to find her.

And so that night, we drank and laughed. We told stories and took pleasure in each other's company.

"Will you play a song for me, Aleksandre?"

With these, her words, I took a well-strung mandolin from the corner of the room and strummed and sang a gentle ode. It was ballad I'd composed about occidental travel and Arabian love... woeful love. It told of two dreamers lost in wandering. Two poetic souls tossed among the continents. While the summer moon swelled beyond the open windowpane, my Arabian melody danced like a winding asp. Nadja wrapped her soft lips around the music and the words, and let her wild hair fall upon my skillful arms as they led my fingers to tame those savage oriental chords; and when the song ended, we embraced and kissed. I took her by the hand, lifted her to her feet, and led her out onto the window ledge so we could look at the night. The sky was clear and full of promise.

"Come out onto the rooftop, Nadja."

"Let me take off my stockings so I don't slip."

"How can you wear stockings in such heat?" I asked her.

"I like to wear them. But now they're off."

With careful steps, Nadja and I climbed out onto the railing of the roof and walked up to the high mansard which overlooked the holy darkened square of St-Germain. We sat down on the edge of the railing and held each other tight. Overhead, the moon hovered swollen and silver, at the peak of its fullness. Beyond us, the city lay in its multitudes, with its branches of lighted avenues and its abysses: dark as the ocean at night.

To tell of the beauty we saw that night!...

While the moon overhead grew in fullness, life grew within us. Our past lay beneath us glimmering like a blanket of sand.

"Tell me of the past," she murmured quietly, curling her hand in the crook of my arm.

"The past is what lives in our dreams and the stories we tell. It sleeps in strange beds and wanders alone like a vagabond. It gambles and begs alms at the door."

I smiled with delight at what I was saying, for I knew that such words were the result of the potent wine and rose liqueur we had drunk.

"And the future?" she asked, "Does it also wander alone like a vagabond?"

"No, the future does not wander. It is not like us."

"What is it doing if not wandering? Is it sleeping in strange beds?"

"No!, clever girl!"

"Is it gambling?"

"No!" I huffed, "The future is not gambling!" I was getting annoyed. Then I settled down... "The future is awake and flourishing. It is beautiful. One would say it is a vibrant garden, hard to reach on foot though it lies and waits to be greeted. Only when we arrive does it close its eyes to sleep."

"Speak to me of this garden… of this garden of our future."

"It is a garden of savage creatures, Nadja, of pleasant orchards, gilded streams, hills abundant of grass, creeping vines. There are also deadly snakes and fierce wasps… There are huge nests of stinging trees…."

"Mmm, huh? Nests of stinging *trees?* Don't you mean nests of stinging *bees?!*"

"Yes, that too," I smiled, the clever girl, "There are also nests of stinging *bees* . . . as well as *singing* bees in the nests of *stinging trees.*"

This made her laugh.

"I want to hear bees sing! And what about the moon overhead?"

"Yes, look at the moon. It's full tonight."

"It's lovely," she whispered, clutching my arm. She then laughed aloud. "It's like a pendant on a string, that moon!"

"*You* are like a pendant on a string!" I laughed at her. Then:

"You are beautiful, Nadja. Be still."

I began to fondle her hips and I caressed her little tummy that was spread out before me. She squirmed and giggled.

"But what about that moon?" she asked me, no longer laughing, but serious and pointing.

"That moon overhead? That moon, one would say is a bowl of silver milk, spilling out over the rooftops of the city."

"That's lovely," she smiled. "I love that moon. Do you too?"

"Yes."

"And I love our past," she sighed.

"We wrote a great mythology in this city together, you and I. It will live on after we are gone."

"Aleksandre?"

"Yes?"

"I will remember you after I leave Paris. And I will remember this moon."

"I will remember you too, dear girl. Fondly, I will."

"Will you also remember this moon?"

"Yes, I will remember this moon. I will remember you, this night, and this moon. One day, long from now, as I am wandering through the flourishing future, alone and strange like a vagabond, I will recall this night in my dreams and in the songs I sing and the stories I tell, and I will say that tonight the moon was a bowl of silver milk."

This was the promise I made to her on that rooftop. And this promise I kept. For always after that, whenever I told the story of my last night with Nadja in Paris, I described her skin as soft and gold, and the moon I described as a bowl of silver milk.

« Parle-moi de cette lune.»

Elle pressa ma main dans la sienne.

« On dirait que c'est un bol de lait argenté

Un jour, on dira que c'était un bol de lait. »

CPSIA information can be obtained at www.ICGtesting.com
Printed in the USA
LVOW12s2134170315

430989LV00001B/192/P